ECHO MURDER

ALSO BY LAURA LAAKSO

Fallible Justice
Roots of Corruption

ECHO MURDER

Laura Laakso

Wilde Investigations 2

2019
Louise Walters Books

Echo Murder
by Laura Laakso

Produced and published in 2019
by Louise Walters Books

Reprinted 2020

ISBN 978 1 999 7809 7 5
eISBN 978 1 999 7809 8 2

Typeset in PTSerif 11pt by Blot Publishing

Printed and bound in Great Britain by Clays Ltd, Elcograf S.p.A.

louisewaltersbooks.co.uk

info@louisewaltersbooks.co.uk

Louise Walters Books
PO Box 755, Banbury, OX16 6PJ

*For my mother, Arja Laakso, thank you for
a lifetime of love, support and belief in my dreams.*

CONTENTS

THURSDAY

1

FIRST BLOOD

'So, how was it?' Lizzie asked.

Tim rested his hand on the small of Lizzie's back and steered her across the road among a crowd. A taxi honked, but the flow of people remained unaffected. All around them, their fellow theatre-goers were talking and laughing; the sound a murmur of joy and excitement.

'You won. I had a good time.'

Lizzie twisted to look at him, a smile lighting her face as they headed up the hill. She seemed oblivious to the people jostling them.

'I knew you were going to like it,' she said.

'The puppets were gorgeous.' Tim wrapped an arm around Lizzie's shoulder. 'I'm really glad you dropped enough hints for me to get the message.'

'By hints you mean anvils, don't you?'

'No wonder they worked,' Tim said with a chuckle. 'I'm not into musicals, but *The Lion King* might have changed my mind.'

'Mission accomplished, then.'

They left the worst of the theatre crowds behind as they weaved through the narrow streets towards the bright lights of Covent Garden. The night air was cool and carried dampness that spoke of rain to come. Lizzie zipped up her coat and inched closer to Tim's warmth.

'Are you tired?' he asked.

'Not really. Do you have something in mind?'

'There's a nice pub near Tottenham Court Road. I thought we could stop there for a drink?'

'Do you mind if we walk? After sitting down for so long, I'd like to stretch my legs.'

'Good idea.'

A car blaring rap music approached them, and Tim switched to Lizzie's other side to put himself between her and the car. She turned her head briefly to nuzzle his shoulder.

They walked through the covered section of Covent Garden and towards the Tube station. The area was thick with tourists gawking at the street performers, and a steady stream of people passing in and out of the many pubs and restaurants. Through a restaurant window, they saw a huge birthday cake being set before an old woman while the staff formed a semi-circle around the table. A door opening to a pub allowed a wave of raucous laughter to roll out. Wherever they looked, the streets were filled with people who were happy and laughing and in love. Surrounded by so much joy, Lizzie reached up to press a kiss on Tim's cheek.

A cluster of homeless people was stationed by the Tube entrance, begging for change. Lizzie dropped some coins into their cups, while Tim watched her with a smile.

The streets beyond Covent Garden were quieter, the shops having closed hours ago. Street lights struggled against the darkness of the cloudy evening, and in places, puddles reflected a pale imitation of the real view.

'I should warn you, I'm going to get lost,' Tim said as he steered Lizzie across the road and turned left.

'Why?'

'Because I always get lost when I try to walk from Covent Garden to Tottenham Court Road.'

'Do you want me to get directions on my phone?' Lizzie asked.

'No, I just thought I ought to let you know.'

'Thanks.' Lizzie's fingers found the hand resting on her shoulder. 'Though getting lost with you doesn't sound like a terrible thing.'

Tim watched her while they walked, and shook his head.

'What is it?' Lizzie asked.

'You are something else, you know that, don't you?'

At the sight of Lizzie's cheeks heating, Tim stopped and kissed her. A whistle from a drunk man staggering in the opposite direction drew them apart, and they continued their walk, both smiling.

A few minutes later, Tim rounded the corner and paused.

'Yep, this is definitely not Tottenham Court Road.'

'Maybe we haven't walked far enough yet,' Lizzie said.

'No, I got lost, just like I said I would.'

'Where are we?'

Tim pointed to a street sign above them. 'Shaftesbury Avenue, near Leicester Square. Somewhere along the way, we should have turned right instead of left.'

'Do you know the way from here?'

'Actually, I do.'

'So all is well. And it's been a nice walk.'

They crossed the road outside the dark windows of a

fancy dress shop and continued walking. Tall trees cast shadows on the pavement and dry leaves floated along in the breeze. Behind them, a man stepped out from an alley and crossed the road.

'How come you know this area of London so well, barring the inevitable confusion over those side streets?' Lizzie asked. 'Did you used to live nearby?'

'No. I enjoy exploring London. I quite often skip the rush hour train home in favour of finding a nice restaurant or pub to try. It's more fun to walk to places because you never know what you'll find along the way.'

Lizzie laughed. 'Next you're going to say that it's the journey that matters and not the destination.'

'As a matter of fact, it's the journey—'

Tim got no further before a man stepped around them and stopped, pulling a knife from his pocket.

'You two, get into the alley,' he said, pointing to a gap between the buildings.

The man was barely out of his teens. He wore a black windbreaker a few sizes too large and he had patchy stubble growing on his chin. His large eyes were darting around, frightened, but determined.

'Take it easy, mate.' Tim put himself between the man and Lizzie. 'We don't want any trouble.'

'Do as I say, and no one will get hurt. Now get in that alley.' The man pointed again for added emphasis.

Still keeping himself between Lizzie and the mugger, Tim stepped into the shadows. The alley was narrow and lined on one side by red bins. The smell of urine mingled with the odours of rotting food and wet cardboard. An emergency exit sign cast a dim light, but Tim had to wait while his eyes adjusted.

'You can take everything I have on me, but please don't hurt her,' he said. Next to him, Lizzie tried to choke back a sob.

'I reckon you give me all your stuff and we're cool.'

'As I said, just take it easy.' Tim removed his watch and handed it to the mugger with his wallet and his phone.

The mugger stuffed Tim's belongings in his pocket. With the knife, he motioned towards Lizzie. 'Now you.'

Lizzie passed him her handbag, but when it came to undoing the clasp of her watch, her fingers shook too much to get a purchase on the metal.

'Hurry up.' The mugger glanced towards the street, waving his knife for effect.

'She's doing her best,' Tim said, trying to keep his voice steady.

'Please,' Lizzie turned to Tim, tears in her eyes. 'I can't do this.'

'Can you leave her the watch? You got everything else.'

'No, I want the watch and the bling. Hurry up.'

Lizzie began sobbing, her whole body quaking. Tim stepped towards her, hand stretched to clasp her elbow, but the mugger got between them.

'Stay back.'

'I'm trying to help her.'

'I said, stay back.' The mugger advanced, raising the knife.

'Can't you see she's scared? I just want to help her give you the watch and the jewellery.'

The knife lowered a fraction, but before Tim could skirt around the mugger to Lizzie, she let out a low wail. The mugger whirled around, pointing the knife at Lizzie's face.

'Shut up,' he said, voice rising. 'Give me the stuff and shut up.'

Lizzie shrank back against the bin while Tim stepped around the mugger to stand between her and the knife.

'You're making it worse,' he said, concern for her overtaking his fear.

The mugger scowled, anger twisting his face. He moved to step forward, and his foot landed on a bottle. Off balance, he collided with Tim, knife first. Lizzie screamed. The mugger stepped back, staring at the bloodied knife, while Tim's hand rose to feel wetness spreading across his jacket. He staggered back.

At the sight of the blood, Lizzie screamed again. The mugger dropped his knife and ran deeper into the alley. Tim slid down to sit on the litter-strewn ground, his back against the bin. The left side of his torso was stained red.

'Get help,' he said to Lizzie, trying to sound calm. 'Call an ambulance and the police.'

Lizzie only stared at him until Tim forced a smile.

'It's okay. I'm going to be fine.'

After a lingering look, Lizzie turned towards Shaftesbury Avenue. Her first steps were hesitant, as if she was uncertain of her balance, but soon concern overrode the shock. She ran. The street was empty of people and cars. Lizzie chose the direction they had been walking in, the heels of her shoes clicking on the pavement.

She was almost at the far end of the street when movement across the road caught her eye. In a small alcove, beneath theatre posters, a homeless man was huddled in a sleeping bag. A skinny dog was lying next to him on a grimy blanket. Lizzie ran across the road and came to a halt next to the alcove, a hand resting on the cool bricks. The dog wagged its tail.

'Please help. We were mugged. My boyfriend's been stabbed. I need to find a phone.'

When the man pushed aside his sleeping bag, the pungent tang of an unwashed body assaulted Lizzie's nose. The man's face was gaunt, his features all but obscured by an unkempt beard, but the eyes that met Lizzie's were sharp and kind.

'Where's your boyfriend?' he asked.

Lizzie pointed along the road, towards the darkness of the alley.

'You find a phone. I'll help him.'

'Thank you,' Lizzie said, her breathing erratic. She allowed herself a moment to watch the homeless man before continuing her search.

The homeless man found Tim still leaning against the bin. Where he was applying pressure to the wound, his hands were slick with blood. At the sound of footsteps, Tim opened his eyes.

'Your girlfriend's getting help. My name's Bob.' He crouched next to Tim.

'Nice to... meet you... Bob,' Tim said. His breathing was shallow and irregular.

'Can you take off your jacket?' Bob asked.

'I don't know.'

Tim tried to shrug off his jacket, but Bob had to help him. Folding the fabric so a dry section was on top, Bob pressed it against the wound on Tim's side.

'What's your name?'

'Tim.' He cleared his throat. 'Timothy Wedgbury.'

'Tim, help is on its way.' Blood seeped through the fabric on to Bob's hands.

9

'How's... Lizzie? Is she okay?'

'Lizzie, your girlfriend?'

Tim nodded and closed his eyes.

'She's pretty shook up, but there isn't a scratch on her. As soon as you're on the mend, she'll be right as rain.' Cocking his head, Bob thought he heard approaching sirens. 'Can you tell me what happened?'

'We were mugged... Just a kid... I tried to... help Lizzie... Kid stumbled... stabbed me... An accident—'

By now, Bob was certain he could hear sirens. He increased the pressure on the wound. Tim's expression did not change.

'Hang on in there, Tim.' When he got no response, he patted Tim's cheek, leaving a smear of blood on it. 'Open your eyes and look at me, Tim.'

The sirens grew loud enough to hurt Bob's ears before they cut off. He heard running footsteps and called out, 'Over here! Help!'

Paramedics rushed around the corner, carrying heavy bags. One of them took over the compression while Bob stepped back. A second paramedic felt Tim's neck.

'I can't find a pulse.'

They manoeuvred Tim away from the bin so he was lying down. The first paramedic bent down to bring his cheek close to Tim's mouth.

'He's not breathing.'

'Start CPR.'

The second paramedic placed his hands on Tim's sternum and then froze. 'What the hell?'

Tim's body was growing translucent, fading from view. Bob noticed that a bloodied knife on the ground was likewise turning insubstantial, and he stumbled back until he collided with the corner of the bin, falling backwards. The paramedics leapt up and one reached for his radio, though he could form no words to describe the nature of the emergency.

In front of the stunned witnesses, Tim, his bloodied jacket and the blood on the ground disappeared, as if they had never been.

SATURDAY

2

HOMECOMING

A heavy silence hangs in the car. More than once, I have opened my mouth to speak, but no words come. After more than a year away from the conclave, I am not certain where to start. After all this time, what am I supposed to say to Dearon?

It has been nearly twenty-four hours since I found him in my home and he declared that my time in Old London was over. When he delivered the summons for me to return to the Wild Folk conclave where I grew up, I could only nod. The case I had just finished had taken its toll, and my body was a mass of fatigue and pain. Despite the physical discomfort, though, what weighed on my mind was the thought of failure. Jonathain Marsh was executed on schedule, even though I had proven him to be innocent. Perhaps another private investigator would have fared better, but I had given the case all I had.

When Dearon appeared, I was in no shape to drive anywhere. I took painkillers, lit a fire and slept the sleep of the dead until hunger woke me. Dearon was sitting in one of my armchairs, watching me with an inscrutable expression. I wondered how much knowledge of my life he had gleaned from the flat. Could he smell Ilana on the sheets; my blood on the hearth stones; the healing poultices of the Paladins of Justice and Lady Bergamon? Could he detect the presence of my Hearth Spirit, Wishearth, watching over me while I slept? Could he sense the depletion of my magic, used freely to solve my first big case and stolen by a Leech?

The silence of my waking lingered while I showered, dressed and prepared us breakfast. Dearon took the offerings without comment, though leftover Thai food was a far cry from the simple meals served at the conclave.

There was no need for me to ask how he had made the long journey from the North Country to Old London. He would have travelled like a Wild Folk should: as a bird, a beast, a fish, the wind and the driving rain. Other than my father, the Elderman of our conclave, Dearon is the strongest among our kind. While I could never hope to match his power, a traitorous thought has suggested more than once that together we could be extraordinary.

For the return journey, I insisted that we drive. Despite the much-needed rest, I was not well enough to travel the Wild Folk way. Even if my magic had been fully charged, keeping pace with Dearon would have been a challenge.

So now we drive, sitting in silence that grows heavier with each passing minute.

As I overtake a lorry, my phone rings in my back pocket, and I shift to get it out. Once my foot has eased off the accelerator, I glance at the screen and see Karrion's name. His call must be in response to a text message I sent him before we left, telling him that I needed to take off for a few days. A few days is optimistic, but it was easier than trying to explain the situation to Karrion in a text. I leave the call unanswered and slip the phone into the small space beneath the handbrake.

From the tilt of his head, I know Dearon is looking at the screen.

'Who's Karrion?'

'My apprentice.'

'The Bird Shaman.'

'How did you know?'

'His scent is in your flat, on you.'

My anger flares at the note of accusation in his voice, but I rein it in. 'Makes sense, given that we work together.'

I imagine a hundred angry retorts he could make. While Dearon says nothing, I can feel the gathering of power around him. Glancing at the dashboard, I see we have only driven fifty miles. It is going to be a long journey.

Summoning up the dredges of civility, I ask, 'How have things been at the conclave?'

'The same.'

'And Ollie? Have his hunting skills improved?'

'Not much.'

My irritation grows at his unwillingness to meet me halfway, and he must sense this. The press of his magic against mine eases.

'Ollie misses you,' he says.

I smile at this. Having to return to the conclave has a silver lining.

'And I've missed him.'

Dearon's eyes burn the side of my face like the midsummer sun. 'You shouldn't have left.'

Old arguments spring to my mind, conversations imagined countless times, but never had. Dearon knew I would leave, though we never spoke of my intentions.

'You didn't forbid me to leave.'

'It was not my place to do so.'

'Not yet, while the old Elderman still lives.' The barb falls from my lips unbidden.

In response, a faint scent of ozone swirls in the car, heralding a storm. Dearon has grown powerful in my absence, and I wonder how much of the Elderman's power he now possesses. Could it be that his magic is stronger than my father's?

It takes another twenty miles of motorway for me to give voice to my curiosity.

'How is the Elderman?'

'You will find him a changed man. The healer rarely leaves his side. His death must be approaching, for he sent me to find you.'

Dearon would never leave the conclave without an order from the Elderman. Do I resent the rigidity of his way of life, or is it disappointment I feel? Did I really think that after the recent years, he would come after me of his own accord? Is this reunion not what I have dreamt of over the past months?

Unlike him, I chose to leave while I still could, knowing it would be temporary. Had I been born into one of the lesser families of the conclave, would I have had the courage to defy the Elderman and our way of life? Had my father been less rigid in following the traditions, would I still have left?

Pain shooting down my leg reminds me that I had reasons other than Dearon for leaving. I rub my thigh, hoping to ease the ache that settles in my bones, and I can feel Dearon watching me.

We stop at motorway services for lunch, though from the way Dearon holds his sandwich, I can tell he has little love for human food. While I too think the bread is stale and the filling tasteless, I eat with more enthusiasm than I feel to annoy him. My rebellion is childish, I know that, but I cannot help myself.

Although only awkward silence awaits in the car, neither of us wishes to linger at the service station. People are staring at Dearon's leather boots and trousers hand-sewn from rabbit hides. Next to him, I blend in with the crowds. For someone used to being the outsider, it is a curious turn of events.

Our journey takes us steadily north on the M1 and later the A1 until we reach wilder country. Each road is narrower than the last as we leave behind large cities, and even villages and farmhouses grow scarce. The scenery changes to fields and forests, and I sit a little straighter behind the wheel, my foot a little heavier on the accelerator. I often roamed across this land in my dreams and memories when the press of Old London became too much. Now I am here once more, in a place where I can run for miles without encountering a road, and where birdsong dominates the soundscape rather than traffic noises. Here I can breathe freely and walk barefoot without the risk of used needles and broken glass.

The canopies are gilded with the last rays of the setting sun and shadows have crept across the road by the time we turn on to the dirt path leading to a clearing in the woods that the conclave uses as a car park. Although our kind prefers to move as natural things move, an element of practicality means that the conclave owns various vehicles. They are kept away from the heart of the conclave; from the clearing, Dearon and I will have to continue on foot.

I park next to a muddy Land Rover and brace my hands against the steering wheel. My heart is hammering and my palms feel clammy. Under the thick canopies, we sit in near darkness, but I know Dearon can sense all of me. I have never been able to hide anything from him, and there was a time when I relished the way he saw me.

'Welcome home.'

With the simple statement, Dearon shows he understands. He knows that as much as I rebel against the role imposed upon me by the Elderman and against the traditions that would see me condemned to a life of pain, I cannot escape the fact that this is where I belong. My power is tied to the wilderness; nature lends me her power, and in return, demands that I respect all that is wild and natural. My whole life has been shaped by this place, by the people I am about to meet for the first time in over a year. Until last week, the conclave and what it represents was all that defined me.

In the dim light, I can just make out Dearon's reassuring smile and I find myself wishing he would take my hand. But I cannot reach out to him for fear of cracking the moral high ground I have built from anger, bitterness and disappointment. Our roles were chosen long ago, and I have never had a say in the matter. This is not the first time I have wondered how different our lives would be if we had been allowed to make our own choices.

But such has been the Wild Folk way of living for centuries: the Elderman's word is the law in each conclave, and few are brave enough to defy the rigid traditions. I have, for a time, and yet here I am.

Was everything I accomplished in Old London a mere illusion; an act of futile rebellion? I failed Marsh because the justice system could only see in black and white. Is it not the same here, where the conclave and the Elderman cannot accept a deviation from tradition and our laws?

It is that thought, that fear that pushes me to open the door and get out. Time to confront that from which I have been running for months.

Dearon follows me out, and side by side, we leave the clearing. The path through the woods is carpeted in maple and horse chestnut leaves. They crunch under our shoes, but neither of us makes the effort to silence our steps. The tang of dried leaves is sharp, dispelling the dullness of upholstery, engine parts and petrol that has clung to my skin during the journey. As I open my senses to the forest, wildness rushes through me. The effect is immediate.

Without needing to reach out to a nearby animal, my sight sharpens until the gloom of the dusk no longer hampers me. My ears pick out the sounds of birds and animals moving around us, the creak of branches and the gurgle of a stream. A child laughs in the distance. I can smell the decay of autumn, the rich soil beneath my feet and wood smoke ahead of us. Some of the ever-present tension leaves my body. I have been stumbling blindly in the city and now I can see once more. My steps slow as I embrace a different kind of homecoming.

During my time in Old London, the clash between nature and man-made has dulled my senses and sapped my magic. I have always seen the power as an extension of who I am: an unseen limb for me to rely on. In the city, it was as though I had to reach through a barrier to access all of myself. I had to drive to the south coast to recharge my powers, to immerse myself in the wildness. Those trips offered a temporary relief, but while they've allowed me to continue treading water, I have had a growing awareness of slowly slipping under. Wild Folk are not meant to live in the city, but I have been too stubborn to accept that. Yet here, immersed in the rejuvenating effect of the forest, I now see what a struggle my life has become.

'You are low on power,' Dearon says.

I bend down to pick up a horse chestnut still in its husk. The spikes prickle my palm. 'A Leech tried to drain me dry.'

Dearon tenses, unease flashing across his face. 'A Leech? Do you mean the enemy of old?'

I search my memory, but I cannot recall a tale about Leeches. 'They drain magic from others and use it themselves. I never knew they existed until one broke into my flat. There was at least one other in Old London, but he was murdered.'

'What happened to the Leech who attacked you?' Dearon's hand grips the hilt of his hunting knife.

'I stopped him. He's in prison.'

I want to tell him the attack left a sense of insecurity simmering just beneath the surface, but the words will not come. It is one thing admitting to Karrion that I am afraid, quite another to say it to Dearon.

As I focus on the tiny threads of power that connect me to the trees, the insects, even to the breeze caressing the leaves, I become aware of the magic flowing in the sap, beating in the chests of animals, and floating through the air with wind and mist and oxygen. Growing up in the conclave, I took this wilderness and the feel of it for granted. But my voluntary exile has given me new perspective.

'This forest has power,' I say to Dearon as I turn a full circle to look around me.

'Yes.'

'You don't understand. This forest feels different. I've

been to plenty of forests in the past year, and none of them feels like this.'

'There are too many humans in the Southern Lands. Much of the wildness has faded. I felt it when I travelled to find you.'

'No, there's more to it than that.' I have felt this kind of power in another forest, one right in the middle of Old London. No wonder it felt like home straight away.

'Like what?'

Some of the haughtiness has gone from Dearon's countenance, and I catch a glimpse of the boy he once was: a boy who was always willing to find out what was under a rotting log or beyond the next hill. Together we explored the conclave lands and beyond, pondered the origins of the stars or the usefulness of slugs. When I asked him a question, he asked one in turn, and together we would find the answer to both. He encouraged me to question everything and to look beyond the obvious answers. It is only now that I appreciate how much he influenced my choice of profession. I have buried the memories of a boy who valued me for who I was, not for who I was to be, but now I miss the simple friendship he once offered.

'I met a woman in Old London, Lady Bergamon. As far as I can tell, she's a Plant Shaman, the only one of her kind. She has created a garden that exists in the middle of Old London, but in a wilder time. What should be a few square feet of lawn is, in fact, miles and miles of gardens, orchards and woods. Seasons happen concurrently there, and everything thrives in perfect harmony. She draws power from the gardens and gives it back again, amplifying the magic of the plants. I've only been there once, but straight away I felt like I had come home.'

What I leave unsaid is that there is another power at work in Lady Bergamon's garden. I sensed hostility from a deep spring, a physical feeling of someone considering me an intruder. During my visit, I was unable to determine who or what was behind that power. Lady Bergamon said I was safe so long as I was with her, but I recall being watched from the gloom of the forest when we headed back to her house. Perhaps one day I will learn more about what else resides in her gardens, for Lady Bergamon offered me access to her domain to recharge my power.

If I am allowed to return to Old London.

'Haven't you just described our way of living? We nurture the land and the land nurtures us.'

'To a point. We draw our power from nature and we are the embodiment of her wildness. Is it that great a stretch to say we leave an imprint of wildness in the places we inhabit?'

'And the conclave has been here for a long time.'

'Exactly.' I nod. 'The longer we stay, the more the land thrives. And the more the land thrives, the more powerful we become. It's a symbiosis. A huge, magic-generating symbiosis.'

Dearon stares ahead and then chuckles.

'What?' I ask.

'You've changed. Before you left, you wouldn't have examined your home in such a detached, analytical fashion. I believe your chosen profession suits you well.'

My first instinct is to tell him that he should not presume to know me or to know where my home is, but I bite back the barb. He has paid me a compliment and, for once, I should make an effort not to throw it back at him.

'Thank you,' I say, the words soft.

Together we continue towards the conclave, the night falling around us. Only leaves and branches obscure the starlight. The darkness holds no menace for me, nor is even the blackest night out here truly dark. I am a creature of the Wild, equally at home in sunlight or darkness. The layers of humanity cultivated in Old London peel away as nature reclaims what is hers.

My resolve to honour old promises lasts until I see the glow of fire ahead. Signs of the conclave have been around us for some time, but at the sight of the flickering light, my steps falter.

'I don't know if I want to do this.'

Dearon pauses by my side, his shoulder touching mine. His hand is inches from mine, and my fingers twitch, eager to bridge the gap. But the gulf between us remains, and I force my fingers to relax.

'Why?'

'I've only just worked out who I want to be, the person I could be, and it's in direct conflict with this place. How can I be Yannia Wilde, Private Investigator in Old London, if I must return here? Has all my hard work been in vain? And what of Karrion? By working with me, he has a chance to do what he loves and to help his family. Will all that potential go to waste because the Elderman feels the need to dictate every aspect of our lives?'

Instead of responding straight away, Dearon turns to me. In the half-light of our enhanced vision, his eyes are hard, the twist of his lips sad.

'For someone blessed with the gifts of nature, your way of looking at the world is remarkably black and white.'

With that, he strides out of the shadows. I hesitate, thrown by his words, and then step into the light.

3

CHILDHOOD SPACES

There are only a handful of people near the fire pit which dominates the clearing. The communal cooking has not yet begun, and people will be in their homes, seeing to the endless tasks that form a part of our way of living. Those who are there glance our way, nod a greeting and return to whatever they were doing. Dearon has been gone only a few days, and I have done something unprecedented. The members of the conclave – the people I considered family growing up – will take their lead from the Elderman. If he welcomes me back with open arms, so will they.

A chorus of yips and barks draws my attention away from the people to a pack of dogs rushing towards Dearon. From their upturned faces, bowed backs and hidden tails, I can tell he has been given the title of the hunt master. The dogs are now his, and they serve him with utter devotion. I cannot help wondering what other titles of the Elderman he now possesses.

The pack, consisting of pointers, spaniels and retrievers, is an integral part of the way we hunt. As the pack circles Dearon, each dog hoping for a touch on the head or along the squirming back, I scan them for a familiar figure. Unable to find it, I begin to worry until I hear a crash from the far side of the clearing, followed by a yelp. A brown dog lopes into the clearing, favouring his left front leg. He does not spot me until he is skirting around the fire pit, at which point he howls and changes direction. A child gets in his way and is knocked over. The pointer does not notice, too intent on reaching me. He crosses the final feet with a leap and lands against me with a solid thump. I take a step back to keep my balance, and after a lick at my chin, he slides to the ground.

'Ollie,' I say with a grin.

At the sound of his name, Ollie leaps up again and dances in front of me on his hind legs. Whines, howls and yelps provide a soundtrack for his excitement, and I laugh.

'How am I supposed to greet you if you don't sit still?'

Ollie cocks his head and sits, though his backside wiggles from the force of his wagging tail. I crouch in front of him, sliding my hands down his neck and over his shoulders. He has filled out in my absence, puppy fat giving way to muscle over his lean frame. His short coat gleams, speaking volumes of the care afforded to the animals at the conclave. The only thing that remains unchanged is the demented look in his eyes, and that is what attracted me to him the moment he tumbled out of the puppy pen behind his mother. He was destined to be the worst hunting dog of the conclave, and that made me love him even more.

'You grew up,' I whisper and glance at Dearon. 'And you have a new master now.'

Dearon is looking at us, and Ollie senses this. He rushes at Dearon, running smack into two of the spaniels, but as soon as Dearon has acknowledged him with a pat, Ollie returns to me and leaps into my arms. The solid warmth of his body is reassuring and familiar, even though his elbow is digging into my ribs and his hind leg is pressing on a bruise on my upper thigh. My balance is precarious, but before I fall backwards, a hand steadies me.

I look up to see Dearon smiling at Ollie. The rest of the pack is lying a few yards away, all eagerly awaiting his command.

'I told you he missed you,' he says, voice low. Before I have a chance to reply, he continues, 'The Elderman is waiting.'

Ollie whimpers a protest when I let go of him and stand, unsteady on my feet. He follows, leaping ahead and around me, until I reach the Elderman's cabin. There his enthusiasm fades, and he licks my hand before prancing off to join the rest of the pack. I envy him as I look at the cabin, steeling my resolve.

When I open the door, the smell of herbs and slow decay washes over me. The main room of the cabin has been converted into a bedroom, and the Elderman is lying on a cot a few yards from the fire. It is stifling in the room, and I shrug off my coat and unzip my fleece.

Even to my human nose, the air is thick with the smell of sweat, urine and vomit. Beneath the other scents is that sickly odour I have smelt in the Elderman's breath for many years. It is some sort of cancer, though our healer has been unable to determine the type. It hardly matters when the outcome is the same. There is little dignity in the gradual decay of disease. If the stories of old are true, the Eldermen used to choose a quick death from the elements over months of frailty and suffering. But as much as our laws still forbid modern medical help, some Eldermen seem less willing to relinquish their power, even to those groomed for the position. That is the case with my father.

Most of the furniture I remember is still in the room, pushed to the far end. The walls are covered in cross sections of trees, and my eyes are drawn to a circle of maple next to the fireplace. Its surface has been worn smooth from my fingers tracing over it. The recording of years ends at thirty-six; my mother was young when she had me and too young when the tree representing her life was felled. There are no photos of her anywhere, and the few charcoal drawings do no justice to my memories of her. I long to remove her circle of wood from the wall and seek to return to a time when she was still alive. Instead, I must face my father.

The conclave's healer is sitting on the hearth stones, grinding herbs in an old stone mortar. He has been watching me with wary interest, but at the twitch of the Elderman's fingers, he rises and leaves the cabin. That is my cue, and I walk to kneel by the cot.

The Elderman has grown frailer in my absence. Each rasping breath is an effort. Pain has etched deep lines on his face, and his brown eyes are cloudy. I stare at the hand resting on a deer pelt, fascinated and horrified by how his skin is stretched taut over the bones. Dearon was right: the Elderman is dying.

'Yannia. You are home.'

'Dearon delivered your summons,' I say, careful to keep a neutral tone. For as much as I rebelled by leaving, I too have been indoctrinated with respect for the Elderman. My anger has been expressed by my absence, or directed at Dearon.

'It is good. Your duties cannot be neglected forever.'

My first instinct is to remind him that I may have other priorities, that I may have found myself a life elsewhere. But it is no use. The Elderman does not see any purpose other than that which serves the needs of the conclave, and he expects similar tunnel vision from us all. For him, this is the only way of being one of the Wild Folk.

A coughing fit raises the Elderman off the bed, and he doubles over. I reach out to steady him, but pull my hand back without making contact. When he finally relaxes back against the pillows, his face is twisted in pain.

'You should rest. I'll call the healer back.'

I am pushing myself up, my knees protesting, when he speaks again. Had I got any further, I would have missed his words. A shame I did not.

'It wounded Dearon deeply that you left. Your place is by his side.'

My temper flares, and an angry retort at his unjustness flies to my lips, but goes no further. Why should my whole life be governed by Dearon and his needs? Am I not of equal value? And why should the Elderman care more about Dearon and the conclave than his daughter?

The answer is simple. To me, he has always been the Elderman, never my father. It was my mother I ran to with a bee sting or when thunder frightened me. I ran to her, or to Dearon. Caught in an impossible situation, I miss my mother for the ways in which she was unlike my father.

Protesting would be a waste of breath. I leave to find the healer. He tells me that there is little he can do for the Elderman now, save for easing his suffering. When I ask for an estimate of time, he says a week, maybe two. I feel a chain closing around my neck.

With the Elderman's words still echoing in my mind and the reality of my situation laid out starkly before me, I cannot bring myself to partake in the communal meal. Instead, I take my bag to my old room in my father's cabin. Either no one was expecting my arrival or no one saw fit to prepare for it. Every surface in the room is covered in a thick layer of dust. I push open the window to air out the musty room and light a candle to regard the cramped space.

By the window are a small table, a single chair and a narrow wardrobe. The bed – a tad short for my adult height – is covered in faded pelts and wool blankets. I take each of them to the window and shake them outside, turning my face away from the clouds of dust. At the foot of the bed is a chest, with trees and flowers carved in the polished surface. It contains the few personal possessions I chose not to take to Old London. Once I have wiped all the surfaces clean and rearranged the bedding, I sit by the chest and open the lid.

A cloying smell of faded flowers speaks of the sort of memories I have stored, and I lift out the remnants of a dandelion garland. Did my mother make it for me or was it Dearon? Beneath is a square of fabric, fastened to a pouch by a length of twine. It contains a handful of shiny stones, a bracelet woven of grass and a few acorns. I smile, recalling the treasures I collected from the woods and proudly carried to my mother. It was she who secured them within the pouch. *It is for a rainy day*, she whispered, *for a sad day, for a day when you need to recall the sun that now shines*. I blink back tears, wishing I could remember the warmth of that summer day as well as the brightness of her smile.

My fumbling hand finds a length of smooth bone, and I lift out a hunting knife nestling within a simple leather scabbard. The blade revealed gleams in the restless light, and I see time has not marred its beauty. Dearon gave the knife to me on my fifteenth birthday, and he carved the handle himself. It was to mark my coming of age, a sign that I was allowed to join the adults on hunts. The knife had seen continuous use until I turned my back on the conclave. I left it in the chest as much to escape a reminder of Dearon as because I had little need for a hunting blade in Old London. Now, I set it on the table next to the candle.

More memories emerge from the chest, and I sit on the floor until my legs grow numb and the night air flowing in through the open window sends a chill deep into my bones. I am roused from my recollections by a soft whine. A rush of blood sends prickling pain to my legs as I stand and lean against the wall to peer outside. The communal fire has reduced to embers, and my eyes cannot penetrate the darkness. Rather than reach out with my magic, I bring the candle closer to the window to reveal a figure lying just outside, looking up at me.

'Ollie,' I whisper. At the sound of my voice, his tail thumps against the wall, but he remains where he is. For all his quirks, he has had the rules of the conclave impressed upon him. No dogs allowed in the cabins.

'Come on, then,' I say, and it is all the encouragement he needs. Ollie leaps in through the window, lands by the door and proceeds to investigate every inch of the room. His tail never stops wagging while I close the window, and strip down to my t-shirt. Blowing out the candle, I fumble towards the bed and slip under the pelts. This time, he awaits no invitation before diving in after me. I laugh until his head connects with mine and I bite my tongue. While I mutter curses, he settles against me with a sigh. Here in my room, we both fit in. He accepts me as I accept him.

Curled up against the solid warmth of Ollie's back, I feel safer than I have for months.

SUNDAY

4

THE TASTE OF FLESH

I wake to the feel of gusts of warm air on my face. The room is grey with the first light of the morning. Ollie is lying next to me, panting. When he sees that I am awake, his tail begins wagging under the pelts. I have become hot during the night, and my t-shirt is clinging to my skin. Dodging Ollie's approaching tongue, I shift the pelts over him and wriggle out of bed. By the time he escapes the covers, I have opened the window.

'Time for you to go, or we'll both get into trouble.'

Ollie takes no offence from being kicked out, and he leaps through the window with his tail still wagging. I watch him disappear around the corner before getting clean clothes from my bag. Once I have dressed, I follow Ollie's example and leave the cabin through the window.

Mist has covered the clearing. Nearby cabins are dark shapes looming out of the whiteness, and my steps leave tiny eddies of greyness dancing in my wake. The air smells of wetness, the forest and smoke. Soon the residual warmth from sleeping has given way to the chilliness of being awake, and I rub my cooling hands together as I head for the fire pit.

At first, I think I am the only one up, but then a figure emerges from the pantry shed. Dearon nods and hands me an enamel mug of tea. It is strong and sweet, just as I prefer. Heat seeps through the metal to chase away the chill from my fingers, while a different kind of warmth settles in my stomach. The mist muffles all sounds, and it is as though Dearon and I exist in a world of our own. When he looks at me, eyes intent under his long lashes, I cannot decide whether what I feel is pleasure or irritation.

'How did you know?' I ask and indicate towards my mug.

'Ollie is not as discreet as he thinks he is.'

I open my mouth to explain, or perhaps to offer an excuse, but Dearon shakes his head.

'It's fine. I've known all along that you and Ollie share a special bond. What reason have I to stand in the way of that?'

Vindictiveness would be reason enough, but I hold back the suggestion. Dearon may be many things, but he is rarely cruel. There are times when I wish he was, for it would make his betrayal easier to accept.

While we drink our tea, I think back to similar moments shared with Karrion. They were simpler, the silences less laden with implied words and unspoken accusations. I miss the comfort of Karrion's presence and the certainty of his affection. It has been only two days since I last saw him and already it feels like I have been away from him for months.

Once our mugs are empty, I take them to the pantry shed. The water there is still warm, and I wash the mugs. Everything is in the same place as before I left, and I find the small detail reassuring. There is predictability to life at the conclave that even I can appreciate. But, I remind myself as I dry my hands, it would be easier to appreciate such things if I was only visiting.

Out of habit, I reach for the phone in my back pocket, only to find it is not there. Phones are not part of the conclave life, and I left mine in my room. In the past year, I have grown accustomed to having it to hand. Now, trying to recall the old routines feels forced, like I have outgrown the mould. How long will it take before I fit back into this life?

'Hunt with me.'

The low words are spoken right behind me, and I jump. Irritated by Dearon's ability to sneak up on me, I turn around and say the first thing that comes to my mind.

'Is that the Elderman's order?'

His eyes flash with anger, and regret washes over me. I am being childish and unfair.

'Forget it.'

Dearon turns to leave, but I stop him with a hand on his upper arm. I try my best not to notice how hard the muscles are, how warm he feels. Even in the cool morning, he is dressed only in a sleeveless leather vest and matching trousers.

'Wait.' He stops, but does not turn to look at me. 'I'm sorry. A hunt would be... nice.'

With a glance over his shoulder, he nods, but there is wariness in his eyes that cuts me deeper than any word he has spoken in anger. I hate that this is what we have become.

Dearon turns and collects strips of dried meat and squares of flapjack into a leather pouch. He hands it and a waterskin to me. I find an empty backpack and fill it with our supplies. While he heads for the weapons store,

I jog back to my father's cabin, swing my legs in through the window to my room and collect the hunting knife I left on the table. Attached to my belt, its weight feels right against my leg.

When I round the corner, Dearon is waiting for me with two bows and quivers. I test the bow and find he has chosen well for me.

On our way out of the clearing, Dearon chooses pointers from the pack. While the rest of the pack waits for a word from Dearon, Ollie creeps up to me.

'We might as well bring him,' Dearon says. 'I doubt he'll stay behind if you're going hunting.'

Ollie bounds along next to me, full of joy. Dearon silences Ollie's excited whimpering with a glance, but there is little he can do about the tail that keeps thumping against my leg.

We head north, walking through the misty forest in silence. The dampness muffles the sound of our footsteps, and even the dogs sense a purpose to our journey, staying behind us. At the edge of the forest, we cut across a road that is little more than a dirt path. There are roads leading through our lands, and by human law, we must maintain them. But the conclaves have no love for humans, and those who stray on to our land are not encouraged to linger. That is why Shamans of all kinds occupy agricultural properties along the edges of the wilderness we own. They act as a natural buffer between us and the humans, and the farms supplement the resources we gather from the forests, moors and waterways.

The sun rises as we wade across a meadow, its rays gilding the mist but not yet burning through it. The beauty of it moves something within me. We eat our breakfast there, standing side by side in an ethereal lake of gold. If I keep my focus on the scene before me, I can almost forget what has been and what is supposed to be.

By the time we move on, I can see the grass beaded with moisture. A gentle breeze is threading through the remaining mist. Drawing on the power pulsing through the soil, the plants, the insects all around me, I revel in the knowledge that every aspect of nature is me and I am it.

Something grey flashes past us. In the time it takes me to identify it as a hare, Dearon has sent an arrow flying. The hare is pinned to the ground with a short scream, and ahead of us, a flock of birds take to the skies in a rustle of feathers. A death has been acknowledged, a warning heeded.

Ollie rushes ahead, and Dearon has to call thrice to get him back. I give him a pet behind Dearon's back, and he leaps up to lick my chin. Dearon hurries to the hare, but its eyes have already glazed over. He pulls the arrow free, lifts the hare into the game bag he is carrying and cleans the arrowhead of blood and soil.

'Nice shot,' I say, my voice low.

Dearon nods, and we continue our walk. My jeans are wet up to my knee, and I am glad I chose to wear my waterproof hiking boots.

'Remember that forest spring you were convinced led to the Fey lands?' Dearon asks, and I nod. 'I reached the bottom.'

I recall summer days spent diving into the pool and all my theories about why the spring had to be a gateway to a different world. Old excitement stirs within me.

'You did? What was at the bottom?'

'I don't know.'

41

'Why not?'

'It was dark. I couldn't see a thing,' he says, his expression serious.

I laugh. He joins in, and I lean against his arm while I catch my breath.

'That's why I should've done it.' I wipe my eyes. 'You probably missed the gateway by an inch.'

'Blind as a fish is a real thing.'

'Keep telling yourself that.'

We come to another forest, this one choked with coils of brambles, and our pace slows. Twice I tear my hand on the thorns, and I lick the blood welling in the scratches. The metallic taste sends my pulse racing, anticipation of the hunt building restlessness in my limbs.

'Do you have a destination in mind?'

'The deer are rutting. Greoff said he saw a group of sika hinds near the lakes three days ago.'

'Any bucks with them?'

'He said not.'

My legs are beginning to ache from the walking, and I regret not taking pain medication before we left. It is too late, and I push the discomfort to the back of my mind. Although Dearon has seen me in pain many times, I am reluctant to show such weakness now.

The mist fades while we walk, and I am beginning to warm when Dearon lifts his face to sample the air. I follow his example, borrowing Ollie's nose, and I catch an impression of musk. Setting down the game bag, Dearon motions for the dogs to stay back, and we creep forward until we reach a copse of ash and sycamore. I call upon the sight of a hen harrier to see better, but even so, it takes a moment before I spot a flash of movement ahead.

A sika buck's grey coat blends well into the dappled undergrowth of the forest, and it is browsing as it walks. Dearon taps my bow, indicating the shot is mine. I estimate the distance to the deer; not impossible, but not easy either. To take the shot, I need to be standing and I back away until I am behind a tree. We are downwind and our approach was quiet, but the buck's vision is tied to movement.

I stand slowly, easing into view. I need not look down to place a shaft on the arrow rest. My muscle memory recalls the drawing of a bow. I aim the arrow behind the buck's shoulder blade and halfway down the side, then adjust for the margin of error that creeps into each of my shots.

Dearon is right behind me, the dogs are waiting for his signal, and the forest is teeming with life. But when my sight is set on a spot in the deer's flank and the bow is drawn, nothing exists but me and the buck. We are connected by the path the arrow is going to take. I smile as I release the bowstring.

The arrow flies too fast for me to track, but the buck rears in an explosion of movement. It vanishes. I crouch. We remain motionless until my legs are aching from the difficult position, both listening for any sign of the buck. The copse is silent, and eventually, Dearon is satisfied. We rise, and I bite back a groan as blood rushes into my lower legs.

'Let's take a look.'

We bring our bows, but leave the dogs by the game bag. While the other dogs obey immediately, Ollie finishes chasing his tail before settling down. There is no sign of the deer, but only a head or a spine shot would have dropped it where it stood. Blood has spattered on the carpet of leaves, and I find the arrow sticking out of the ground and pull it free. The blood on the shaft is pinkish red, and I see several air bubbles.

'A lung shot,' I say.

'It shouldn't have got far.' Dearon sweeps his arm to cover half of the copse. 'Which way did it go?'

I return to the shot site and inhale, borrowing the dogs' sense of smell. The scents of blood, buck and adrenaline guide me. A short whistle from Dearon calls the dogs, and by the time they catch up with me, I have found another splatter of pink blood on the ground. I dip my fingers in it, drinking in the scents of hunt and prey and flesh. My stomach growls, and a primal part of me whispers that this is right, this is my way of life. I could be a creature of instinct and hunger, forsaking all pretence of civility. All I have to do is embrace the Wild.

Standing up from my crouched position, I find Dearon watching me. His eyes shine with the same hunger, and a new layer is added to my temptation. We could be the doe and the buck, the hen and the cock, the alpha pair. Together we would be extraordinary.

But what would be the price of giving in to him?

The answer is obvious, and yet I refuse to confront it. Instead, I move on, already scanning the ground for the next splash of blood. Dearon follows.

Even with the help of the dogs, it takes considerable time to follow the deer's trail. The tracks take us out of the woods and across the open moors until we find the buck bedded down in the shelter of a boulder, his fur all but blending into the heathers. I can see the bloodied hole in his side, and his nostrils and muzzle are stained pink.

We take a moment to stand before the buck. Each death begets life; that is our way and the way of nature. The deer will feed us, and one day we will feed the land.

Fingers brush against my hand, and I turn it to feel a light stroke across the sensitive skin of my palm.

'You have blood on your cheek.'

I move to wipe it off, but he shakes his head.

'Leave it. Your wildness is captivating.'

He accepts all of me. As we face each other, I see that and more in his expression. There is desire there, as dark and intense as Dearon himself. I remember what it felt like to be immersed in that desire. A surge of yearning leaves me trembling, and he leans closer. My eyes are drawn to his lips, but before I have a chance to kiss him, I am knocked sideways by a solid shape colliding with me.

'Ollie,' I groan at the dog standing over me, tail wagging and tongue lolling out. As I speak his name, he licks my face.

'He likes you,' Dearon says, his affection clear. The hunt master loves his hounds, and the feeling is mutual.

'I'm surprised you've kept him, given how hopeless he is as a hunting dog.'

'I keep him because you love him.' He helps me up, while I try to find a response.

The temptation to kiss him has passed. We move a little more easily around one another as we roll the deer from his final resting place and lay him on his side in the heather. Handing me his bow and quiver, Dearon pulls the buck across his shoulders and stands. The buck must weigh at least a hundred pounds, but Dearon lifts him like he is no bigger than a hare. As strong as Dearon is, I feel the slow expansion of his magic, like frost spreading across a pond. To carry a deer for any distance, even the strongest among us will need to rely on our power.

We pick up the game bag, and then follow a more direct route back to the conclave. As we walk, I notice that the pull of Dearon's magic gradually increases. The sika buck is heavy even for him.

'Let me take a turn,' I say after a while.

'No need.'

'It's my kill. I should do my fair share of the carrying.'

'You're sick. You shouldn't have to carry a deer.'

I jump in front of him, a finger pointed at his sternum. 'Don't tell me what I should or shouldn't do.'

Startled by my reaction, Dearon takes a step back.

'Just because you're healthy doesn't mean you get to make my choices for me. It's not up to you to decide whether I can carry a deer or walk to the shops or do any of the dozens of tasks I do every day. The choice is mine and mine alone.'

'I'm sorry.'

It is my turn to be surprised, and I watch him with wary eyes.

'I thought I was being considerate,' he says and sets the deer down.

'You weren't. What you were implying was that my physical illness makes me less capable of making choices. It's condescending.'

'That wasn't my intention. All I wanted was to help.'

'Offer me the choice. Give me options. But don't tell me what I can't do.'

'Shall I lift the buck on to your shoulders?'

'Yes.' I remain wary of him, but his regret looks genuine. 'Please.'

I turn around and lift my hands to accept the weight. Although I was expecting it, my knees buckle when Dearon rests the deer on me and I have to take a step forward. He maintains a hold on the carcass until I indicate that I have regained my balance. As soon as I can focus my mind, I borrow the strength of nature to remain upright and moving.

This would never be possible in Old London. I would deplete my inner power reserves in a matter of minutes with no way to supplement them from the world around me. Yet, I have chosen to live in the city, determined not to let it tame me. But as much as the thought of the city defeating me is terrifying, perhaps what I fear even more is the conclave and Dearon taming me.

The thought keeps me occupied as I pick my steps carefully along the path, maintaining a slow but steady pace. I am out of breath in no time. A wet patch forms across my shoulders from leaking blood, and the fabric of my shirt chafes the skin raw. Where I am holding on to the deer's legs, the bones press against my collarbones and send a throb down my arms. I increase the draw of magic from around me and struggle to push the lesser pains to the back of my mind. To carry one's kill is a source of pride among my kind. I have never killed a deer this big and I want to be able to walk into the conclave with my head held high. But when we descend the side of a steep hill, my knees protest, and Dearon holds out a hand to steady me.

'I've rested. Shall we swap?'

'I don't mind carrying it a little longer,' I say even though every step feels like someone is hammering nails into my knees.

'There's no shame in accepting help freely offered.'

When I frown past the deer's haunches, he continues, 'Please let me take the deer for a while. Rest assured, I have no desire to present it to the conclave on your behalf.'

'Fine.'

Dearon takes the deer, and I rub my collarbones. Walking unburdened eases the pain in my knees, but fatigue weighs on my limbs. Now I wonder how wise agreeing to a hunt was, for reasons that have nothing to do with Dearon. For someone eager to choose for myself, I should take better care in considering the consequences of my choices.

We are within sight of our home forest when Dearon lowers the carcass back on to my shoulders and I whisper a thank you. The others within the conclave give me a far more enthusiastic welcome when I walk into the clearing carrying a sika buck. Dearon hangs the hare in the larder shed and goes to greet his dogs, leaving me to answer questions about the hunt.

His reaction puzzles me, and I find myself turning back to it as the deer is taken off my shoulders and prepared for butchering. When the current Elderman was the hunt master, he would always relate the tale of the hunt and his part in it. Dearon seems to want none of the glory, even though he knew where we might encounter the deer.

To avoid spending the day over-analysing every move Dearon makes, I volunteer to help with the deer carcass. My clothes get splattered with gore and the smell of intestines makes me gag, but there is a certain satisfaction in the process. I shot the deer, tracked it, and it is only right that I should prepare it for consumption. Nothing is wasted, from the blood to the coils of intestines, and many members of the conclave participate in the preparation. All the while, the hunger I awoke earlier gnaws at my insides. It is there when I lick flecks of blood from my lips, when I bite into fried deer liver, and when I look up to see Dearon watching me. It demands to be sated, and yet food cannot dull its edge.

My muscles are shaking from exhaustion when I sink into a hot bath. The blood on me turns the water pink, much like it did when I washed my clothes. Most were salvageable, but my white t-shirt will go to the rag pile once it is dry.

The heat eases some of the ache from my bones, and the painkillers I took blur my perception of the agony in my limbs. I had forgotten how demanding the conclave life could be, how physical the existence is here. Yet, despite my fatigue, a restlessness remains within me, and I rise from the bath sooner than I would prefer. I return to my father's cabin only to slip out of the window again.

I pause by the communal fire pit to pick up an offering and to whisper a dedication to my Hearth Spirit. Although I am hundreds of miles from Old London, I would like to think he is still listening. Distance is no matter to a spirit like Wishearth. Only the Hearth Spirit and the drowsy hounds witness my stepping up to Dearon's threshold.

He is waiting. When I slip in through the door and close it behind me, he stands from a seat by the window.

I am wearing a knee-length tunic, which I pull over my head. In return, he lets his grey robe drift open and fall into a pool of fabric at his feet, revealing that he is likewise bare underneath. We stare at each other in the dim moonlight.

We move at the same time, meeting halfway in a kiss violent enough that our clashing teeth cut my lip. He sucks it into his mouth and licks the blood. The next kiss is no less fierce. Our tongues carry a metallic edge, but it only fuels my desire. Deer's blood may have awakened the hunger, but Dearon stokes it until I am lost, starving for his touch. My hands are in his hair to keep him close, and strong arms lift me off the ground. His grip causes small blooms of pain, but I am unable to ask him to stop, unwilling to make him stop.

Dearon nips a path along my jaw and down my neck until his teeth reach the line of stitches across my shoulder. The twinge of pain triggers panic in me. I recall the chill of my bedroom, the sound of Ilana choking and the sour stench of a Leech. The memories take me back to a different dark room and to the brief battle fought in the dying light of embers. Bile rises in my throat, and my hands shake when I turn Dearon's head so our lips can meet. Let his touch burn away the memory of Jans's hunger. It is not a memory I wish to retain.

Our lovemaking is desperate, bordering on violent. The urgency with which we grasp at each other, the need to be as close as we can, is a culmination of many months apart. Although we spent only one night together, our bodies remember the fire we awoke. It has been lonely out there in the cold. But we are also Wild Folk and, in this unguarded moment, can give in to our most primal urges. Coupling in nature is rarely slow and tender.

Afterwards, his hold on me remains tight while sweat cools on our skin and our breathing evens out. With the darkness of the cabin forming a barrier between us and the rest of the world, I find a small measure of peace in his arms.

5

SECOND BLOOD

'That cheese board might have been a mistake.'

'You mean after a plate of ribs and a slice of chocolate cake?' Lizzie laughed.

'What can I say? My greediness is in a class of its own.' Tim joined in the laughter, patting his stomach with the hand that was not resting on Lizzie's shoulder.

'Are you that enthusiastic about anything else in life?'

'You?' Tim chuckled when Lizzie blushed. 'Come here.'

They stopped under the white awning on Bishop's Square, and Tim cupped Lizzie's face. She tilted her chin up, eyes fluttering closed in anticipation, and he kissed her. Each brush of his lips was unhurried until it was Lizzie who deepened the kiss. One of her hands was buried in the thick hair at the nape of his neck, while the other brought their bodies flush against one another. Tim groaned against her lips, and she chuckled, low and sensual.

'If tomorrow wasn't Monday, I'd take you home right now and keep you in bed all day.' Tim spoke next to her ear.

'All in good time,' she replied, peppering her words with pecks along his jaw. 'We agreed to take things slow.'

'I know and I'm good with that, but you'd make a sinner out of the most devout of saints.'

'When we do spend a night together, it will be all the more special because we've waited.' Lizzie looked away, sadness clouding her expression. 'I want this to be different.'

'It is, this is different.' Tim used gentle fingers to coax her to look at him. 'I'm not an arse like your ex. I'm never going to hurt you.'

'I trust you.' Lizzie smiled and the shadows lifted from her eyes. 'You've been so good to me.'

'You deserve nothing less, honey.' He kissed her again.

A cold wind tugged at their coats, and they both shivered. The square was empty, and the dark shops gave the place a desolate feel. Lizzie looked around and shifted a little closer to Tim.

'Shall we get going?' he asked.

'Let's.'

They rounded the corner to Brushfield Street, and Lizzie glanced back.

'We should come back when more of the market stalls are open. I've heard there's some interesting art and enchanted items for sale here. Though it's no One Magic Change.'

'Shopping. Sounds fun.' Tim winked.

'You're such a man,' Lizzie said, her tone mocking. 'Besides, we've already established that you think with your stomach so I can park you near the food stalls. By the time I've investigated the market, you will have had a chance to eat your way through most of them. What could be better than that?'

'I don't only think with my stomach. Though perhaps you're not far off. And you've made shopping sound a lot more appealing. With a plan like that, how could I refuse?'

Lizzie grinned. 'I was hoping you'd say that. Though I must warn you, you're only a short step away from spending your weekends shopping on Oxford Street.'

He groaned. 'Great.'

Brushfield Street ended at Bishopsgate, and they turned left. Ahead, the side entrance to Liverpool Street Station was brightly lit against the October gloom.

'Are you catching the Tube home?' Tim asked as they stopped at a red light.

'No, a bus is quicker.' Lizzie nodded towards the bus stop a few hundred yards away.

'Do you want me to wait until the bus comes?'

The lights changed, and they crossed the road.

'No need. The stop is just there, and the streets aren't deserted.'

'Are you sure? I don't want you to feel unsafe.'

'What time's your train?' Lizzie asked in turn.

Tim glanced at his phone. 'In seven minutes.'

'Don't miss it because of me. It'll already be late by the time you get home. I'll be safe enough.'

'Fine, but promise to text me when you get home so I don't worry?'

'Of course. I'll want to say goodnight anyway.'

'Something for me to look forward to, then.'

'If that's the most exciting part of your evening, I worry about you,' Lizzie said with a grin.

'Oh no, the most exciting part of the evening is still happening. But getting a text from you when I'm staring at the walls of my flat is the next best thing.'

'If that's the case, why live out in the sticks instead of the city?'

'I've been wondering the same thing. Who knows

what'll happen in the future.'

Lizzie glanced at her watch as they stopped opposite the station entrance. 'I'm no fortune teller, but I foresee you missing the train if you don't go soon.'

'I can't go,' Tim smiled, 'I haven't said goodbye yet.'

Lizzie rose to tiptoes and wrapped her arms around Tim's neck. She leant closer so their lips almost touched and smiled. 'Goodbye.'

'Nice try.' A hand at the back of her neck kept Lizzie close while he kissed her. 'That's a proper goodbye.'

'And there I was thinking I'd leave you something to look forward to.'

'You did promise to text me.' He kissed her again. 'And this is fantastic.'

'It is. Now go, or you'll have to run to catch your train.'

Tim let go of her and stepped between two parked taxis, ready to cross the road. In doing so, he turned back to Lizzie, a wide smile spreading across his face.

'Hey, Lizzie? I'm falling in love with you.'

Lizzie opened her mouth to reply, but her eyes were drawn to a van approaching Tim. He never saw the driver turn in his seat to fumble with his phone, never saw the van swerve towards him as he stepped out on to the road. His eyes were fixed on Lizzie until the collision flung him through the air. He landed on the road in a heap: a puppet whose strings had been severed all at once. The van ploughed into the back of a parked taxi.

For a few seconds after the crash, everything was silent. Then Lizzie screamed, the van driver pushed open his door, and passers-by ran to where Tim was lying motionless on the road.

'Shit, shit, shit,' the van driver mumbled. His hands

shook so much he dropped his phone, and the screen blossomed in a pattern of cracks.

A crowd gathered. In the press of people, Lizzie and her screams faded into the background. Sirens heralded the approaching ambulance, the flashing lights turning the street into a strobed series of dark and blue stills.

Tim regained consciousness when the paramedics leant over him, opening their first response kits.

'Lizzie?' he asked, his face contorted in agony.

'Try not to talk.'

One of the paramedics checked Tim's wrists for a medical alert bracelet and then pulled out his wallet to search for a medical ID card. Finding none, he checked the driver's licence.

'Victim's name is Timothy Wedgbury.'

'His pulse is thready,' the other replied, gloved fingers pressed against Tim's throat.

They were still taking stock of his injuries when Tim's eyes rolled back and his spine bowed. He began to convulse, but before the paramedics had a chance to administer an anti-seizure shot, his whole body went slack.

'No pulse.'

The paramedic moved to begin chest compressions and then swore.

'What the hell?'

Before their eyes, Tim's body and the blood pooling beneath him faded from view. The paramedics shrank back. A few moments later, they were kneeling on the road amidst the debris of a car crash with no victim.

MONDAY

6

A REALITY CHECK

The world is grey with the new dawn when I slip out of the door and head for my father's cabin. As much as I would have liked to fall asleep with Dearon, the official consummation of our union should wait until the mating ceremony. Or, that is the excuse I gave him when I disentangled myself from his hold. In truth, I am not certain how wise sleeping with Dearon was and I need solitude to sort through my feelings.

I return to my own bed for a brief rest, body aching from hours of lovemaking. Ollie follows me to the bedroom window and whines to be allowed in. This time, I refuse him entry and crawl under the covers. Sleep eludes me, and I end up staring at the ceiling while my body relives the night with Dearon. His fingers and teeth have left many bruises, but they will fade far more quickly than the maelstrom of confusion our night together has re-awoken in me.

For as long as I can remember, Dearon has been a presence in my life. As a young boy, he held my hand on dark forest paths, spun me around until I was squealing with joy and put himself between me and anything I found frightening. When I tripped and fell, he was the one to pick me up and wipe away the blood and dirt from my skinned knees. During thunderstorms, he told me stories of sky serpents battling amidst the storm clouds, their blows sending lightning across the sky. If sleep eluded me, he sat next to my bed and sang the stories of old, of how our life used to be.

We explored the forests together, swam in lakes and stayed up all night to watch a herd of deer on a moonlit meadow. In the evenings, we would sit by the communal fire, listening to the Elders telling stories or singing songs passed down from generation to generation. We grew close enough to spend hours in each other's company without the need to talk. More often than not, he knew what I was about to say even before I said it.

I thought things would never change. I wanted them never to change.

We come into our powers with puberty, and while I was dealing with the physical and magical changes, my mother died of an illness that wasted her away over several years. In hindsight, I know it was cancer. Mourning her and learning to control my powers took up most of my attention for the better part of two years. During that time, I was aware that Dearon was always there on the edge of my vision with a ready smile and supportive words. He had already come of age, had taken his place as a full member of the conclave, but whenever I was free, he found time away from his duties to go for a walk with me.

Once, I was sitting by the communal fire with a mug of tea first thing in the morning when Dearon stepped out of his cabin. It struck me then that I had never noticed how tall he had grown or how broad his shoulders had become. I was seeing him anew, and the discovery was bewildering. His eyes found me across the clearing, and a broad smile lit his face. A warmth shifted within me.

From there on, we were bound together by an unseen force. Wherever he went, my eyes followed him, even as I focused on my duties and training. When we sat side by side, I was aware of our shoulders brushing or his leg pressing against mine. As I stared at his fingers preparing the offering to the Hearth Spirits, heat pooled in my stomach. When he looked up from his task, his eyes were dark and I had to look away for fear of losing myself.

It was not long afterwards that my father took me aside and explained that the future of our conclave had been decided the night I was born. Dearon was to become the next Elderman after my father, and I was to be Dearon's mate. With my studies almost complete, it was time I began to learn the duties of the Elderman's wife. My role would be one of supporting the new Elderman. It had all been worked out for me, other than the specific timing of the mating.

I reacted with all the composure and grace of a teenager. How long I wept alone in a forest meadow, I cannot be certain, but it was Dearon who found me there. When I confronted him, he admitted to having known about the arrangement for many years. I lashed out. He was the first and most logical target for my rage. To me, our friendship had been a fraud from the beginning, and he had merely been doing his duty by being kind and considerate to his future mate. I said many hurtful things that day, mostly to make him leave. In the end, I succeeded.

Nothing was the same after that. I kept my distance from Dearon. It was much harder to rebel against my father, and I had little choice but to attend the lessons he set.

Even after the emotional turmoil dissipated, I was left with a growing sense of disappointment that I had no say in my future. Around the same time, an ache in my hips, which had begun as an occasional niggle after a long day of physical labour, grew into steady pain. Given my bleak view of life at the conclave, the pain established a hold within me that few things could break. I became hollow as I went through the motions that were expected of me, all the while allowing the pain to consume me. Whenever I looked up, Dearon was watching me, always with a frown. But I held on to an old grudge long after the wound had scabbed and scarred, too stubborn to admit that I missed him and cared for him.

I did not go to him until the night before I left the conclave. My growing disquiet about the conflict between who I was and what I was expected to be, compounded by the relentless pain, drove me to choose an unknown future away from everything familiar. Dearon was the hardest to leave, and I think he guessed more about the inner workings of my mind than I appreciated.

I slipped into his cabin after the conclave had retired for the night. He said nothing as I closed the door and crossed the room to him. I did not trust my voice and I kissed him instead.

He took me into his arms and into his bed. I refused us sleep, desperate to memorise as much of him as I could. Perhaps he sensed the reason for my desperation, for I fancied that I could see a hint of sadness in his eyes as we moved together.

At dawn, when I drove away from the conclave, a fallow buck kept pace with me in the woods until I passed beyond our borders.

My thoughts are no clearer when I rise to confront the new day. Sore from yesterday's hunt and from a night of rough sex, I choose to spend the morning tending to the Elderman. A desire to avoid Dearon plays a part in my decision.

So, I change soiled bed sheets and wash my father's skeletal limbs, the smell of urine and vomit clogging my nose. I find it strange that I cannot remember tending thus to my mother during her final months. Someone must have done it, yet I cannot imagine the Elderman washing sheets or spooning herb broths past parched lips. It saddens me that I have not retained more memories of my mother's last years. I recall her when she was well and I recall kneeling in the grove of memories, holding vigil over her remains while nature reclaimed what was rightfully hers.

Looking at my father, I find it difficult to see beyond the suffering to the Elderman I remember. As much as the healer tends to him, the herbs he uses have little or no effect. Our healing traditions go back centuries, but our healers are no Plant Shamans.

When I return to my room at lunchtime, I see that I have a missed call from Detective Inspector Jamie Manning. He has left a voicemail asking me to call him back. Unwilling to do so from the cabin, I slip my phone into the back pocket of my jeans and exit through the window. I head for the privacy of the forest and let my feet choose a path without conscious thought. There are no phone masts nearby, but I have just enough signal to make the call.

'Manning,' Jamie answers, and I remember his kindness in reassuring me that Jonathain Marsh's execution was not my fault.

'Jamie, it's Yannia. You called?'

'Can I stop by later with someone? I have a potential client and a case for you.'

I know Jamie specialises in magical crimes because he wishes he too had power. I see it in the longing in his expression whenever we meet. Karrion and I impressed him with our work last week, and he promised to help us in the future. Now, that aid seems to extend to drumming up business for me. I am not complaining, but my current situation complicates things.

'I'm actually not at home. Could you come tomorrow instead? Preferably in the evening?'

'I'll make a call and let you know.'

'Thanks, Jamie. Anything else you want to share at this stage?'

'No, this is something you need to hear from both of us.'

I am intrigued, but get nothing further from him. When we end the call, I see that my meandering path has taken me to the grove of memories. The meadow forms an almost perfect circle deep in the woods. The grass is still tall, but wildflowers have given way to rosehips, which glow red in the sunshine. Towards the middle of the grove, a section of grass has been stamped down. Greagorey, one of the conclave Elders, mentioned that his sister had died recently. Creatures great and small will have fed from the body until only bones remained. They will be buried somewhere in the area to further nourish the soil.

My mother's bones were likewise interred after my father and I watched over the body while nature fed. Dearon hovered on the edge of the clearing during our vigil, but our laws prohibited him from joining us. He was not family then. He is still not family.

Turning away from the grove of memories, I wish everything was that simple.

7

A REPRIEVE

'You're not staying, are you?'

Jamie texted to say that tomorrow evening is no good for the prospective client, but that they could come to see me first thing in the morning. We agreed on eight thirty, and I continued walking in the woods, pondering my dilemma and turning a potential solution round and round in my mind. It may work, but I will not know for certain until I have spoken to the Elderman.

I must have been staring at the path to the cars for some time for Dearon to have found me. He comes to stand next to me, our shoulders touching. He, too, looks towards the path, his jaw set. Anger radiates from him, searing me like fire. I can see that our night together has changed nothing for him. Did it for me?

'I can't. There's a potential client I need to see, someone who needs my help.'

'And you think we don't need you here at the conclave?'

I shrug. 'There's nothing I can do that others here can't, most likely better than me.'

Dearon's laugh is laced with bitterness. Another man in his position might claim he needs me, but not Dearon. He is never going to say that because it would not be true.

He wants me, but he does not need me.

'The Elderman is dying.'

'But he's not dead yet. You won't become next Elderman until he does.'

'It's only a matter of days now. Why else would he have sent me to find you?'

'I might be able to help him. There's a healer in Old London I could consult.'

'You know our laws about doctors.'

'Lady Bergamon's healing comes from plants.' I glance at Dearon and away again. 'She might be able to brew a medicine to help the Elderman.'

'To what purpose? To help the Elderman, or to prolong his life so you may remain in Old London?'

My anger flares at the accusation. The thought has occurred to me too, and I hate that Dearon reached it straight away. Even after all these years, after all the time I have spent pushing him away, he still knows me.

Digging my nails into my palms, I force my voice to steady. 'Do you think prolonging my stay in Old London is worth causing my father additional suffering?'

'Perhaps.' He looks at me for the first time, his expression dark with anger and frustration. 'I don't know you anymore.'

I recoil from him, the words dissipating my anger.

'And whose fault is that?' I whisper.

Instead of replying, he walks away. I watch him go, already regretting my harsh words. Why is it that the two things I do best with him are fighting and sex? How are we ever supposed to live together, let alone present unified leadership to the conclave? The childish part of me thinks that the Elderman should have thought of that before promising me to Dearon, but it is a futile thought.

I return to the Elderman's cabin and ask the healer to give me a moment alone with my father. Once he has left, I photograph all the herbs in the room. I have a basic understanding of our healing, but there are some among the pots that I do not recognise. The first step in Lady Bergamon helping the Elderman is her knowing what has already been tried.

My father stirs as I kneel by his cot, and I offer him a cup of water. He is too weak to take it so I tilt his head forward and hold the cup to his lips. Some of the water runs from the edge of his mouth and down his neck. I dab it dry with a rag. When he signals that he has drunk enough, I lay his head back on the pillows.

'I would like to consult a healer in Old London regarding your condition, Father.'

'You know our laws, Yannia. Human medicine has no place in the wilderness.'

'Lady Bergamon is neither human nor a doctor. She is a Plant Shaman.'

The Elderman coughs and licks his lips. 'Plant Shamans are a race of old. They disappeared countless generations ago.'

'All, but one.'

'It is impossible. A Plant Shaman could never survive in a city.'

I am tempted to ask how he could possibly know that since he has never been to Old London, but antagonising the Elderman will not get me what I want. Instead, I shake my head.

'She has not only made Old London her home, but she thrives there. Much like I do.'

'My daughter, thriving in a city. It is abhorrent,' he whispers.

'Just because it hasn't been done before doesn't make it abhorrent. Wildness exists in places other than these unspoilt lands. Nature is versatile. Why shouldn't we be the same?' I am struck by a need to explain, to make him understand. 'In Old London, I have a chance to help people. I can make a difference, solve crimes others can't because I'm one of the Wild Folk and it is nature herself that lends me her power. There is no one like me in the city.'

'Your duties are here, by Dearon's side.'

He will not listen, regardless of what I say. But I may still be able to buy time.

'I want to ask the Plant Shaman to help you. I think she might be able to find the right combination of herbs to slow the progression of the disease and to ease your suffering.'

'Our healer is most capable.'

'Yes, but he is not a Plant Shaman. If a different natural remedy is available, would you not wish to try it?'

'And if her medicine works, then what?'

'You continue as the reigning Elderman. It is what you want, isn't it?'

Even crusted and yellow, the Elderman's eyes still bore holes through me. I shift, sending needles of pain into my legs which have gone to sleep during the conversation.

'And what of you, my daughter?'

Digging my nails into my palms to steady my nerves, I meet his gaze. 'When the time comes, I will take my place by Dearon's side.'

It is the bargain we struck when I first left. It was enough then, and I hope it will still be enough.

The silence that follows lasts long enough that I wonder if the Elderman has fallen asleep. Perhaps he does drift off briefly before a violent fit of coughing raises him from the pillows. I offer him water, and we repeat the earlier steps.

Once he is lying down again, the Elderman nods. 'If the Plant Shaman's herbs can help me, you may return to Old London.'

I exhale my relief, but keep the triumphant smile off my face. 'Thank you.'

When I rise, blood rushes down to my legs and I take a faltering step to the side, wincing at the tingling pain. Before I get a chance to leave, the Elderman speaks, his eyes closed.

'Your mother passed you her spirit, but I had hoped that you might have inherited some of my sense of duty.'

He does not understand. I have his sense of duty, but it does not stop me from rebelling against what I view as unfair decisions made for me. My mother must have shared some of that feeling of injustice. Why else did she leave me a bank account and a car?

'What did my mother think of your decision to mate me to Dearon?'

'She said you had loved Dearon since the moment we placed you in his arms as a baby.'

'What about Dearon?'

'He knew from the beginning that you were precious. It pleased your mother a great deal.'

'But?' There must be a "but". Why else would she have given me the means to escape?

'She knew you were independent, stubborn. It concerned her, and she often said that she would have to broach the subject of your future gently with you.'

'But she didn't. She never said a word about it.' In hindsight, I wish it had been my mother who'd broken the news. Perhaps I would have taken it better. Then again, perhaps the betrayal would have been even greater.

'The time was never right.'

'Time is never right for the important conversations.'

The Elderman nods. 'Her condition deteriorated far quicker than anyone expected. It was left for me to explain the decision to you.'

'I remember.' Some of my anger seeps into my tone.

He surprises me when he says, 'I regret causing you so much anguish.'

'But not enough to change your mind?' I need to know.

'The choice I made is best for the conclave.'

After all this time, the statement was to be expected, but I cannot help the disappointment that wells within me. This is why I promised myself I would not go over old arguments with the Elderman. The only possible outcome is more pain for me.

With that in mind, I should bite my tongue, but I cannot. 'What about me and Dearon? Did you ever pause to consider what was best for us?'

'Benefiting the conclave is best for us all.'

'Yeah.' I shake my head, unwilling to rise to the bait any further. 'I'll return when I have medicine for you.'

It takes only minutes to pack my bag. In the two days I have been at the conclave, I have never unpacked. Perhaps I was hoping all along that I would find a reason to leave again.

70

Once more, I climb through the window and shut it behind me. Skirting around the edge of the clearing, I head to the car park without speaking to anyone. It is a coward's exit, but I have little desire to explain myself to the others. Helping to clean the deer carcass yesterday went some way towards easing their wariness, but they have not yet accepted me back into the conclave. Leaving now will undo the progress, even if I return in a matter of days. I should feel guilty, and yet all I feel is relief.

As I walk along paths covered in dry leaves, I draw in the power of the forest. I feel stronger than I have for many months, but I know that as soon as I return to Old London, my magic will begin to deplete. It is the price I pay for a different way of life, a price I did not attempt to explain to the Elderman. But even as I ensure my magic is charged, my thoughts are already steering towards practical matters.

I will need to call Karrion about tomorrow and pay a visit to Lady Bergamon. It will be too late to see her tonight. At some point soon, I will also need to visit Wishearth. I have missed his smoky presence and his sharp humour, even if I would never admit it to him. He will know I have been away, of that I am certain, but I am curious to see whether he will ask about my time at the conclave. Perhaps he already knows everything of importance.

I am putting my bags in the car when I hear someone approaching at speed. Ollie crashes through the bushes and yelps when he sees me. I turn just in time for him to leap into my arms and bang his head against my chin hard enough that I bite my tongue and taste blood.

'Ollie,' I protest, and he leaps at me again.

Pushing him away, I crouch and hug him. He squirms at the feel of my arms around him and twists his head to lick my ear. I close my eyes and allow myself to be suffused with his uncomplicated love. When I look up, I see Dearon standing on the path, partly obscured in the shadow of a towering ash tree. From the distance, I cannot tell whether his expression is one of anger, disappointment or sadness. My imagination conjures all three possibilities and mixes them into a scowl that leaves me feeling far less optimistic about the reprieve I have negotiated for myself.

Ollie whimpers in my arms, and I turn my attention back to him. I see hope in his eyes and I press a kiss on his forehead.

'I'm sorry. You can't come with me.' He nudges my neck, gentle all of a sudden. 'Your master is here, your place is in the pack. There are no rabbits to chase in London, no space for running. You belong at the conclave, where you can be wild and free.'

Does the same not apply to me?

I stop stroking Ollie and shake my head. The choice has been made, and it is time for me to return to Old London.

'Go,' I whisper. 'Go to him. I'll see you soon.'

At my urging, Ollie leaves. Every few steps, he pauses to look behind, but he does not stop until he reaches Dearon and lies down at his feet. I open my car door and raise a hand, hoping Dearon will say something. Instead, he turns and strides away. Ollie slinks behind him, his tail between his legs.

I slip into the car. As I drive away, I feel the burn of Dearon's silent anger long after I have left the conclave lands.

It takes me several hours of driving to find my equilibrium. When I do, I stop at a service station to get petrol and buy a coffee. Leaning against my car at the furthest corner of the car park, I call Karrion. He picks up after just two rings.

'Yan!' He sounds out of breath.

'How are you?'

'Where have you been?'

'I had to go back to the conclave for a few days.'

'Are you still there?'

'No, I'm on my way back.'

'What happened? Did you have to sneak away under cover of darkness?'

'Karrion, the sun is yet to set. I drove north, not to another time zone.'

'Point. But you didn't answer my questions.'

'No, I didn't sneak away.' That may be stretching the truth a little, but I am unwilling to offer a longer explanation at present. 'I'll tell you more about it tomorrow.'

'What happens tomorrow?'

I grin for the first time since leaving the conclave. 'Tomorrow we go back to work.'

'We have a case?'

'Jamie is bringing a potential client to meet us tomorrow morning. Can you get to mine by eight?'

'I'll be there at six if you wish.'

'Don't, or I might throw a log at you.'

Karrion laughs, and the sound eases some of the lingering anger within me. 'With your aim, I don't think I need to worry.'

The banter continues a little longer before we end the call. I am smiling as I carry the coffee cup to the nearest bin and navigate the maze of lanes back to the motorway.

It is late by the time I arrive in Old London, and sleep weighs heavily on me. I stretch my legs next to the car, and my eyes are drawn to the windows of the flat above mine. They are dark, which is to be expected. Jans is in prison, and it will no doubt take the landlord a while to find a new tenant. Whoever my new neighbour will be, the first thing I will do is make sure they are not another Leech. But even knowing that the flat above mine is empty, I hesitate before descending the steps to my front door.

The flat is cold and the office downstairs damp after days of having stood empty. I leave the lights off as I fumble my way upstairs. Before I attend to my nagging bladder or unpack my bag, I build a fire in the lounge fireplace. A clay bowl by the log basket holds short lengths of dry fir. I light one of them and, when the flames are licking my nails, let it fall on to the fire.

'Hearth Spirit, ward this home and its inhabitants. We thank you for the light you offer and for the protection you give.'

Five minutes later, when I crawl into bed – nothing more than a double mattress on the floor in front of the fireplace – I fall asleep safe in the knowledge that Wishearth is guarding my rest.

TUESDAY

8

A Prospective Client

Hunger wakes me at dawn. I roll on to my back with a groan, but the hollow feeling in my stomach makes it clear that sleep is no longer on the cards. It is only now I remember that the fridge was empty when I left.

I recall the taste of deer liver and the smell of fresh meat, and my hunger takes on an edge of wildness. Food should be gathered from the woods and rivers, not purchased from a shop, and the emptiness in my belly should be all the motivation I need to hunt. But that does not happen in Old London. That is not my life here.

The sadness welling within me forces me up. The fire has reduced to ash, and the chill of the autumn has returned to the room. I waste no time getting dressed and splashing cold water on my face, which chases away the last vestiges of sleep. I pull my hair into a ponytail and pick up a coat on my way out.

As soon as I climb up the stairs from my front door, the noises of the rush hour hit me. Even without any hearing enhancement, the sound is too loud and I shake my head. The stink of the city overwhelms me. My wilder side recoils, urging me to flee back to where I belong. But I take in a few deep breaths, focusing on the movement of my lungs rather than the smells. When I look around,

I concentrate on the spell sprayed on the pavement, on the poster advertising potions affixed to a lamp post, and on the thrum of magic all around me.

Old London – covering the City of London borough – where magical races co-exist peacefully with the humans of New London has a very special feeling of power. It is not the same natural flow of magic I sensed at the conclave, but centuries of spells have left their mark on Old London. I feel it in the buildings, taste it in the air, hear it in the echoes of those who have been before me. Some claim this area of London is haunted, but I say it is a side effect of so much magic concentrated in one area. We gather here because of the magic, and our magic feeds the lure that pulls us to congregate here.

The echoes of power ground me while I walk to a corner shop and pick up basic provisions for breakfast. I know the owner well enough to exchange pleasantries, but today I choose not to linger for a chat.

I am a yard from my flat when a pigeon lands on the iron railing and I grin. Sure enough, when I turn, Karrion is striding towards me with a grin that matches mine. Even the presence of the pigeon does not bother him. Without preamble, he pulls me into a hug that crunches something in my back. I grunt in pain, and he lets go of me.

'Sorry, Yan.' He looks embarrassed. 'Also, hi.'

'Morning.' I set the shopping bag down and stretch my arms back. The hug does not appear to have done any damage.

Karrion's plumage consists of piercings, hair dyed black and clothes adorned with studs and chains, and the sight brings another smile to my face. In keeping with the image, his preference is to associate only with ravens and crows, but pigeons are drawn to him. It frustrates him for he does not yet see that the pigeons represent elements of himself: courage, perseverance and love.

'Did you get stuff for breakfast?' he asks and picks up the shopping bag.

'Yes.' I follow him down to the door, and he opens it with his set of keys. 'The fridge is empty.'

'That doesn't surprise me. Mum sent some stuff she baked yesterday after church.' On his way through the office, Karrion switches on the electric radiator and glances at me. 'Might as well make this place a little more habitable before the prospective client arrives.'

Together we unpack the groceries, and Karrion adds a tin of homemade bread rolls and a ginger cake from his bag. I am touched by his mother's thoughtfulness.

'Why don't I cook breakfast while you take a shower?' Karrion sniffs my shoulder. 'You smell of smoke and other outdoorsy things.'

'Do you think I can trust you with a frying pan?' I do my best to keep a straight face.

'Hey, I'm a lot better cook than you are, Miss Can't-Even-Boil-A-Potato.'

'I'm not that bad,' I protest, but at the twist of his lips, I have to concede the point. 'Though I'm not great either.'

I head downstairs to the shower. Standing under the hot spray, I reach for my shower gel. It will wash away those outdoorsy smells Karrion mentioned, but I cannot help wishing it would also cleanse me of the anger I carry. That anger has no place in Old London and in the life I want to lead. As much as I struggled to fit back into the conclave life, so too have I brought something back with me in the form of the bitterness I still harbour. It is not part of Yannia Wilde, PI working in Old London, but I am not certain how to set it aside. Every word I spoke in anger, every hurtful comment my father made swirls around my mind until I am all but lost and I long for the distraction of a case. If I can throw myself into work, perhaps I will be able to regain the sense of purpose I found last week.

By the time I return from the shower, still braiding my hair, the smell of beans, bacon and toast is filling the flat. I follow my growling stomach to the kitchen and notice Karrion has filled my log basket. He learned early on that the easiest way to help me is not to ask if I need him to do anything, but simply to do things for me. I tried to object at first, but he has never made a big deal out of it and I have come to value his quiet support.

Karrion hands me a plate of food, and we sit in the lounge. While we eat, I fill him in on the reason for my hasty departure and what happened at the conclave. I leave out the hunt with Dearon and the night I spent with him, but I do explain about the bargain I struck with the Elderman. If he notices the omissions, he says nothing.

When our plates are empty, we head downstairs. The office has warmed up. Karrion switches on my laptop and opens a blank document, ready to take notes. I am about to wonder out loud whether Jamie is likely to be punctual when the doorbell rings.

'Our prospective client is early.'

I open the door to find Jamie waiting outside. Another man is standing on the first step up, looking towards the street and the side of the building. When I move aside to let them in, I cast my senses out to the garden, searching for an animal. Sure enough, a hedgehog is sniffing for slugs under a blackberry bush. I borrow its nose and inhale, focusing on the stranger. Beneath aftershave, deodorant and laundry detergent are only natural pheromones. He is human.

Jamie nods a greeting and motions to the other man. 'This is Tim Wedgbury. Between us, we have a curious tale to tell.'

'Yannia Wilde,' I say, offering him my hand. Tim shakes it with a frown.

'I know.' He gets out his wallet. 'I have your card.'

'You do?'

Karrion comes to stand behind me, craning his neck to look over my shoulder. The business card in Tim's hand is mine, from stock I had printed about a month ago.

'A man gave it to me last week and said something about this address having the finest hearth in Old London.'

From the dawning understanding on Karrion's face, I know he has jumped to the same conclusion as I have. He takes the card from Tim, turns it over and even smells it. As a last resort, he gives it a vigorous shake. Nothing happens.

'Why would Wishearth have one of your business cards?' Karrion asks and gives the card back to Tim.

'Who knows? Maybe it's the sort of thing fairy godmothers like to do.'

Karrion snorts.

Jamie has been listening to the conversation with open curiosity. 'Who's Wishearth?' he asks.

'A friend,' I say. On the off chance that someone is eavesdropping, I add, 'One who likes to meddle.'

I introduce Karrion to Tim, and we all sit down. A week ago, a North Mage and a Feykin were sitting across the desk from me; now two humans. But what would a human want with a private investigator in Old London?

'Tell me your curious tale,' I say while studying Tim.

He is tall and lanky, dressed in a suit that looks to be off the rack, but not cheap. His dark brown hair is cut short, functional rather than fashionable. Brown eyes watching me are cautious and there are dark circles under them. He is tired and sceptical. Where did Wishearth find him?

'Someone has killed me twice,' Tim says.

Next to me, Karrion makes a disbelieving noise and then casts an apologetic glance across the desk.

I fix my attention on Jamie. 'I'd say that's impossible, but there's been a lot of that going on recently.'

Jamie nods. 'But this is weird. Last week, paramedics were called to a scene of a mugging off Shaftesbury Avenue. A male victim had been stabbed and before he died, he told them his name was Timothy Wedgbury. The body, the blood and the knife he'd been stabbed with all faded away, right before the paramedics' eyes.'

'Faded away, as in magic?' Karrion interrupts.

'That's what the Mage at the scene said. He didn't get there until the next day, given that the case was considered a low priority. The opening of the alley contained magical residue, but not enough for him to identify a spell. He concluded that Mages from Old London had decided to play a prank on humans.'

'Where do you fit in?' I ask Tim. 'Other than sharing a name with the man who faded away.'

'The investigating police sergeant ran the victim's name through the DVLA database and found a driver's licence for a man matching the description,' Jamie says. 'The police paid Tim a visit and found him to be very much alive. It was that, together with the Mage's report that led to the case being dismissed as a prank.'

'What changed New Scotland Yard's mind?' Karrion asks.

'It happened again,' Tim says.

'You were stabbed and died?' I frown.

'No, this time it was a car accident outside Liverpool Street Station. A man got hit by a van and died at the scene before fading away. Once again, the victim was identified as Tim Wedgbury and he looked like Tim. Yet, Tim's alive and well.'

'And that's where you come in?' I say to Jamie.

'Yes. I heard talk of the case and requested the files. Officially, the only crimes committed have been wasting public resources. Unofficially, something doesn't feel right. The Mage attending the second crime scene concluded a Feykin spell had been responsible. If the people dying in these pranks were different, I might think they were the work of a couple of bored magic users. But the same man dying twice feels targeted, even if the casters were different. Besides, he wasn't alone the second time, and I worry there are more people, Tim included, who are in real danger.'

'That's why Detective Manning suggested that we turn to you for help.'

From what little they have told me, I am intrigued. The stakes of the case are different from the Marsh investigation. Last time, an innocent man died. Now, an innocent man has died twice already, and yet he lives. But this time, the price of success should not be a further failure. That alone tempts me to accept the case. And even though Marsh was executed, it was the Paladins' decision. Karrion and I proved ourselves capable of solving an aristocratic cover up. Time to build on that.

'I'll take the case, and we'll do what we can.'

Karrion's magic flares at the inclusion, and his knee nudges my leg. I detail my charges to Tim, and we go through the formalities of paperwork. Jamie watches me, satisfaction evident in his relaxed posture.

'I have a few things for you to get started.' Jamie opens his briefcase and passes me a cardboard wallet.

'Case files?' I hazard a guess.

'And CCTV from the second death.'

'You have CCTV?'

'Yes, though you'll see that it's of limited use.'

Now I am curious, but I force myself to set the wallet on the table and focus on Tim.

'Why don't you tell me a little bit about yourself?'

'I'm an investment manager in the City. I live in Braintree in Essex and catch a train to Liverpool Street every morning. My office is a short walk from the station. I'm single, have been for a while, and live with my mother. She's... not well.'

'Can you think of anyone who'd want to harm you, in particular, anyone living in Old London?'

'No. My life is completely ordinary.'

Karrion and I exchange a sceptical glance. Seeing this, Tim shakes his head.

'It's true. I go to work, I catch the train home, and I look after my mother. On weekends, I just look after

Mum. I have no hobbies that would take me out of the house, no real friends and certainly no enemies.'

'So why you? Of all the people who pass through Old London every day, why target you?'

'That's what you'll have to figure out. I hope you're up to the task.'

'I am,' a glance to my left, 'we are.'

'Do you have any clients at work who might bear a grudge against you?' Karrion asks.

'As you can appreciate, some of the investments we make for our clients are high risk and they incur losses as well as gains. But when an angry client calls to have a go at someone, it's usually one of the directors, not me.'

'Are there any who blame you personally for their losses or who've sent you threats?'

'No. I have a good, or at least fair, relationship with all the clients I look after. I can't recall a client ever being angry enough to threaten me, or anyone on my team.'

'And your colleagues, do you get along with them?' I ask.

'Yes,' Tim says. 'I don't like all of them, but I make a point of keeping my personal feelings separate from working relationships. Plenty of people in the office meet socially, but I haven't been able to do much of that recently because of Mum.'

'Have you noticed anyone following you on your way to or from the train station?'

'No.'

'Has a stranger approached you and tried to threaten or scam you?'

'No.'

'Have you noticed anyone paying particular attention to you on the train or in Old London?'

'No.'

'Have you felt unsafe without being able to pinpoint why?'

'No.'

'How about your neighbours? Is there anyone you don't get along with?'

'Mum and I keep to ourselves for the most part, but when she last went missing, everyone on the street joined the search party.' Tim tugs at his left sleeve. 'Although—'

'Although?'

'A couple of months ago, Mum wandered off and got into our neighbour's house. The woman who lives there was doing some gardening and the door was unlocked. Mum doesn't understand electric kettles, and she put it on the hob to make tea. She started a fire, but luckily it was caught quickly. I paid for the damages, of course, but Janet doesn't like us much.'

'We'll check it out. What's her address?'

Tim gives us the house number, and Karrion adds it to his notes.

'Do you know if Janet has magical blood?' I ask.

'As far as I know, everyone living on my street is human.'

It is a tacit reminder that we see the world in a different light. In Old London, the assumption is that everyone has power. Outside our borders, the assumption is that everyone is human. All magic users grow up knowing that humans outnumber us a thousand to one.

I glance at Karrion, and he shrugs. We are both out of questions.

Tim stands. 'Unless there's anything else, I need to get to the office.'

'We'll review the case files and the CCTV,' I say. 'I'll keep in touch about the progress we make and with any further queries we have for you.'

'Thank you.' Tim shakes first my and then Karrion's hand. He is almost at the door when I jump up.

'Wait. This may sound strange, but has anything else odd happened to you recently? Anything at all?'

Tim considers the question, a hand resting on the door handle. Karrion had already closed the notes file and now opens it again.

'Sunday evening, I thought there was a car crash outside my house. That's what it sounded like. But when I went outside to check, I found a quiet street and no crash.'

'Any glass on the ground?'

'Nothing. I assumed I either imagined it or a neighbour had turned the volume of their TV right up and then down again.'

'Do you recall what time it was?'

'About nine, I think.'

'Thank you.'

We say our goodbyes, and I close the door behind Tim. Jamie has remained sitting and has leant back in his chair, crossing his feet at the ankles. He seems emboldened, as if we are meeting as equals for the first time. The longing for my magic still lurks beneath the surface, but perhaps it matters less.

'You've handed us quite the mystery,' I say as I return to my seat.

'This could be my way of conducting a job interview.'

'If that's the case, you'd have to hire us both.'

'I haven't ruled it out,' Jamie says and leans forward. 'Seriously, though, I'm glad you're on the case. This one gives me a bad vibe.'

'As I said to Tim, we'll do what we can.'

'I know. And whatever help I can offer, you need only to ask. Unofficially, of course.'

'We appreciate it.'

Jamie takes his leave, but he turns at the door, his expression serious. 'As much as you say Wishearth is meddling, I'm glad that you have people keeping an eye on you. Your chosen profession isn't without its dangers, and you're beginning to make a name for yourself.'

He sees himself out.

9

LITTLE TO GO ON

Karrion stares at the closed door, a frown creasing his brow.

'A feather for your thoughts?' I ask.

'I get that Jamie is concerned with your wellbeing, but what a ridiculous comment to make. As if you can't look after yourself.'

I smile, flushed with affection for Karrion. 'Reliable back-up never hurt anyone.'

He crosses his arms. 'There's a difference between having back-up and needing someone to take care of you.'

'You're right. And out of the two of you, I'd rather you got that than Jamie.'

'I do.' I see uncertainty in his eyes. 'And you must know that although I insist on helping you out, it's not because I think you can't manage on your own.'

'Karrion, I know that.' I laugh out loud, feeling the corners of my mouth twisting into a wicked grin. 'Can you imagine what Jamie would say if he knew I'm sick and have EDS? No way would he send work my way, if he already thinks I need you, Wishearth and him to protect me.'

Karrion joins in the laughter. 'I won't tell him if you don't.'

'Deal.'

Pointing towards the papers Tim signed, Karrion asks, 'Shall I run to the bank?'

It is another parallel to last week when the first task I gave him as my new apprentice was cashing a cheque. This time, the balance on the office account is further from red and there are other matters that are more pressing.

'Not yet. I want to go through the case files first and figure out a plan for the next couple of days. And I'll need to pay a visit to Lady Bergamon. She's expecting a full account of last week's investigation, and I need to ask her about possible herbal medications for the Elderman.'

'There must be something I can do on Tim's case while you are chatting to Lady B about herbs.'

'Lady B? Since when have you started abbreviating her name?'

'I thought I'd give it a go.'

'I don't recommend doing so in her presence. We don't know her well enough to be sure she won't take offence.'

'Of course not.'

'Good. Let's go upstairs and see what Jamie brought us.' I lean over to switch off the radiator. 'It's getting stuffy in here.'

We move upstairs, and I build a small fire to ward off the autumn chill. At the back of my mind lingers a thought that Wishearth may want to see that the nudge he gave Tim worked. At least, this is what I assume Wishearth intended. Hearth Spirits are not mortal, and their way of looking at the world is different. From what I have gathered, Wishearth cares nought for the lives of mortals, except those he considers his friends.

I fall into that category, and I consider him a friend too. Ours is an easy companionship, and on the rare occasions that he touches me, the heat of his fingers lifts some of the pain that never goes away. Still, we are by no means close, and Wishearth remains an enigma.

When I empty the contents of the cardboard wallet on to the table, my optimism regarding the case fades. In the Braeman murder, the file was enormous. The two reports concerning Tim have barely enough information to fill three sheets of paper.

'Which one do you want?' I hold up the files. 'Death by white van, or a mugging gone wrong?'

'Van.'

I pass Karrion the second file, and we both focus on reading. It does not take long for him to look up from the papers, but he remains silent until I, too, have finished.

'Anything interesting in the file?' he asks.

'Not a whole lot. In the little time they had with the victim, the paramedics noticed a single stab wound to the left side of the torso. They think the knife hit the liver and punctured his left lung. The victim would have gone into shock and died from internal bleeding. They saw no other injuries on him. As Jamie said, the knife faded away alongside the body and all the blood. There was nothing else in the alley that seemed to relate to the crime or prank, whichever it was.'

'And the Mage report?'

'Three lines is hardly a report. A South Mage stated that there was magical residue present in the alley, but it was too faint for him to determine which spell might have been used, beyond that it had been cast by a Mage.'

'So we have nothing?'

'We don't have a lot. But there is something in the report worth following up. The paramedics said there was a homeless man at the scene when they arrived and he was administering first aid. It was he who told the paramedics the victim's name and that Tim had been mugged.'

'Maybe he left something out?'

'That's what I was wondering. The paramedics weren't interviewing him to establish the particulars of the crime, only to find out who the victim was. It's possible he saw or heard something else.'

Karrion taps his papers against the desk. 'It's not going to be easy finding a homeless man in either London.'

'No. He gave his name as Bob and he was near Shaftesbury Avenue late at night. It's not much, but it's a start.'

'That's something I could do this afternoon, isn't it? I can try to track down Bob.'

'That may be best attempted in the evening.' I set my papers down. 'That's what I've got to share. How about you?'

'Not much. A lot of what's in this file is the insurance companies of the van driver and the taxi he crashed into arguing over who's liable. The main argument seems to be that a crash resulting from a magical prank cannot be the van driver's fault.'

'What of the victim?'

'Suffered injuries consistent with a vehicle collision: broken bones and a head injury. Lots of cuts and bruises. The specific cause of death was undetermined because the body disappeared. All the stuff the paramedics used was left behind, *sans* any blood.'

I lean back in the chair. Karrion notices my expression and pauses his summary.

'If the body and blood disappeared, but the items used on the victim remained, it means that the spell was limited to the victim alone. I say victim because I'm not yet convinced he truly was Tim. In any case, the victim could interact with the real world until the spell wore off, at which point he vanished, but any consequences of his actions remained.'

'Do you know of a spell that could do that?'

'No, but I'm no Mage. We'll need to find someone to help with that aspect of our enquiries.'

'Should we turn to Lord Wellaim Ellensthorne for help?' Karrion asks with a crooked grin.

I snort. 'Oh, I can see that happening. The First among the Shadow Mages probably hasn't got anything better to do with his time, especially now that he's looking to use the High Council of Mages to advance his elitist agenda.'

'Plus, you made such a great impression when you accused him of murder.'

'There is that. Shame the police did nothing about the blackmail.'

'But you know about it. That information might come in handy someday.'

'Are you suggesting I stoop to Ellensthorne's level?'

'Not at all,' Karrion says. 'But he doesn't know that.'

'You'd make a fine politician, Karrion. Nevertheless, I think we'll have to find another Mage to help us. Ilana blames me for her father's death, so she's out too.'

'What is it about you that alienates Mages?'

'Must be my charming personality.' I roll my eyes. 'Back to the case.'

'Right. The sequence of events went like this: a man walks between two parked cars, turns to speak while stepping on to the road. He never sees the white van or the driver fumbling with his phone and gets hit side on. The victim is flung further on to the road, and the van crashes into a taxi. Bystanders call an ambulance, which arrives in record time. The paramedics have maybe a minute to administer first aid before the victim dies and fades away.'

'What did the Mage report say?'

'She couldn't get any clear trace of the spell. Like with the first event, the Mage was there too long after the accident. But she did think it was Feykin magic.'

'Which is why the police thought the pranks were unconnected,' I say.

'Lucky for Tim, Jamie was more on the ball.' Karrion jots a note on the margin of the paper he is holding. 'But I do think it's odd there were two casters doing pretty much the same thing to Tim.'

'It would be logical to assume they were doing it together.'

'Or could it be an attempt to throw the police off the caster's scent?' Karrion asks.

'What do you mean?'

'Is it possible for a Mage or a Feykin to cast a spell that makes their magic appear like it comes from a different caster?'

'It's an interesting point, but it does show a level of premeditation that worries me. We'll add that to the list of ideas to explore.'

Karrion gets a small notebook out and scrawls on an empty page. The notebook is identical to the one I carry with me, and I duck my head to hide a smile.

'What about the other person?' I ask. 'Jamie said the victim was with someone.'

'Yep. She was there when the victim was hit and then she vanished.'

'Vanished as in faded away like the victim, or simply disappeared in the general chaos that followed? Could she be one of the casters behind all this?'

'I don't know. Maybe the answer is on the CCTV Jamie gave us?'

'Let's find out.'

I open a folder on the memory stick. Jamie appears to have done most of the work for us, and the video clips are numbered. Choosing to view them in order, I open the first clip.

It affords us a view of a square, which is partially covered by a white canopy. After a few seconds, I realise it is Bishop's Square next to the Spitalfields Market. There are a few people hurrying across the square, but no one is sitting on the benches. If the weekend was as cold in Old London as it was at the conclave, I am not surprised the benches are unoccupied.

'Whoa,' Karrion says.

On the screen, two figures have appeared in the middle of the square. My first thought is that the man is Tim, my second that I am not certain. Both figures are blurred, like an out-of-focus photograph. The effect is strongest around the faces, but one of the people is a woman. All I can tell is that her hair is down around her shoulders and her build is slender. I squint, my eyes watering.

'Is it my imagination, or are those two blinking in and out of view?'

'Play it again,' Karrion says.

I do so, and this time I keep my eyes fixed on the centre of the square. The figures appear out of thin air, already in motion. As before, they are not in focus.

'Do you reckon the blurriness only affects cameras?' Karrion asks.

'Mixing magic with technology is unpredictable. It wouldn't surprise me if the illusion the Feykin used was only designed for mortal eyes.'

'If that's the case, we're lucky we can see anything on tape.'

The couple stops by the awning, just in view of the camera as they kiss. I glance at Karrion.

'Tim said he was single,' I say.

'Maybe he's into casual sex,' Karrion says, though he does not sound convinced.

'From the little he told us of his life, I doubt it. Besides,' I point at the screen, 'does that look like casual sex to you?'

'No. It's a shame we don't have audio.'

'Most of that looks like flirting.'

Despite the blurriness of the figures, their expressions seem clear to me. It is odd, given that I cannot describe either of them.

We watch as the couple kiss for a little longer and then head towards Brushfield Street. The clip ends after they have walked out of view. I call up the next one, and they turn towards Liverpool Street Station.

'It looks like the woman is heading for the bus stop whereas Tim is catching a train,' Karrion says, eyes fixed on the screen.

'Which means that whoever the Feykin illusionist is, they know Tim well enough to know where he lives.'

'Or at least how he travels to and from London.'

On the next clip, the couple walks along Bishopsgate and stops across the road from the station entrance. The rest we already know. Tim walks between the parked taxis and turns. He says something as he steps out on to the road, and the van hits him. The van driver stumbles out, drops his phone, and a crowd gathers around Tim.

When I shift my focus to the woman, she is nowhere to be seen.

'Wait. Where did the woman go?'

Karrion rewinds the clip, and this time I keep my eyes on the woman. She appears to notice the van right before it hits Tim and raises her arm. After the impact, she covers her mouth while people rush past her. With her line of sight to Tim broken, she fades from view.

'She disappeared first,' Karrion says and plays the clip again. 'What does that mean?'

'I'm not sure. I can't even tell which of them is the focal point of the spell.'

'That depends on the Feykin's intentions. Was Tim meant to get hurt?'

'Maybe they are simple accidents.'

'Two accidents involving an illusion of the same man? That seems unlikely.'

'I agree. But how can we be certain they are illusions?'

'That's what the Mages said in their reports,' Karrion says, finding the right spot in the car crash report and showing it to me.

'True, but that doesn't mean they were right. They only had faint magical residue to analyse. I doubt they could say anything definitive.'

'What else could it be? Homunculi?'

I cock my head. 'Homunculi?'

'They're an urban legend, like Leeches or Lady Bergamon. Mages are supposedly able to create artificial helpers out of bones and human skin and mandrake root. They're like miniaturised humans, and their maker has complete control over them.'

'It's an interesting theory, but the versions of Tim were fully grown. Although it's hard to judge from the CCTV, I'd say the man on the screen was the same height as the real Tim.'

'Maybe they were golems instead. They're human size or a bit larger. And rumour has it, they're made of flesh.'

'Even if they were constructed out of flesh, I doubt they'd bleed like humans do, let alone present the right sort of injuries following a vehicle collision. Besides, how many Mages do you know who have a golem?'

'I'm willing to bet Lord Ellensthorne's house is full of them. And we never went down to the basement of the Braeman residence.'

'Here I was, thinking that you had to construct golems in the loft to be close to thunderstorms,' I say, holding back laughter.

'No, you're confusing golems and Frankenstein.'

'Monster.'

'What?' Karrion drops his pen and bends to pat around the floor. When he rises, he catches the side of his head on the edge of the table and winces.

'Frankenstein was the scientist. The construct was his monster.'

'Right. Why was that important again?'

'I was trying to make the point that I don't think whatever was hit by the van was a golem. It acted like a human and reacted like a human. Or an illusion of one.'

Karrion thinks for a moment, and his expression brightens. 'Got it. Someone is killing Tim's doppelgängers and hiding the bodies under an invisibility spell.'

'And what? The bodies disintegrated upon turning invisible so the paramedics could find no trace of them?'

'Vampires. Invisible bats. It explains everything.' Karrion bites his lip to keep a straight face. He fails.

'Need I remind you that vampires don't exist?'

'You're the one who said last week that there are unexplored places in the British Isles and beyond. Who's to say vampires can't be living in coastal caves with their pet bats?'

'True. But as amusing as your suggestions are, none of them is viable. Other than an illusion, what else could cause copies of Tim to walk around London?'

Karrion's grin fades into concentration. 'I was going to suggest that a Feykin and a Mage are murdering people and using glamour to make the victims look like Tim, but that wouldn't explain the disappearing bodies.'

'It's possible there were two spells in effect: one to make the victim look like Tim, and the other to make the body disappear.'

'If that's the case, the casters must have been nearby. There was nothing in the paramedics' report about a spell caster, was there?'

I check my share of the file and shake my head. 'It's something we should ask Bob about. Could the paramedics have missed the Mage while they were attending to Tim?'

'And the Feykin. If they're in cahoots, they were both there.'

'It's hard to miss two casters, even in a darkened alley.'

'There's always invisibility spheres,' Karrion says. 'What about the car crash? It would have been easy to cast a spell from the crowd.'

'Lucky for us, we have CCTV.'

We spend half an hour going through the clips. Plenty of people are watching the paramedics and taking photos, but we cannot spot anyone casting a spell. We watch the footage again to see if anyone is acting suspiciously. Again, we gain no new insight.

'Could the answer be something different?' Karrion asks.

'Such as?'

'Could they be using an artefact?'

'We saw no one pointing a staff or a rod at the victim.'

'That's not what I meant. They could have planted an item on Tim, or whoever the victim was, and triggered it with a command word. Abracadabra, the body goes poof.'

'I'm pretty sure no self-respecting magic user would ever say Abracadabra. But it's a good point. If Mages can imbue warding magic into heart copper and true silver symbols, why shouldn't they be able to use objects as conduits for other spells?'

'I couldn't have put it better myself.'

I nudge his shoulder. 'We need to add talking to a Mage to our list of things to do.'

'Just as soon as we find a Mage that stays on good terms with you.'

Ignoring the jibe, I turn my attention to the time stamp on the screen. 'See that?'

'It says nine fifteen. What of it?'

Pausing the footage, I call up the notes Karrion took earlier and scroll to the end. I was right.

'Look, here. Tim said he heard a crash outside his house about nine on Sunday night.'

'So? He doesn't live anywhere near Bishopsgate.'

'No, but don't you think it's odd that while an illusionary version of him, or whatever the spell is, gets hit by a van in Old London, he hears a car crash in Essex?'

'You think they're related?'

'I do. He found no trace of a crash on the street. Perhaps the cars involved simply faded away because of more magic, or perhaps the explanation is more complex than that.' I close the notes. 'But it already tells us something.'

'What's that?'

'If the two incidents are connected, it wasn't caused by a magical prank. Something bigger is going on.'

'But why target a human?'

'We don't even know Tim is the target, though perhaps it's a safe assumption for now. But if the casters are using magic to make other people look like Tim, the victims could be anyone.'

'And since they keep disappearing, we don't know for certain.'

'Nothing like a simple case to get us back into investigative mode.' We laugh.

'What's the plan, boss?'

'You did say something about running to the bank.' I grin at his look of surprise. 'It's one task for you, but another is more urgent. I want you to go through this footage and get as clear a screenshot as possible of the woman. Email it to Tim and see if he recognises her.'

'You want me to contact Tim? By myself?'

'You're more than capable.'

Karrion's chest puffs with pride, and I feel the change in his magic as a thousand downy strokes against my aura. He pulls the laptop to him.

'When you've emailed Tim, go to the bank to cash his cheque. The second half of Ilana's payment is in the top drawer. Take that with you as well. You know where the paying-in book is for the office account.'

'Will do, Yan. Give Lady Bergamon my best.'

Having fetched a basket of dishes Lady Bergamon left me last week, I leave Karrion to the video footage and head over to Ivy Street and another era of Old London's history.

10

LADY BERGAMON'S GARDEN

From the outside, Lady Bergamon's house looks almost like all the others along the street. Almost, because her paved driveway is covered with a wild array of potted plants. The organisation of them is different from last week, and this strikes me as curious. It must have taken a great deal of effort to change the arrangement of pots when they are so tightly packed.

A narrow path wends around some of the larger pots on its way to the door. I brush my hand on leaves, feeling the low hum of magic that comes from life and growth and rot. It is my kind of magic, which is why I have felt kinship with Lady Bergamon since we first met.

Today, I reach the front steps without the door opening. Wishearth may have warned her of my visit, but then again, how would he know? It is unlikely that he spends all his time keeping tabs on me. I knock and turn back to survey the plants as I wait.

The pots are the first hint of the wonders that lie beyond the door, and they are a subtle show of a Plant Shaman's power. If Lady Bergamon is in her garden, it may take some time for her to reach the door. But as large as her domain may be, she must have an awareness of it all, including the house and the front door. It will be a matter of being patient.

My thoughts are interrupted when the door opens, and my smile brightens when I turn to greet Lady Bergamon. Tall and thin, her frame belies the strength of an oak tree. White hair cascades past her shoulders, and her cornflower blue eyes are filled with affection as she regards me. Just like her magic, she is filled with vitality and wisdom. Simply by being in her company, I have my patience rewarded many times over.

'Yannia. This is a lovely surprise.' She beckons me in.

Although her scent remains fresh in my memory, I borrow the nose of a cat snoozing in the house and inhale the aromas of dark soil, nectar, fresh green shoots and rotting plants. The heady brew relaxes me, reaffirming the connection I feel with Lady Bergamon.

'I brought you back your dishes.' I hand her the basket. 'And I hope I haven't caught you at a bad time.'

'Not at all. I was wondering when you might visit.' She closes the door. 'Go through to the garden. It rained earlier, but the sun should have dried the table and chairs by now. I'll put the kettle on. How's the pain today?'

I smile, a little uncomfortable with the question despite her quiet compassion.

'It's manageable.'

'I'll prepare something for it, then. And your shoulder? Has the wound healed?'

'Barely noticeable now.'

'Good.'

Lady Bergamon is like Karrion in that she does not wait for me to ask for help. I am disconcerted by it, as I was on first meeting her when she read me like an open book. Meanwhile, I thank her with a nod and walk out of the back door. When I step over the threshold, my vision goes blurry and I am no longer in the same Old London as before.

Past the small patio covered with more plant pots, the garden stretches far beyond the few square feet the houses along this street should have. The air is heavy with the fragrance of flowers and grass, and the only sound I can hear is birdsong.

Walking further from the back door, I unzip my coat. The rest of Old London may be having a damp, overcast day, but here it is still late summer, and the sun feels warm on my face. Seasons appear to have little meaning in the garden, and plants of all seasons flourish concurrently. But I do note that the leaves of the nearby apple and cherry trees are beginning to turn yellow and red when last week they were in full blossom. Or am I thinking of an orchard elsewhere in the garden?

While I wait for Lady Bergamon, I crouch on the edge of the lawn to observe bees swarming around a cluster of rapscallion roses. A curious bumblebee abandons its pollination to buzz around my face. I extend my hand, and it lands on my fingertip. The hairy body and spindly legs tickle my skin while it explores. When it has satisfied its curiosity, it flies off to resume feeding.

'They are such sweethearts,' Lady Bergamon says as she sets a tray on the table. 'The bees are so friendly, I have no need for protective clothing when I collect the honey.'

'I imagine the honey your bees produce is unlike anything sold in London.'

'Or anywhere in the country.' She smiles. 'Now, come and sit. You're just in time for lunch.'

Her words remind me that I said nothing to Karrion about lunch and I get my phone out only to see that I have no signal. Of course. Where I am standing, phone masts will not be invented for several hundred years. I have to trust Karrion will raid my fridge if he gets hungry.

Lady Bergamon has prepared a large bowl of salad for us, together with a pot of tea for herself and a smaller tea infuser for me. She removes a cloth covering a bread-board and cuts slices of dark, crusty bread.

'I make the bread myself from grains that grow wild on meadows here.'

She passes me a slice and a butter dish and fills two wide bowls with salad. No doubt everything in the salad, the chicken included, has also been grown by her.

'Are you self-sufficient?' I ask.

'For all basic provisions, yes, other than milk. I once kept a few cows, but I found the work too much. These days, I let the milkman do the work for me. I shop once a month for more exotic items, such as oranges and pomegranates. I blame Wishearth for those.'

'How so?' Every answer she gives fuels my curiosity.

'He brings them as gifts sometimes, spices too. He claims he spent a few centuries as a djinn in Arabia, but I'm not sure I believe him. Wishearth says a lot of things.'

Ducking my head, I hide my grin and butter the slice of bread. 'Is it wise to call a spirit a liar?'

'I've called him many things over the years and liar isn't the worst of them.'

'I'm intrigued.'

Lady Bergamon's face lights with mirth, but she says nothing further as she pours me pale amber tea and adds

106

a spoonful of honey. I accept it with a grateful smile.

The bread has a rich, nutty flavour and is full of seeds. I can taste the simple ingredients and enjoy it all the more for them. As much as I have grown used to the varied cuisine of humans, I miss the foods of the conclave. Lady Bergamon lives by many of the same self-sufficient principles as the Wild Folk, except I presume she must hunt less. I have no idea how many, if any, game animals live in the garden.

'Last time we met, you were in the middle of a case,' she says. 'Will you tell me how it all ended?'

Over cups of tea, salad and, later, carrot cake, I tell her everything. I tell her of the flaw in the justice system and of the Paladin General's choice to execute Jonathain Marsh to protect the citizens of Old London. Everyone present at the meeting was sworn to silence, but I trust Lady Bergamon. It is a relief to be able to unburden myself, to share my doubts and regrets with her.

When I finish, Lady Bergamon sets her fork down.

'I don't envy the Paladin General,' she says. 'The price of power is having to make the difficult decisions.'

The arguments we made in that meeting spring to my mind, and the memory of Ilana's pleas for her father still sting with the bitterness of failure.

'As much as I understand the reasons behind it, I'm not sure I could have condemned an innocent man to death,' I say.

Lady Bergamon dabs her mouth with a napkin. 'That is the benefit of insignificance; we will not be called upon to make such choices. What a shame Ilana Marsh couldn't understand that.'

'You don't like her.' I had sensed Lady Bergamon's disapproval of Ilana when she came to offer her healing in the aftermath of Jans's attack.

'I'm sure she's perfectly lovely, but you were never going to be able to give her what she craved from you.'

'And what's that?'

'Wildness. Freedom. The courage to make your own way in this world.'

'It's not as easy as it seems,' I say.

'But she was never going to understand that. To her, you were the embodiment of everything she wanted to have, but couldn't.'

My expression must betray the sadness within me, for Lady Bergamon reaches across the table to cover my hand with hers.

'It's not a criticism of you. People like that will come and go, there'll always be someone who wants something you can't give. Every relationship should be an act of giving, without seeking to measure that which is held back. In my experience, the true satisfaction is in the exchange, in the knowledge that you have received what is freely given and nothing more.'

'Thanks.' I drain the last of my tea, eager to change the subject. 'There was another reason I came: a request for assistance.'

Her nod encourages me to continue, and I tell her about the conclave, of the Elderman's illness and the agreement made regarding my future. Lady Bergamon listens without interrupting.

'I take it you have some idea which herbs the healer is currently using to treat the Elderman?' she asks.

I show her the photos I took and describe the smells

and appearances of the herbal brews I helped feed my father. When I fall silent, Lady Bergamon fixes her knowing eyes on me.

'There may be something further I can brew, some other treatment that may help your father. However, you must understand that anything I make will be a temporary fix. I can treat the symptoms, not the cause.'

'I know.'

'And you are happy to prolong his suffering?' Before I have a chance to respond, she continues, 'I may be able to ease his pain, but my healing cannot work miracles. It will grant him more time, but he will suffer.'

The full implications of what I am asking of her dawn on me, and my cheeks heat. The price of my continued freedom is my father's pain. I could argue that this is payback for all the anguish he has caused me over the years, but I harbour no hatred for him. I had hoped Lady Bergamon could offer more than time. I had hoped she could cure my father.

But even as my conscience twinges, I recall my musings about the Eldermen of old. My father has clung to life and power over years of illness, and he continues to resist death with all his will. He supports my being here, and receiving Lady Bergamon's healing brews will advance his own agenda.

'My father gave his blessing for this visit. He knows the price of the medication you offer, and it is his choice to take it or not.'

'Very well,' Lady Bergamon says, but I can see that our decision troubles her. 'It will take me a few days to brew the potions. Some of the herbs need time to steep. I'll make enough to last for several weeks.'

'Thank you.' I make no effort to hide my relief. 'What sort of payment would you like?'

'The gift of healing should be freely given, and so it shall be.'

I thank her again, and Lady Bergamon stands.

'I'll begin collecting the herbs straight away. If you would like to run in the garden, you are more than welcome to do so. Last time, the effect of your brief visit was quite remarkable.'

It is an offer I cannot refuse.

'A word of warning. You may drink from the springs and streams, but don't go in the water. It's not safe for you.'

The warning raises yet more questions, but as she says no more, I must accept that Lady Bergamon does not wish to explain herself. So I will follow the advice.

I leave my jacket on the chair and remove my shoes and socks. It feels wonderful to have warm grass under my feet, to sense the contours of earth and to connect with the land. I take the path I remember, past the small orchard and the vegetable plot to the well. Ahead of me is the clearing where Lady Bergamon works her most potent magic. Beyond that, uncharted territory. As I walk, my pace gradually quickens, and by the time I reach the forest's edge, I am running. Opening my senses to the garden, I embrace the wilderness.

For the next hour or two, I lose myself to the ever-expanding landscape and the steady rhythm of my strides. And if at times I think a grey horse keeps pace with me, radiating hostility, surely it must simply be another quirk of the garden?

11

PROGRESS

When I return home, feeling optimistic and brimming with power, Karrion is on the phone. He greets me with a wave, and paces across the lounge. While I listen, he confirms a time and a place and promises that we will see the caller there. At least, I assume I am included in his "we".

'How did it go?' he asks as he slips his phone into the back pocket of his jeans. I wonder if I copied the habit from him or vice versa.

There is a plate with half a sandwich next to my laptop. Karrion stuffs the sandwich in his mouth and takes the plate to the kitchen. I decline the offer of a slice of his mother's cake, but suggest he puts the kettle on. He does so and returns with dessert for one.

'It went well,' I say, once I realise I never answered his question. 'Lady Bergamon thinks she can help the Elderman, and I got a chance to explore her domain further. It's a wondrous place.'

I tell him nothing of the horse. This is not the first time I have seen signs of a horse in Lady Bergamon's garden, but she has never broached the subject and I have not asked. She is entitled to her secrets, and I will learn them if she chooses to trust me.

The kettle boils, and I head over to the kitchen while

111

telling Karrion about a hen harrier pair I observed as I lay on a wildflower meadow and rested. My tea bag jar has only one remaining, and I reach for the top shelf to get a new box. As I do so, the sleeve of my fleece slips down to reveal most of my arm. I barely notice until I hear Karrion gasp behind me. When I turn, he steps forward with a frown and touches my arm just under a series of finger-shaped bruises.

'Did... did Dearon cause these?'

The bruises are deep purple against my pale skin. If Karrion is concerned about these, he would be horrified to see the rest of the marks on my body.

'Yes.'

'Did he hurt you?' Each word is forced out through clenched teeth, but I can see that he is trying not to jump to conclusions.

'Technically, yes, because I am bruised. But it was all consensual, and I left my fair share of marks on him.'

Karrion's posture relaxes, but his frown remains as he stares at my arm. 'If you're sure.'

'I am. I bruise easily, and it had been a while for both of us. We got carried away.'

'Fine.' Karrion pauses. 'Actually, it's not fine. He should take enough care not to hurt you during sex.'

'What if I like it rough?'

I keep my expression neutral while Karrion blushes. He opens his mouth to speak several times, but no words come out. Unable to contain the laughter bubbling inside me, I hug him. Karrion stands stock still at first, and then he wraps his arms around me, far more gently than this morning. I remain in his embrace for a moment before stepping away to get the milk from the fridge.

'It's all good, I promise. I get bruises from walking into things all the time. Occasionally, it's nice if I enjoy the activity.'

'Okay. I just hate seeing you get hurt.'

My smile slips away as I consider him. My mind made up, I tell him something I have never revealed to anyone.

'Karrion, with the connective tissue disorder I have, sex always hurts.' His eyes widen, and I hurry to keep talking. 'My hips are permanently damaged. Sometimes, the pain is so bad all I want to do is curl up and be sick. Other times, I can't walk afterwards.'

'That's terrible.' It is Karrion's turn to hug me. His friendship lends me strength when I would otherwise falter.

'Yes, but you must understand, it's my choice.'

From Karrion's expression, I see he does not understand.

'When I sleep with someone, I make a conscious choice to do so despite the pain. I accept the consequences of my actions because more often than not, the pleasure outweighs the pain. But it's always my choice to make, not someone else's. So you see, bruises are of little consequence in the context of the other pain.'

Karrion presses a kiss to my temple, and I step back to make the tea.

'Thanks for telling me, Yan. You rarely talk about your illness.'

'What's there to talk about? I'm in pain every moment of every day and I've had to accept that. Complaining won't help, and it's easier to just get on with my life.'

'As long as you still look after yourself,' he says and puts the milk back in the fridge.

'There's a difference between not dwelling on the pain and not taking steps to manage it. I meant the former.'

'I know. You've come a long way from the time we first met and you were still angry with the world and with your body for the illness.'

'We all get our fair share of complications in our lives. Mine just happens to be a bit more painful than most people's.'

Karrion nods and picks up our tea mugs. 'True. Now sit down, and I'll tell you about my productive afternoon.'

Once we are sitting in the lounge, Karrion gets to the point. 'I found a decent enough still of the woman and emailed it to Tim like you asked. He replied while I was at the bank. The poor quality of the photo meant he couldn't say anything for certain, but he did think the height and build of the woman bore some resemblance to his ex-fiancée, Carol.'

'Now we're getting somewhere.'

'There's more. Tim said he hasn't seen Carol in a couple of years, but he had a phone number and an email address for her. She also works in the City. I checked the email address, which was for an insurance broker, but she's not there anymore. Lucky for us, she's kept her number and she's willing to meet us tonight at six.'

'Good work. I knew I kept you around for something.'

Karrion grins. 'My good looks, of course.'

'That must it be it. If the meeting isn't until six, we have time to check out Tim's neighbour.'

'Are we driving?'

'Taking the train is probably wiser, otherwise we'll get caught in the evening traffic.'

'We can go straight from Liverpool Street Station to the Holborn Bars.'

'A meeting at the border of Old and New. Why did you pick that spot?'

'I didn't. Carol suggested it. I think she works there.'

'Fair enough.'

The train out of London is half empty, and we pick seats in the middle of a carriage. As the scenery changes from houses to fields, I try to imagine doing the commute twice a day, every day. The idea is abhorrent even when the train is empty. Being crammed in with a carriage full of humans would be intolerable.

In Braintree, we walk along wide roads until we reach Blenheim Street, where Tim lives. The semi-detached and detached houses are all made of the same sandstone coloured brick. Spacious front gardens are decorated with shrubs and flowers that still linger despite the cooler weather. A faded green Nissan Micra is parked on Tim's drive.

'So this is how the other half lives,' Karrion says as he looks around with open curiosity.

'Tempted?'

'Not really. It must be nice to have all this space, but the idea of living among humans just seems weird.'

'Imagine how weird it must be for those humans who choose to live in Old London.'

'I'd never thought of it from that perspective. Did you think being surrounded by Mages and Paladins and Shamans was strange when you moved to Old London?'

'Yes, at first. But I soon got used to it. Old London has a vibe that makes all magic users feel welcome.'

'Is detecting vibes one of your Wild Folk super-powers?' Karrion asks, the corner of his mouth twitching.

'As a matter of fact, it is.'

While Karrion laughs, I look around. Tim's house is no different from any along the street, except the front garden on both sides of the driveway is laid out to lawn. I expect it is for easy maintenance. The house next to his is owned by Janet, and that is where I lead Karrion. There are no lights on inside, but an Audi is parked on the drive.

'How do you want to play this?' Karrion asks.

'Just follow my lead.' I get a clipboard, a stack of papers and a pen out of my bag and knock on the door.

A middle-aged woman dressed in jeans and a pink cardigan opens it, a mug in hand. I catch the scents of fresh coffee and milk before I focus on the woman, and smile.

'I'm sorry to disturb you, but I'm conducting a survey for the council and I wondered if I could take a few minutes of your time?'

The woman is staring at Karrion, disbelief written in the curve of her eyebrow and the tilt of her head. 'He doesn't look like anyone I've met from the council.'

'David is doing work experience with us this week, and my boss thought he could do with some fresh air. I think she finds his piercings disconcerting.'

My gamble pays off, and the woman smiles. 'I can see why.'

'I'm Yannia, by the way.' I offer her my hand.

'Janet Fenchurch. Come on in.'

When she turns away, I call upon the mouse I sense in the garage and smell her. The blend of perfume, fabric softener and bleach tells me what I already suspected: she is human.

Janet takes us through to a lounge decorated in pastel colours. A small dog with a curly coat and a friendly disposition rushes in from the back garden and leaps at our feet, tail wagging. Karrion bends down to make a fuss of it, and I can see some of the lingering stiffness leaving Janet's shoulders.

'What's the survey about?'

'We're looking to find out what percentage of people in this area are aware of the fire safety checks offered free of charge by our fire department.'

'In this house, you're preaching to the converted. I have smoke detectors in every room, a carbon monoxide alarm in the kitchen near the boiler, I have clear escape routes in case of a fire, and I even have a rope ladder under my bed in case I need to get out through the window. Someone from the fire department was here last month going through it all with me.'

'It sounds as though you're doing everything right already. Is everyone else living in this household aware of all the safety precautions?'

'There's just me and Molly these days.' She points to the dog. 'My husband passed away a few years ago, and our daughter lives in New Zealand with her family.'

'Fair enough. Can I ask how you found out about the fire department's services? Was it in response to the leaflets we circulated in the spring, or have you been to one of their open days?'

'No, there was a fire a couple of months ago. The old lady next door wandered in and tried to make tea with an electric kettle on the cooker. Fortunately, the smoke alarm was working and I managed to put the fire out before anyone, my neighbour included, was hurt. The fire marshal that attended to the fire suggested I have the comprehensive checks done.'

'That must have been awful for you. I suppose your neighbour isn't used to modern technology.'

'It's not that. She's gone doolally.' Janet taps her knee, and Molly abandons her position at Karrion's feet and leaps on to her lap. 'I know it's not the politically correct term, but that's the truth.'

'Well, I hope she doesn't wander off again,' I say, and stand. 'Thank you for your time. I'll fill in the survey to show that you're doing everything right already. If only there were more people like you.'

Janet sees us to the door, still holding Molly in her arms. 'My daughter worries, and this has gone some way towards allaying her fears. Besides, I'd hate to see Molly getting hurt in a fire. Firemen don't always think to check for pets.'

'There's a sticker you can get,' Karrion says, turning on the threshold. 'It warns firemen that you have a pet and that they should also be rescued in the event of a fire.'

'Thanks. I'll look into it.' Janet smiles and closes the door behind us.

Out on the street, I glance towards Tim's house and notice a pale face staring out from one of the downstairs windows. I wonder if she is watching us, but upon sharpening my sight, I see that the eyes are unfocused. She must be Tim's mother. My curiosity piqued, I wonder if we ought to talk to her. What stops me are the memory of Tim's concern for her, and Janet's words. If she is that confused, it would be best not to speak to her without Tim.

'That was pretty awesome,' Karrion says, drawing my attention away from the window.

'What was?'

'Your story. Did you make it up on the fly, or did you plan that?'

'A bit of both. I figured that as someone who'd recently dealt with a fire, Janet would be a receptive audience for any discussion on fire safety. And I assumed she'd be up to date with it now, meaning that I wouldn't have to run her through an imaginary survey.'

'Did they teach you that at the Holmes Academy for Private Detectives?'

'No, at the Poirot Night School.'

We laugh as we head back the way we came. I step off the pavement briefly to look at the road surface, but I see no marks from a car braking suddenly or any other signs of a car crash.

'This was a wasted trip,' Karrion says, stuffing his hands in the pockets of his long leather coat.

'Not quite. We've eliminated a lead, and it's useful to see where Tim lives.'

'I guess. This place looks too ordinary for anything bad.'

'Most streets are like that. Except for Murder Alley and Larceny Lane.'

'Murder Alley would be a great place for a PI's office. I bet you'd get tons of business.'

Before we turn a corner, I glance back. The street is quiet, and I can no longer see Tim's mother in the window. Could the people behind the illusions be living out there, blending in among humans?

*

Back in Old London, we pick up coffees from a vendor outside Liverpool Street Station. We have plenty of time and we opt to walk to the Holborn Bars.

Holborn, or the A40, runs along the border between Old London and New London. One side of the road is steeped in echoes of spells, rituals and the residual power from magic users living in close proximity. The other side is adorned with gym posters and fast food flyers. I find stepping from our world to the mundane disconcerting, even though I do it on a regular basis. The background power is of no use to me, but just sensing it is reassuring. Despite being filled with people, buildings and machines, human cities are lifeless and empty.

Karrion does not feel the same sense of discomfort in the human London, which is to be expected. His power is tied to birds, his sense of magic far narrower than mine. Wild Folk have the ability to sense power in others, just as we can identify other magic users by their scent. It is something that I came to appreciate only once I moved to Old London, where I come into contact with Mages, Shamans, Paladins and Feykin every day. While I need to be careful with my enhanced senses to avoid a sensory overload, they give me an edge in my chosen profession.

Our destination, Holborn Bars, is an imposing terracotta building. As we cross the road to New London, I crane my neck to take in the Victorian architecture. On an overcast day, the brightness of the facade is less striking, but the building is nevertheless beautiful. Although I've never been inside, I imagine the interior is opulent.

We are still approaching the main entrance when the enormous double doors open and a young woman in a pale grey business suit steps out. She is buttoning a long white coat, and a grey scarf is draped around her neck in a carelessly stylish fashion. Her brown hair is twisted back in a chignon, but I can see why Tim thought she could be the woman on the CCTV. The details, however, are wrong. Carol appears right at home in a suit and high heels, whereas the woman caught on tape was dressed casually in jeans and a wool jacket. There was nothing wrong with the mystery woman's clothing, but it conveyed an image of someone not overly concerned with their appearance. I may be jumping to conclusions, but Tim's ex-fiancée does not fit that description.

Karrion has also spotted the woman and he approaches her.

'Carol Peters?'

'Actually, it's Carol Wright these days.' She lifts her left hand, and I see a solitaire diamond ring. 'I got married.'

'Sorry, Tim didn't mention that.'

I hear uncertainty creeping into Karrion's voice, but I resist the temptation to intervene. He can navigate social niceties, possibly better than I can.

'I never told him.'

'Fair enough. I'm Karrion Feathering.' He offers his hand. 'We spoke on the phone.'

They shake hands, and Karrion introduces me. When I step forward to greet her, I spot a Chihuahua being carried in a beige handbag near us. I borrow its nose and breathe in Carol's scent. All I get is an understated floral perfume, almost overpowered by the smells of the street. But it confirms what I already suspected: she is the not the woman we are after.

Carol frowns at me; she must have caught the flicker

of change across my face while I used my power. Her smile is polite, but when I hand her one of my cards, the frown deepens.

'What has an Old London PI got to do with Tim?'

'He's connected to a case we're working on,' I say, unwilling to reveal that Tim is my client.

'Is he in some sort of trouble?'

'That's what we're trying to figure out.'

'Why did he give you my contact details?'

'Because of this photo.' Karrion gets out his phone and calls up the still of Tim and the mystery woman. 'I asked if he recognised the woman in the photo and he thought it could be you.'

Carol squints at the screen and gets a pair of glasses out of her Louis Vuitton bag. She takes the phone from Karrion for a better look and shakes her head.

'Perhaps that could have been me a few years ago. Now,' she motions to her clothes, 'less so. But I guess Tim wouldn't know that.'

'Do you have any idea who the woman in the photo is?' Karrion asks.

'No, the quality is too poor. It looks like the faces are blurred deliberately. I barely recognise Tim and I was engaged to him.'

'When was that?' I ask.

'The engagement? Four years ago. We'd been together forever and the plan was to get married the following autumn. But then Tim's mother got diagnosed with Alzheimer's, and we had to postpone the wedding plans. Margery deteriorated quicker than the doctors expected, and eventually, Tim had to move back home to look after her.'

'But you didn't?'

Carol's eyes grow unfocused as she dips her chin. 'No, I broke up with him.'

Karrion and I exchange a glance, but Carol continues before either of us has a chance to say anything.

'You have to understand, I was twenty-seven. My career was going places, I had a great guy, and Tim and I were talking about trying for a baby after the honeymoon. It may have been selfish of me, but I wasn't willing to trade all of that for years spent spoon feeding a woman who couldn't remember my name.'

I shrug. Carol's life choices are of little interest to me given that it is clear she has no connection to the spell casters or the woman we are looking for. Unless it is by association.

'Do you spend a lot of time in Old London?' I ask.

'Some. It is across the street from my workplace. Some of the lunch places and bars I go to with my colleagues are on that side of the road.'

'Do you know many Mages and Feykin?'

From the corner of my eye, I notice Karrion watching me. His brow is furrowed, and no doubt he is trying to unravel my line of questioning.

'A few, none of them very well. They work at the Holborn Bars, though mostly in different areas from me. I wouldn't go as far as saying they prefer the company of their own kind, but we do move in different social circles.'

The implication is clear. As much as we live side by side with humans, the power we possess remains a divisive factor. Our laws on the use of magic to commit crimes are strict to a point where the punishment for killing with magic is death. They are designed to demonstrate to humans that we can police our own. For the same reason, our justice system relies on the Heralds of Justice, otherworldly beings summoned by the Paladins of Justice. No amount of magic can fool the Heralds, but as I discovered last week, there is a way to convict an innocent man.

'When did you last see Tim?'

'About two years ago. We sold the flat we owned together and had to sign all the paperwork for the sale. The flat was too big for me, and by then he'd been living with his mother for some time. I gather his share of the sale proceeds went towards modifying the house to be safer for Margery.'

'Do you know if he was seeing someone else?'

'I don't think so. We didn't talk much, but I got the impression that between work and looking after Margery, he didn't have time for anything else.'

'Can you think of anyone who would want to hurt Tim?'

'No, he's a kind, gentle man. Not many men would choose to look after a relative at home rather than dumping them in the first available nursing home.' Her expression grows troubled. 'Why? Is someone trying to hurt him?'

'That, too, is something we're trying to figure out.' Carol looks like she would like to pry more, and I continue, 'Thank you for agreeing to talk to us. We won't take up any more of your evening.'

'You're welcome,' Carol says, hesitant all of a sudden. 'If there's anything else I can help you with, give me a call. Despite our relationship not working out, I want nothing but the best for Tim.'

We say our goodbyes, but we have got no further than a few yards when Carol calls out after us.

'If you see Tim, would you say hello to him? Would you tell him that I wish him every happiness and that I'm... just tell him I said hi.'

I nod, and we leave her standing outside the Holborn Bars while we return to the London where we belong.

12

ON THE STREETS

Once we are back in Old London, I glance at Karrion.

'Thoughts?'

'I believe her when she said it wasn't her in the photo,' Karrion says.

'Why?' I ask, keeping my tone neutral.

'The clothes don't fit, but more importantly, her demeanour doesn't fit. She's too confident and self-assured.' He nudges me gently. 'Besides, your question about whether she knows any spell casters implies that she isn't one.'

'Very good, Karrion. And you're right. Carol is human.'

'I suppose it would have been too easy if we'd solved the case on the first day.'

'True. And nothing Carol said made me think she bears a grudge against Tim. If anything, it should be the other way round. She was pretty shit to him.'

'Poor Tim.'

'Life is rarely uncomplicated.'

'What's next on our list? You seem to know where you're headed.'

I point towards the Chancery Lane Tube station. 'While we're up and about, we might as well see if we can track down Bob.'

'Finding a homeless man in London is not going to be easy.'

'No, but it's the right time of day for it. The way I figure it, the homeless are likely to move around during the day, depending on what their needs are. I've been to Shaftesbury Avenue, and if my memory serves me, the part where the stabbing occurred is relatively quiet. For a homeless man begging for change, there are better streets nearby, like Charing Cross Road, or even Leicester Square and Covent Garden. However, the area is ideal for finding a quiet place to sleep.'

Karrion nods. 'And that's why you said we were better off doing this in the evening.'

'If we're lucky, Bob will have settled down for the night and we'll have no trouble locating him.'

'Are you feeling lucky?'

I smile. 'Sometimes.'

We take the Tube to Leicester Square, and I get through the journey by fixing my eyes on the row of piercings on Karrion's left ear and by breathing through my mouth. Living in the city has been an adjustment, and I have learned to tolerate it. But travelling deep underground in a confined space evokes my flight instinct. I try to remind myself that earthworms and moles and other creatures spend their whole lives underground, but the fear goes deeper than that. This must be what a caged animal feels like, this instinct to hurl myself against the confines of my prison until it yields or I bleed.

When the carriage doors open at the station, I am the first to leave. Karrion hurries after me, doing his best to keep up while dodging fellow passengers.

'We could have taken the bus,' he says when he catches up with me on the escalator.

'It would have taken forever.'

'So what, if it would make you feel more comfortable?'

'Maybe on the way back.'

We go through the turnstiles and choose one of the exits leading to Charing Cross Road. We emerge next to a casino. China Town is behind us, and with a whisper of magic, I smell fried meat, star anise, rotting rubbish and the stink of cars. People are everywhere, overwhelming my senses, and it is the press of the crowd that forces us forward. We cross the road, but instead of turning left to continue along Charing Cross Road, I choose one of the narrow side streets. Karrion's expression registers confusion, but he follows without a word.

I soon find what I am looking for: an independent cafe that is still open. A bored teenager lounges behind the counter, but his countenance changes when I rattle off my order. When he sets about preparing everything, I turn to Karrion.

'Do you want anything?'

'From the sound of it, I'm going to need both hands to help you carry the bags.'

I sit at the nearest table, and Karrion follows suit. The laminated menu is sticky, and I lean back to keep my arms off it. Behind the long glass counter, sandwich fillings, cakes and a selection of fruit salads are on offer. I wonder if I should have ordered something for us as well, but I am still full from lunch.

'You aren't hungry, are you?' I ask.

'No. I figured we'd be pretty busy today so I ate quite a few of the rolls Mum baked you.'

The teenager places the first paper bag on the counter and adds a handful of napkins and wooden forks.

A second bag joins the first on the counter, and we watch as the boy places takeaway cups of tea in cardboard holders and stacks them in two more bags. I pay with my credit card. Karrion takes the bags with the cups, and I take the other two.

Out on the street, I retrace our steps to Charing Cross Road and we head towards Shaftesbury Avenue.

'Are you going to explain our little detour?' Karrion asks.

'The homeless have little reason to trust us, let alone help us. We could bribe them with money, but I don't think that's right given how common substance abuse is. I'd much rather give them a warm drink and something healthy to eat.'

'Hence the sandwiches and the fruit salads.'

'Yes.'

Karrion nods, and the warmth of his smile insulates me from the chill in the wind.

Turning right towards Shaftesbury Avenue takes us from the bright lights of the Palace Theatre and the fast food restaurants dotted around the square. The first homeless person we encounter is huddled next to a bin at the start of Earlham Street, a sleeping bag wrapped around him.

I approach him. 'Would you like a cup of tea and something to eat?'

'Yes.' The man peers at us from under a woollen hat. 'What do you want?'

'Information.'

At my signal, Karrion hands the man a cup of tea. I get

a tuna baguette and a fruit salad from my bags, together with utensils. My heart clenches as I watch the man carefully wrap the fork in the napkin before tucking them into a pocket of his coat. The two packets of sugars he asks for go the same way, and he puts the food in another pocket. He cradles the teacup with both hands, and I can see grimy knuckles peeking through the holes in his gloves.

'What do you want to know?'

'We're looking for a homeless man called Bob. He may be spending nights in this area.'

'Why do you want him?'

'He helped someone who'd been stabbed last week, and I'd like to hear his account of what happened.'

With one hand holding the teacup and the other tugging the sleeping bag across his chest, the man shakes his head.

'I don't know any Bob.'

I thank him for his time, and we pick up our bags. He looks relieved that we are leaving, but calls out to us.

'Hey, lady.' When I turn, he raises the cup. 'Thank you.'

'You're welcome. Stay safe.'

As we make slow progress along Shaftesbury Avenue and its side roads, we have several conversations with the homeless that yield no information. Where the people we meet have a dog with them, I give them an extra sandwich so their pets will not go hungry. One woman is moved to tears, and she hides her face in the neck of a large Labrador cross. The dog leans closer to its mistress and licks her ear.

When we return from a futile foray into Neal Street, we come across a homeless woman trying to fix a broken cardboard box from which her possessions have spilt on to the pavement. While I speak to her and offer her food, Karrion jogs back the way we came and returns shortly with another box for her. The woman insists on us not touching her things, but she is grateful for the food and the help. When I ask her about Bob, she points towards the way we were heading.

'I think he was bedding down by the church.'

We thank her and hurry along, turning left where Shaftesbury Avenue meets High Holborn. The lit windows of St Giles-in-the-Fields and its darker grounds are easy to spot, and I notice two figures huddled against the wrought iron fence.

'Hi,' I say as I walk closer. 'Would you happen to be Bob?'

A scruffy grey dog next to the man whines and wags its tail.

'I am. Who's asking?'

'Yannia Wilde. I'm a Private Investigator.' I offer him my hand, and he takes it, his grip firm. As he withdraws his hand, I notice a blood stain on his coat sleeve.

'If that's the case, shouldn't you be wearing a trench coat and a deerstalker?' he asks, and I see a twinkle in the dark eyes regarding me from under bushy eyebrows.

'It's my laundry day,' I say, and he laughs.

We offer him food and tea, both of which he gladly accepts. He unwraps his ham sandwich and breaks it in half, offering one part to his dog and tucking into the other himself. It is clear he is ravenous, and I get another sandwich out for him. This one he hides away among his belongings like we have seen several times this evening.

Once he is sipping his tea, Bob offers us a smile that reveals stained teeth. 'I'm going to guess that you didn't seek me out just to hand out food, as nice as this has been.'

'We need your help.'

Bob splutters a laugh and wipes drops of tea off his scraggly beard. I offer him a spare napkin, and he uses it to dry his hand. He is not wearing any gloves, and his nail beds are caked black.

'You don't often say that to a homeless man, I bet.'

'I do if it's true.' My gaze never wavers when it meets his. I crouch in front of him.

'How can I help you, Yannia?' He falters over the pronunciation of my name.

'I gather you witnessed a stabbing last week? A man called Tim Wedgbury died at the scene.'

'He did, poor lad. But I didn't see the stabbing. By the time I got to him, Tim was already in bad nick. The first I knew of anything amiss was when the girl came running down the road, screaming for help.'

Karrion looks at me, a question in his eyes, and I shrug. There was nothing in the police report about a girl.

'What girl?' Karrion asks.

'Tim's girlfriend, Lizzie.'

'Who's Lizzie?'

I shake my head at Karrion and say to Bob, 'Why don't you start from the beginning and tell us what happened?'

'Right. I had settled down for the night near Neal Street when I heard someone calling for help. A woman came up to me and said her boyfriend had been stabbed. They had been robbed, and she was looking for a phone. I said I'd go and see to her boyfriend while she kept looking. I found Tim leaning against a bin, trying to apply

132

pressure to a wound on his side. I took off his coat and used that as a compression. My hands weren't clean, you see. A few minutes later, an ambulance arrived at the scene, and Tim died shortly after. When he disappeared, I thought someone had spiked the coffee I'd bought earlier that evening. But a police patrol came and declared it all a magical prank. I gave a statement and then went back to Plato.'

'Plato?' Karrion asks. Bob points at his dog.

'While it was just you and Tim, did he say anything?'

'He told me his name. He asked whether Lizzie was okay, he was really concerned about her. And he said the mugger was just a kid and that the stabbing had been an accident.'

'So we have two accidents,' Karrion murmurs, and I shake my head at him again. This is neither the time nor the place for speculation.

'When you were in the alley with Tim, was there anyone else around?' I ask.

'It was just us.'

'Are you sure? You didn't see any movement in the shadows, or hear someone speak? It may not have been much louder than a whisper.'

'I can't say I paid much attention to anything other than Tim, but I don't remember noticing anything.'

'Do you remember what Lizzie looked like?' Karrion asks.

'Brown hair, brown eyes. Average build. I think she was wearing a black coat and maybe jeans. She was pretty enough, but there was nothing remarkable about her.'

From the description Bob gives, it is possible the mystery woman from the CCTV is Lizzie. But who is she

133

and what is her connection to Tim?

'Did anything strike you as odd about the events you've described?' I ask.

'Other than the victim magically fading away?' Bob thinks while he finishes his tea. 'Yes. The girl, Lizzie, never came back.'

'What do you mean?'

'She was in a blind panic when she spoke to me, barely coherent. If she was that concerned about Tim, why didn't she return to the scene after calling for help?'

'Maybe she was told to stay by the phone?' Karrion suggests.

'Nothing the emergency services might have said would have kept me from returning to my other half.'

I sit back on my haunches while I replay our walk along Shaftesbury Avenue. Something about the street has been nagging me at the back of my mind, and I finally know what it is.

'Wait a minute. Why did Lizzie have to come all the way to Neal Street to find a phone? There's a Thai restaurant almost opposite the alley where Tim was stabbed. Why didn't she go in there?'

Bob considers the question, his brow furrowing until his eyebrows meet in the middle. 'That's a good question. But the answer doesn't make any sense.'

'Meaning?'

'Meaning you'd think I was crazy if I said that on Thursday night when Lizzie was running towards me, there was no Thai restaurant on Shaftesbury Avenue. Or if there was, the lights were out and the windows boarded up.'

'But how's that possible?' Karrion asks. 'We just walked past, and it's open for business.'

'I said you'd think I was crazy.'

'No, we don't think you're crazy,' I say. 'What you've told us is impossible, but we've seen a lot of that recently.'

'Perhaps it happens in the other London, but here a street's a street and a restaurant's a restaurant.'

'Magic has no concept of boundaries drawn on a map or of laws that restrict its use. That is up to the wielders.'

Bob shifts as he looks from Karrion to me. When he gets no reaction from either of us, he opens the lid of the fruit salad and wolfs down chunks of pineapple and mango.

'Another cup of tea?' I ask as I stand. At Bob's nod, Karrion hands him a second cup. A flock of pigeons that has been hovering nearby takes to flight.

'Thanks. For this and the food.'

'You're welcome. Thank you for your time and the information.'

'I hope it was helpful.'

'It was.' I smile, my free hand in my pocket. The street light nearby stretches my shadow to that of a giant. 'We now have a better idea of what sort of magic we are looking for.'

13

BEYOND AN IMPOSSIBLE CRIME SCENE

Stopping by Neal Street, I look down Shaftesbury Avenue and try to imagine it as Bob saw it last week. The stabbing occurred late at night after all the shops had closed. There is a cinema nearby, though perhaps there were no screenings last Thursday. Or, perhaps the cinema also did not exist while a version of Tim was dying.

'What are you thinking?' Karrion asks.

'It's possible Bob was distracted and missed someone casting a spell, but I'm inclined to think he and Tim were alone in that alley.'

'I wondered if you were going to say that. But what does it mean for our theory?'

'That perhaps New Scotland Yard's Mages were right and we are dealing with illusions after all. Especially in light of what Bob just told us. If Lizzie was the caster responsible for making the bodies disappear, it doesn't make any sense that she vanished before they did.'

'What now?' Karrion asks.

'Thai restaurant or the alley first?'

'Are you hungry?'

'No. I want to ask them about last Thursday.'

'But Bob just said the restaurant was closed.'

'Bob said the restaurant either wasn't there or it was

closed and boarded up. Neither seems likely, given it's open now. What I'm looking for is an alternative point of view to the events of the night.'

'You think what Bob saw wasn't real.'

'I don't know. But we think we're dealing with some sort of an illusion. I want to know how far that illusion extends. Or can you think of another way a caster could make a restaurant disappear for half an hour and then reappear?'

'No. In which case, restaurant first.'

We continue along the left side of the street and enter the restaurant. Aromatic scents of lemongrass, coconut milk and ginger wash over us, and my stomach growls. Karrion grins.

'Sounds like you're hungry after all.'

'It wouldn't hurt to have dinner,' I say and survey the restaurant. Half the tables are occupied, and the food looks good.

A waiter comes to us with menus, and I ask for a table by the window. From my vantage point, I can see the alley where Tim was stabbed. Anyone seeking help would have to be blind not to try the restaurant first.

When the waiter comes to take our drinks order, I ask if he was working Thursday night and offer him one of my cards. He says he was not, but several of his colleagues were, and he promises to ask one of them to come to us as soon as they are free.

True to his word, our drinks and a bowl of prawn crackers are delivered by a Thai woman with a wide smile and curious eyes.

'You have questions?' she asks after we have ordered our meal.

'I understand you were working last Thursday?'

She nods.

'Did you notice anything strange happening out on the street that night? It would have been right around closing time.'

'There was an ambulance, and a police car followed a little later.'

'Did you happen to notice what time the ambulance arrived?'

'Maybe ten to eleven.'

'Were you busy that evening?'

'Yes, though most people had left by then. Only a group of businessmen stayed until closing time.'

'Did you notice anything else strange that evening, especially shortly before the arrival of the ambulance?'

'No, I was busy. No one said anything to me. We talked about the ambulance before our shift on Friday, but there was nothing in the local news about an incident. I'd forgotten all about it until now.'

'Thanks, that's helpful.'

She looks like she wants to ask the reason for all my questions, but instead, she flashes us a smile and leaves. I take a sip of my mango juice and straighten my legs under the table. It feels good to sit down and give my muscles a break. It's too soon for more painkillers, and I do my best to ignore the throb in my ankles and knees.

'The restaurant was open on Thursday,' Karrion says.

'It was. That must mean that the street Bob saw was part of the illusion.'

'But how did the customers get to the restaurant if it looked shut from the outside?'

'Tim was stabbed just before eleven, too late for anyone coming in for a meal. I doubt it looked any different earlier that evening.'

Karrion takes a sip of his beer. 'My head hurts. Why would the casters exclude a restaurant from their illusion?'

'That is a mystery. I can think of two possible reasons: either the restaurant didn't fit the illusion or the casters didn't know the restaurant existed.'

'I'm not sure I follow the second option.'

'Let's say I give you a random street in Old London and ask you to draw it from memory. If you haven't been there recently and you're not allowed to do any research, what would you do?'

Understanding dawns on Karrion's face. 'Add in the detail I remember and fill in the blanks with whatever I think fits the street.'

'Exactly. If our illusionists weren't here when they created the illusion, it's possible all they could recall was that there were shops along the street and they imagined only dark windows.'

'That rules out Lizzie as one of them,' Karrion says and bites into a prawn cracker. White flakes float on to his black t-shirt.

'Perhaps it does, perhaps it doesn't. All it would mean is the real Lizzie wasn't here when the spell happened.'

'There's something I don't understand about the illusion: if the caster wasn't here overseeing every detail of it, how is it that Lizzie was able to ask for Bob's help and also to call an ambulance? We know both Bob and the ambulance were real.'

'Perhaps the main characters within the illusion,

namely Tim and Lizzie, had a degree of autonomy in their interactions with people and things outside the illusionist's control. But the basic premise was dictated by the illusion, including erasing this restaurant for its duration.'

Our food arrives, and we pause the conversation while we thank the waiter and sample our chosen dishes. Everything is delicious.

Stealing a forkful of stir-fried vegetables from my plate, Karrion continues, 'I just find it hard to get my head around the fact that someone can create illusionary people capable of interacting with the real world.'

'That's what concerns me,' I say, and take a piece of his fish. 'So far, the only person who's been hurt has been a version of Tim. What happens if one of the characters in the illusion decides to attack a real person?'

'Surely the illusion can't extend that far.'

'I don't know. Think about the sound of the car crash Tim heard outside his house. If that was a side effect of what was happening in Old London, who knows what else the casters can do?'

Karrion frowns. 'If that's the case, shouldn't we be out there trying to stop them instead of having dinner?'

'We have too little to go on at present. I have a few avenues I'd like to pursue tomorrow, but unless Tim knows who Lizzie is and we find that she is one of our spell casters, there's not much we can do at present. We need more information, more leads to follow.'

'Are you saying that we need this to happen again before we can solve the case?'

I look down, raking my fork through the sauce on my plate. 'I'd rather it didn't, but I fear it must and it will.'

'As long as the illusion doesn't become reality.'

'This is where we need all the luck we can get. The protection of a spirit or two wouldn't go amiss either.'

'At least you've got one of those already.'

Looking down on my plate, I offer no reply. Wishearth is known for his unpredictable nature. He cared nought for the dead Paladin we discovered last week, so why would he care about a human who is unlikely to believe in Wishearth's existence? He has already directed Tim to me. Does that mean I am now expected to take care of the rest?

We finish our meal without rushing, but neither of us wishes to linger over coffee and dessert. I put my credit card down to settle the bill and silence Karrion's objections by reminding him that we are still working. With the hours we keep, the least I can do is make sure that we take regular meal breaks.

The night air feels cold after the warmth of the restaurant, and I zip my coat up. Karrion waves away a pigeon and nudges my arm.

'The alley next?'

'Yep.'

Street lights on Shaftesbury Avenue cast a pool of light as far into the alley as the nearest bin. Beyond that, the darkness is impenetrable until I borrow the sight of a cat and other shapes materialise out of the blackness.

'Can you use your magic to see in the dark?' I ask Karrion.

'Yes. I'll just channel my inner owl. But I can't do it for long, or else I'll start vomiting owl pellets.'

'I'd pay good money to see that,' I mutter and crouch to inspect the ground by the bin.

As expected, there is no sign of blood, nor can I detect any when I inhale through the nose of a rat. The bins overpower all other smells, but if blood has been spilt here, I should be able to detect a trace of it.

'Anything?' Karrion asks, hovering next to me.

'Nothing.'

'What about magic? Can you detect the illusion?'

'No, but I could have told you that without ever setting foot in this alley. I can sense magic in others, but not spells that have been cast. That's a Mage ability.'

'Shame.'

We spend a few more minutes searching the area without finding anything relevant. By then, my sinuses are aching from all the smells, and I am glad to relinquish the threads of my magic and return to the dull senses of a human.

'Are we taking a bus back?' Karrion asks when we head towards Charing Cross Road.

'Yes. One Tube ride a day is all I can handle.'

'Works for me. If birds were meant to be underground, we'd have developed paws instead of wings.'

I nod, but my thoughts linger on Karrion's words while we drop the final sandwich off with the first homeless man we spoke to and continue our walk. I have often heard it said that a Shaman possesses a soul that is neither human nor animal, but something in between. The magic in their blood allows them to bridge the divide, to find solace with the animals that are a part of them. They are also granted aspects of their animal side: endurance for Horse Shamans, keen nose for Dog Shamans and innate sense of direction for Bird Shamans.

'Here's something else I don't get,' Karrion says while

142

we wait for a bus. 'Neither of us is a Mage. Even if we're lucky enough to come across one of these illusions while it's happening, how are we going to identify the spell casters?'

'We need a Tinker.'

'Do you know any?'

'No, but I know where to find one.'

Karrion nods. 'Time to go shopping at One Magic Change.'

'Tomorrow.'

'What's the plan for tomorrow? Other than Tinker hunting?'

'I'm going to email Tim and see if I could meet him when his train gets to London. It would be useful to observe his morning routine and see where he's most likely to come into contact with Mages and Feykin.'

'He works in Old London. There could be all manner of places.'

'True, but we need to narrow it down somehow.'

'Do you want me to join you?'

I consider the question while we get on the bus and find seats on the upper deck. 'I think it's best if I go alone. Two of us following Tim around would be more conspicuous. Besides, we've worked all day and you deserve to have a later start tomorrow. Why don't we meet up at mine around ten?'

'Works for me. I can pack lunch for Robin, Wren and Jay and walk them to school.'

'So much for the lie in I'd envisaged for you,' I say with a smile.

'Not many chances for those with our brood, but I don't mind. It gives Mum an easier morning.'

I squeeze his hand. After the chill of the evening, my fingers are stiff and cold. Karrion takes my hand between his and rubs it until blood begins flowing. He repeats the process with my other hand.

'I was thinking, what we did tonight felt good. Maybe we could make it a regular thing? Buying food from a cafe is expensive, but we could get thermos bottles and cups and maybe make soup or stew at your place. Something warm anyway, what with the winter coming. What do you think?'

My expression causes his ears to turn pink, and he looks away, teeth worrying his lip piercing.

'I think it's a fantastic idea. Were you thinking of helping the homeless here or in Old London?'

'In New London. There aren't as many homeless people in Old London, and the Paladins run a soup kitchen.'

'I expect people already in a vulnerable situation would feel uncomfortable in an area known for magic.'

'You're probably right. But I do know that I want to help. I never realised how many people are homeless. Or perhaps I never paid attention.'

'It would be nice to do something. Perhaps Funja might be willing to donate leftover food.'

'Sure, we can ask him,' Karrion says, but I hear reluctance in his voice.

'It would just be for cheap supplies. We'd still have to do most of the hard work.'

'I'm okay with that.' Karrion's expression brightens. 'Look at us, fighting crime and saving the world.'

'We're the modern superheroes,' I say and rest my head on Karrion's shoulder. He turns his so it leans against mine.

Back in Old London, Karrion picks up his bag from my flat and then leaves. I write the intended email to Tim and glance at the clock. My intention was to stop by the Open Hearth for a quick drink and a catch up with Wishearth, but it's getting late. Better to commune with Wishearth through my fireplace and have an early night. Perhaps tomorrow I will have dinner at the Open Hearth.

As I am undressing in front of the fire – an act that feels intimate despite my being alone – my thoughts turn to the night ahead of me. Will I dream of an attacker cloaked in shadows or of two wild creatures chasing prey? Or will a man with flames in his eyes grant me a night of oblivion in return for my faith?

WEDNESDAY

14

TRACING A LIFE

I meet Tim at the top of the stairs leading out of Liverpool Street Station. The smile he greets me with is forced, and the circles under his eyes seem darker than yesterday. A rolled up tie is just visible in his shirt pocket, and his collar is undone. Nothing about him stands out, nothing that would single him out as a target for the illusions.

Why Tim?

It is a question I keep coming back to, and I hope I will soon have the answer. Here is a client as burdened as Ilana, and I will not fail a second time.

'How's the investigation going?' Tim asks in lieu of a greeting.

'We're making progress. Yesterday, we tracked down an eyewitness to the stabbing, and he said that when you were mugged, you were there with your girlfriend, Lizzie.'

'I already told you, I don't have a girlfriend.' Tim frowns. 'Lizzie?'

'Yes. Do you know anyone called Lizzie? Or Elizabeth?'

'Well, I'm guessing the Queen isn't trying to kill me. There was an investment director at work called Elizabeth, but no one dared call her Lizzie. She moved to Edinburgh about six months ago to head our new office.'

'Which means she's unlikely to be the Lizzie in question.'

'Agreed. There may have been a Liz at school, but no one I specifically remember. Sorry.'

'It's not your fault. I suppose it would have been too easy if you'd identified the woman without a second thought.'

'But you think this Lizzie has something to do with what's been going on?'

'I do. You see, Detective Manning thought the prank had escalated with the inclusion of a woman on the second occasion, but someone else was there both times. Based on the description provided by the eyewitness, it was the same woman. Lizzie.'

'And do you think she's the Mage behind the pranks? Or the other caster?'

'We think she's connected somehow. And whatever is going on, I believe it extends beyond a simple prank.'

Keeping my voice low, I explain about our theory that the car crash in Old London and the one Tim heard outside his house are connected. When I have finished, he rubs his eyes.

'Who is Lizzie? And why is she after me?'

'I'm going to find out. One thing is clear: the woman caught on CCTV wasn't Carol.'

'You've seen her?'

'Yes. She asked me to give you her regards.'

'How did she seem?'

'Fine, I think. Hard to say since I don't know her.' I hesitate. 'She's married.'

'To whom?'

'She didn't say, and I didn't ask.'

'Right.' Tim's posture sags, and he glances at his watch. 'I need to get going if I'm to be at work by nine.'

'Of course. Do you have a morning routine you follow?'

Tim leads me out of the station and down the steps to Liverpool Street. The area is crowded, and I dodge around commuters, flyer distributors and cyclists. Tim follows the flow of people, clearly moving on autopilot, whereas I find the thought of having to do this on a daily basis claustrophobic. People go to bizarre lengths to earn a living.

'There's not much to it,' Tim says once we can walk side by side. As we pass a lamp post, my attention is drawn to a poster seeking information about a missing Shaman girl. 'I get off the train, stop by at a cafe to pick up a coffee and breakfast, and then walk to work.'

'Is it always the same cafe?'

'Yes, Amici, around the corner.'

'What do you do about lunch?'

'I work through lunch and eat at my desk so I can leave at a sensible time.'

'Do you bring food with you, or is it delivered?'

'Mostly I bring lunch. If Mum's having a bad day, I don't always get a chance to pack something. On those occasions, my secretary gets me a sandwich from wherever she goes for lunch.'

'How about after work?'

We reach Bishopsgate, and I look left along the street. Double-decker buses obscure my view of the crash site. Tim, oblivious to my concentration lapsing, turns right, and I have to hurry to catch up with him.

'I take a train home,' he says.

'How about drinks with colleagues or other social events?'

He stops outside a cafe. 'Like I told you yesterday morning, I have no life outside of work. I rush home every day to minimise the time Mum spends alone and to check that she hasn't hurt herself. Even the groceries are delivered to the house.'

'I'm sorry,' I say as Tim holds a door open for me. Aromas of coffee and pastries waft out, and the hiss of an espresso machine provides a backing track to the many conversations that are going on inside.

'It's my choice,' Tim replies and stops at the back of the line.

I nod, but my attention is drawn away from him. There are a dozen tables dotted along both sides of the path to the counter, and most of the tables are occupied. A steady stream of people is getting takeaway coffee, and the line we have joined remains a constant length. I keep an eye on the people at the tables and on those queuing with us, but no one seems to pay attention to Tim. In a crowded, confined space like this, my enhanced sense of smell would be of no use, but I feel magical auras brushing along the edges of mine. We are in the presence of spell casters, but I cannot identify any of them.

'Do you want anything?' Tim asks as we near the cash register.

So far, I have not spared a glance at the blackboard menus mounted above the espresso machine, but after a brief deliberation, I ask for a hazelnut cappuccino. The cakes on display behind the counter turn my stomach; too early for anything that sweet.

A caress of power sends my eyes roaming over the crowd, and sensations akin to cool spring water, a gentle evening breeze, a tendril of mist upon heated skin cause me to whirl around. I find an older man watching me. Although his clothes are nondescript, the high cheekbones, the hair tinted with copper and the radiant purple of his eyes tell me he counts the Fair Folk among his relatives. The Feykin tips an imaginary hat in my direction and leaves.

The Fey would be little more than bedtime stories and cautionary tales were it not for children born with inhuman grace and beauty. They are known as Feykin, and their glamour and magic make them masters of manipulation. It is well known that they have no regard for the feelings of others so long as their personal agenda is advanced. Feykin make for poor allies and dangerous enemies. That one of them recognised me is not unusual. Nature grants us both power, and our magic responds to that connection. But I feel no kinship with them like I do with Lady Bergamon; rather the Feykin are wild tempests that I respect from afar. Even the most powerful among them are faint echoes of the beings that gave them life. I have never met one of the Fair Folk, but I have felt their presence in the unspoilt wild places on moonlit nights, during summer solstice or the Samhain. Wild Folk legends are filled with the Fey, but none can say whether they still inhabit our world, or whether they have become infrequent visitors.

The encounter with the Feykin occupies me enough that I miss Tim stepping up to the counter and have to hurry to catch up. The server smiles at Tim, finger poised over a tablet.

'Hi, Tim. How was the train this morning?'

'On time, for a change. How are you?'

'Fine, thanks.' The young woman – there is no tag pinned to her apron – looks like she wants to say more, but a flush creeps up her neck and she focuses her attention on the tablet. 'What can I get you? The usual?'

Tim orders a latte and porridge with steamed fruit for himself. The woman is already saying the total cost when Tim adds the cappuccino for me, and this causes her to accidentally cancel the order. While they start again, I turn to survey the cafe once more. There is nothing out of place with the other customers, and I sense no hostility from anyone. The baristas all seem friendly and absorbed in their work.

Our order is called out by a man whose tag identifies him as Pavel. When he passes me my cup, our fingers brush and Pavel winks. Tim, oblivious to this, thanks him by name, and we leave. The walk to his office takes no longer than five minutes, and during that time, we pass at least a hundred people. Any of them could be the illusionists I am after, and yet none look at Tim twice.

Outside his office building, I stop to survey the layout. The glass front offers an unobstructed view of a security desk, turnstiles and the lifts beyond. While I cannot see any cameras, I expect the coverage is extensive.

'What's the security like?' I ask.

'Anyone working in the building needs a key card to get through the turnstiles. Visitors have to sign in at the front desk and sign out when they leave the building. The lifts have cameras, but once you're in the building, you can go to whichever floor you wish. There are reception desks outside the lifts on all of our floors, and anyone not known to the reception staff has to wait there until someone comes to collect them.'

'Other than employees, who visits your floor regularly?'

'Cleaners, though I leave long before they start their work. There are often contractors attending to this or that, but they're always accompanied by one of our internal maintenance staff. Unless something needs fixing in my office, I see only colleagues and the occasional client. IT support is in-house.'

'What about post?'

'It's delivered to the security desk downstairs, and the secretaries pick it up from there.'

'And on your way back to the station, do you take the same route?'

'Yes. I'm normally in a hurry to catch a train.'

'Okay. Thanks for letting me follow you around. It's been helpful to get a better sense of your routines.'

'Do you think this will help you figure out who the casters are?'

'I do,' I say, though I choose not to elaborate. Instead, I offer Tim a smile filled with confidence I cannot feel and wish him a good day.

My feet remain rooted to the spot long after I have watched Tim go through the turnstiles and disappear into one of the lifts. The coffee, too sweet for my taste, grows cold in the cup while my thoughts run through the brief walk time and time again. Mornings are the likeliest time for Tim to come into regular contact with a Mage or a Feykin in Old London, and yet there are other possibilities. Could it be a neighbour or someone on the train? Perhaps I am missing something, but I cannot for the life of me figure out what it is.

Now what?

15

UNEXPECTED VISITORS

Self-doubt and frustration slow my steps, and it is past ten when I round the corner to my home street. There is no sign of Karrion so he must have let himself in. My conscience twinges at not having texted him to say that I would be late, but I cannot bring myself to care. If he was concerned, he would already have called me.

Distracted by the dark thoughts, I barely notice a black Tesla with tinted windows parked a few doors from my home. Even the sound of car doors opening behind me does not elicit a reaction, but a familiar drawl jolts me out of my thoughts.

'Ms Wilde.'

Turning around, I see Lord Wellaim Ellensthorne stepping away from the car and engaging the lock over his shoulder. Instead of a rumpled suit, he is dressed in tight jeans and a leather jacket. The lanky locks of hair and crimson spectacles all but hide his searching eyes, but I have already taken the measure of him. He is a dangerous enemy: a ruthless politician who will stop at nothing to realise his goals. From our previous meetings, I know he considers Shamans vermin and me a curiosity who should not linger in Old London.

'For a struggling PI, you are a hard woman to find,'

Lord Ellensthorne says and raises his chin. His tone and the twist of his lips speak of disapproval.

If he expects me to apologise, he has underestimated me or overestimated himself.

'Who says I'm struggling?' I ask instead, my earlier frustration turning into irritation.

Lord Ellensthorne shrugs. 'Marsh's money won't last forever, and I doubt Ilana paid you generously. The fee was tied to skill level, was it not?'

'My charges are private.'

'At least you've grasped one of the principles of your profession.'

'Why are you here?' I ask. Today is the wrong day to be butting antlers with an arrogant Mage.

'I have a business proposal for you, though I rather expected we would be discussing it in your office.' Lord Ellensthorne makes a show of looking up and down the street. 'You do have an office, don't you?'

My first instinct is to tell him where he can shove his business proposal, but I bite my tongue. As much as it galls me to admit it, Lord Ellensthorne is right. The fees from Ilana and Tim will only keep my business afloat for so long, and I doubt angering the Speaker of the High Council of Mages would do my business any favours. As much as I dislike the man, it is wisest to remain civil.

'Of course,' I say and start towards my front door. 'This way.'

It is only then that I realise another man is trailing behind Lord Ellensthorne. I would guess he is a bodyguard, but his short, bulky stature suggests otherwise. He grips the handrail as we descend down to the front door, but he looks around with the same arrogant disdain as Lord Ellensthorne.

I hold the door open, and they step in to survey my office. Neither man seems to find Karrion's Wanted posters amusing. It is their loss.

Lord Ellensthorne motions to me. 'Yannia Wilde is the only Wild Folk living in Old London.' The man nods as if this explains something, and Ellensthorne continues, 'And this is Mr Whyte.'

As I step forward to shake his hand, I draw upon my magic, and a familiar scent of velvet darkness tickles my nostrils. Another Shadow Mage. It explains the arrogance.

'That's ironic.'

'As you can see, she's good,' Lord Ellensthorne tells his colleague. 'Unoriginal, but good.'

Footsteps sound above me, and I track them down the stairs. The door to the rest of the flat opens.

'Hey, Yan, I was starting to get wor—' Karrion spots my visitors. 'Oh. I didn't realise we were expecting company.'

Lord Ellensthorne smirks, and I watch him jump to the obvious conclusion. It matters not, and my posture remains relaxed as I indicate that Karrion should join us.

'Karrion, you remember Lord Ellensthorne. Mr Whyte, this is my apprentice, Karrion Feathering.'

'He's a Bird Shaman,' Lord Ellensthorne tells Whyte, who makes a disappointed noise.

Karrion's temper rises with his magic; an unkindness of ravens taking to flight. I shake my head a fraction, a warning enough for him to see, and he bites back whatever angry retort is at the tip of his tongue. Lord Ellensthorne thrives on pushing people's buttons, and Karrion is an easy target.

'Take a seat,' I say and sit behind the desk. Karrion fetches my laptop from upstairs while the Shadow Mages accept my invitation. Lord Ellensthorne slouches back in his chair.

'How can I help you?' I ask, trying to keep my tone neutral.

'I want to hire you.'

'For?'

'You, Ms Wilde, possess a unique ability in Old London. Given Reaoul Pearson's arrest and subsequent death, I assume you are fully appraised of my predecessor's true nature.'

'Reaoul Pearson is dead?' I sit straighter, shocked by Lord Ellensthorne's words.

'You hadn't heard? Pearson died in Paladin custody. Apparently, he ate something that didn't agree with him.'

'That's—' Karrion says, but he does not finish the sentence. He is as troubled as I am.

'That's clearly news to you.' Lord Ellensthorne pushes hair from his face, satisfaction curling his lips upwards. 'It just goes to prove the old adage that you learn something new every day.'

As much as I am thrown by the news, it is a matter for another time. I doubt Lord Ellensthorne descended from his Old London mansion to mingle with the commoners simply to rattle my cage. But what he has done is place the control of the discussion firmly in his own hands. Time to take some back.

'I'm aware that Braeman was a Leech.' I find a small measure of satisfaction in the way Whyte flinches. Lord Ellensthorne also notices his reaction and tuts.

'There's no need to be coy, Mr Whyte. This is a confidential meeting, and it wouldn't do to tiptoe around the issue at hand, no matter how sensitive it might be.'

While I am tempted to point out that I have not agreed to keep anything confidential, my curiosity overrides the desire to antagonise Lord Ellensthorne. At the very least, I can put that desire on hold until I find out the reason behind this visit.

'Did you come all this way to tell me that you, too, know about Braeman's true nature?' I ask. 'Because I would have thought our last meeting made that clear.'

'You'd be none the wiser had I not pointed you in the right direction.' Lord Ellensthorne steeples his fingers and rests his chin on them. 'You're being obtuse, Ms Wilde. It is most unbecoming.'

'Alright, I'll bite. What is it that you want from me?'

'You are the only one in Old London capable of detecting a Leech, when they're not draining you dry. I want to utilise your unique talent.'

'To do what, exactly?'

'I'm the newly appointed Speaker of the High Council of Mages. The Circle of Shamans follows my lead, as they should. Old London and her inhabitants look to me for guidance and leadership. They need look no further. I will be a proper leader of our community.'

'Unlike Gideor Braeman.'

'Braeman was a fool. I doubt he realised how close to destroying us all he came with his quest for power.'

'As much as I share your view on Braeman, you still haven't explained what you need me for,' I say.

'If a Leech is able to assume the positions of the Speaker of the High Council of Mages and the First among the Light Mages, there's no telling how many others are masquerading as Mages and Shamans at the top of our political hierarchy. I want you to vet the High Council and the Circle, to flush out any Leeches that are trying to follow Braeman's footsteps.'

'I'm happy to run background checks on everyone, but there's no guarantee that doing so will allow me to spot a Leech. Braeman was hiding in plain sight for years.'

'That's not the sort of vetting I'm after. I'm hiring you for your nose, not for your ability to check addresses and family trees.'

Karrion's hands become still on the keyboard, and I can feel the feathers of his magic ruffling; a sparrow preparing to take on a crow. I share his affront.

'If it's a Bloodhound you're after, I suggest you search online for a suitable kennel. You might get lucky and find a dog that's already trained.'

Lord Ellensthorne's eyes narrow. 'No dog, not even one bonded to a Dog Shaman, could ever rival a Wild Folk's ability to identify people with magical blood.'

It is my turn to lean back as the corner of my mouth lifts. 'Isn't that a shame?'

'I will have nothing but the best, and you are the best.'

'The best?' I cock my head. 'Or the only?'

'Either way, you're ideal.'

'I'm also busy.'

'I doubt you're too busy to accept my assignment. It would mean good fees for you.'

'Tempting though it is, I'm nobody's sniffer dog.'

Lord Ellensthorne rises and leans forward to place his palms on the edge of my desk. My hackles rise at the sign of dominance, and I meet his stare full on, refusing to be intimidated.

'I don't think you quite grasp the full implications of your refusal. Flushing out the Leeches from our social and political hierarchy will offer a degree of protection to all inhabitants of Old London. Can you imagine what would happen if the general population found out what Braeman did? Or worse yet, if the humans got wind of the Leeches and their power?'

I open my mouth to offer a clever rebuttal, but none is forthcoming. As much as I hate to admit it, Lord Ellensthorne has a point. The secrets Karrion and I agreed to keep last week were for the same reason: to protect our kind. I may dislike Lord Ellensthorne as a person, but I cannot disclaim his desire to keep Old Londoners safe.

'No,' Karrion says, shaking his head. 'Yannia is a person, not a tool.'

Lord Ellensthorne dismisses Karrion's words with a wave. 'There's no shame in being a tool if you're used by those better and smarter than you.'

'That discounts you, then.'

I bite back a laugh at Karrion's audacity, while Lord Ellensthorne's neck flushes. It is the first rise we have got out of him. All the glory to Karrion.

'You may wish to teach your apprentice some manners.'

'Karrion's manners may be lacking, but his heart is where it should be.' When Karrion tries to speak, I stop him and continue, 'However, I admit that you have a point. We have kept Braeman's origins a secret for a reason, and it's possible others may be attempting a similar charade. Who knows, Braeman may even have manoeuvred other Leeches into positions of power.'

'In his position, that is precisely what I would have

done,' Lord Ellensthorne says. 'Do we have an accord?'

'Yes, I'll vet the High Council and the Circle for you.'

'Once you have done so, there may be others I will want you to check, potential replacements for the Council seats and other prominent figures.'

'Fine, I'll fit the work around my other cases. I should warn you, the case I'm currently working on remains a priority.'

'Excellent. Mr Whyte will provide you with a list of people, including addresses, family members, whatever we have on file for them. I assume you will apportion your daily charges between the work you do for me and any other clients.'

'I'll make it easier for you. How about I charge you by the hour?'

'Eminently sensible. How much is your time worth: fifty pounds an hour?'

'I was more thinking five hundred.'

The anger in Lord Ellensthorne's face makes up for all his insults. I remain relaxed in my chair while he reins in his temper.

'That seems rather steep.'

'You did say I'm unique and the only one able to perform the job you outlined.'

'Taking advantage of your position? That's very calculating of you.'

'I have a business to run, and if I'm not mistaken, you'd do the same in my position. Besides, I doubt you'll be footing the bill for this vetting exercise yourself. The High Council must have a budget for incidentals.'

'Very well, but I expect to see an itemised account of the time you bill me for.'

'Of course.'

'In that case, we are in agreement.' Lord Ellensthorne offers his hand, and I stand to shake it. His is a limp fish in my grip, and once I am back sitting, I wipe my hand on my jeans. 'Give Mr Whyte your contact details, and he will email you the list. He will also organise payment of your fees in due course.'

I pass Whyte my card, and he places it in his wallet. They stand. As I escort them to the door, I should thank them for their custom, but the words get stuck in my throat. I force a smile instead and promise to be in touch when I have something to report.

The door closes behind them, and I am struck by the thought that light having faded, shadows are coming out to play.

16

ONE MAGIC CHANGE

When I turn away from the door, Karrion is tugging on the row of hoops in his ear. His expression belies his youth as he turns to me.

'Why are we working for him?'

'You heard the reason.'

'But he thinks the likes of you and me are vermin. My mum wasn't even good enough to scrub his floors.'

'Think of your siblings.'

'I am,' Karrion says, and stands. His chair falls backwards with a clatter. 'I don't want them growing up believing they're less than a Mage.'

'On the other hand, I doubt you want them to grow up fearing humans.'

Karrion starts to speak, but stops, his brow creasing.

'I know both of us have, to some extent, lived removed from humans. There's safety in that separation, but also danger. Wishearth warned me about this last week. We need to be able to demonstrate to humans that we can co-exist in harmony. That is what will keep us safe.'

'They wouldn't go against us in Old London.'

'But what of those who live in the rest of the country? There's no protection in numbers there. And I doubt you'd want to live your life isolated in the middle of human London.'

Karrion stuffs his hands in his pockets and walks to the row of posters on the wall. He stops next to one showing a blank square and the text "Invisible Man still at large".

'Lord Ellensthorne doesn't care about the Shamans out there, or the Wild Folk, or Mages from poor bloodlines,' he says.

'Not directly. But without the lower classes that make up the majority of the population, he'd have few people to lord over.'

My words have the desired effect, and Karrion's lips twitch. But he is not ready to drop the subject.

'That doesn't make him any less arrogant or obnoxious.'

'No, it doesn't. But those things also don't make him evil. As much as I dislike him, he's right about this. If another Leech shares Braeman's ambitions, they need to be stopped.'

'I just wish it had been the Circle of Shamans that reached out to you. Or any other Mage.'

'That's why we're charging him a premium fee.' I grin. 'Something has to make up for his unpleasantness.'

Karrion smiles, and his shoulders relax. 'You know just what to say to make me feel better.'

'I try.' I motion towards the door. 'Shall we get going?'

While we wait for a bus, I recount my morning with Tim. Although I voice none of my doubts, Karrion picks up on my frustration. The reassurance he offers rings hollowly in my ears. We both know that at present, we are at a dead end. Even if this shopping trip is a success, it will only give us the means to react. We need a lucky break before Tim or anyone else gets hurt.

One Magic Change is a structure of glass and steel next to St Paul's. It is the largest magical shopping centre in Old London and it attracts humans and non-humans alike. Tourists come to gawk at the gaslights, the flames of which take on the shapes of gryphons and dragons, and to breathe in the aromas of potions. The locals stock up on spell ingredients, further their research and come to find a community.

For me, a visit to One Magic Change is a chance to observe the lighter side of magic and the sense of wonder it evokes in those without the gift.

We cross the road near St Paul's, and Karrion draws my attention to a group of Paladins in front of the corridor leading into the shopping centre. The Paladins are checking everyone going in, and the air shimmers with their spells. Scanning the crowds, I spot a familiar figure staring at the Paladins with a look of speculation.

Fria senses my eyes on her and turns in unison with the three cats keeping her company. Her expression betrays hesitation, which she covers with a smile and a wave. The movement draws Karrion's attention away from the Paladins, and he frowns at the sight of the cats.

'Hi,' Fria says as she approaches. A tortoiseshell cat leaps into her arms and climbs to balance on her shoulder, fixing its eyes on Karrion.

I feel his magic responding to the challenge, like a bird ruffling its feathers to appear bigger in the face of a predator. That he is a giant compared to the cat is of no consequence to the instincts of a Bird Shaman.

'Fria, hi.'

Karrion's frown deepens as he connects the dots. But

I notice he cannot help taking in the jeans accentuating Fria's athletic build, the short leather jacket and a bob of hazelnut brown hair that frames her face. He will complain later about what a travesty it is that such a beautiful woman was born a Cat Shaman.

'What's going on here?' I ask into the silence.

Fria shrugs. 'Someone was robbed last night, and the Paladins think the stolen goods are going to be sold here.'

'I see.'

'Who?' Karrion asks, his tone brusque. 'Who got robbed?'

'Lord Ellensthorne, the First among the Shadow Mages.'

At this, Karrion laughs and claps a hand over his mouth when he realises how loud the sound is. His hostility forgotten, his eyes shine as he checks my reaction.

'How strange that he failed to mention that,' I say with a grin. 'What was taken?'

'The Paladins didn't say, but if they're out in force, it must have been something valuable.'

Fria's expression betrays nothing, but I get the impression she is a little too non-committal. Karrion seems to have reached the same conclusion, for he regards her with something resembling approval.

'I take it you're not a fan of Lord All Shadows?' Fria asks. The cat on her shoulder mirrors the tilt of her head exactly.

'We've had a couple of... meetings with him.' My reply is diplomatic, and Karrion snorts, no doubt keen to express his true feelings regarding Lord Ellensthorne. I dislike the man as much as Karrion does, but I prefer to keep my personal opinions private.

'I guess your investigation didn't go so well,' Fria says, 'given that Marsh was executed last Friday.'

As I hesitate, Karrion's temper flares once more. He is keen to defend me and set the record straight, but I stop him with a shake of my head. The official story is that Marsh was guilty and received his just punishment. I may have trusted Lady Bergamon with the truth, but that is as far as I am willing to break the Paladin General's confidence.

'No, it didn't quite go according to plan.'

My tone is a hint for Fria to drop the subject, and her attention drifts back to the Paladins. She seems to be staring at the jewelled swords the Paladins carry, and a speculative gleam returns to her eyes.

'I wouldn't,' I say.

'Wouldn't what?'

'You'd need more than nine lives to break into the Brotherhood of Justice.'

'Good to know.' Fria stretches, mindful of the cat on her shoulder. 'What brings you to One Magic Change?'

'We need the advice of a Tinker in our current case.'

'Do you have someone in mind?'

I get the impression that as much as Fria sounds bored, she is keeping a close eye on my body language.

'No. I figured we'd go upstairs and pick one at random.'

'Go see Tinker Thaylor. If you tell her I sent you, she'll give you a fair deal.'

'Thanks. I appreciate the recommendation.'

Fria nods and sends a final lingering glance in the Paladins' direction. The two cats on the ground lose interest in us and head out, but not before the black one has rubbed against Karrion's legs. Karrion swears and jumps back. I am certain the cat grins at Fria, who has the good sense to keep her expression neutral.

'I'll leave you to it,' she says, and leaves.

Once he is certain Fria is out of earshot, Karrion huffs. 'Someone that hot should not have been born a Cat Shaman.'

'I knew you were going to say that.'

'It's true.'

'Next time I see her, I'll tell Fria you said so.'

'Don't you dare.'

I laugh and leave Karrion to ponder whether to glower after me or Fria. The Paladin I walk up to appears puzzled by my wide grin, but she is too polite to question my amusement. She explains the reason for the search, and I empty my pockets when asked. Once she has checked my belongings, I step forward into the area of the spell. Magic slides along my skin, as real as a person touching me, sinking into my bones and through them. It leaves me feeling like I am breathing underwater, and I wipe my hands on my jeans, even though I am not wet. At the far side of the spell, the feeling dissipates with the caress of morning mist.

'Paladin magic is weird,' Karrion says when he emerges next to me. He rubs his face and runs a finger along my shoulder.

'Says the man who can speak with pigeons.'

'With crows and ravens. Pigeons are just an unfortunate side effect.'

'Keep telling yourself that,' I say and dodge the poke aimed at my ribs.

Shops of all kinds are situated around the central staircases. A group of schoolgirls gives way to coils of orange smoke snaking out of an apothecary. I can smell sulphur, tin and pine, and wonder what sort of potion is in the making. Karrion looks around with delight.

'I remember when I was a kid and Mum gave me pocket money in return for chores. Every month, I came here and spent it on spell crackers. But only the ones that turned into a phoenix. I'd even walk here so I could afford an extra cracker.'

'Not much has changed since last year, huh? At least you have a bus pass now.'

'As funny as you think you are, maybe don't give up your PI business just yet.'

A young man is standing near the stairs, juggling four glowing balls. One falls through his fingers and shatters on the ground, sending out a wave of blue flowers. They fade away, leaving only an aroma of lavender. A group of tourists claps and drops coins into a copper cauldron in front of him.

'Mages are always showing off,' Karrion says, but his gaze lingers on the remaining balls.

'Theirs is a different kind of magic, you know that. Mages draw their power from the weather patterns, from the memories of the bedrock, from the cycles of the tides and from the flicker of flames. But they will never share a connection with living things like you or I do.'

'I know that, Yan. I'm part of every bird I meet, and they are all within me. There's nothing Mages can cast that trumps knowing what it's like to soar across the sky or feel wind through my feathers. I just can't help thinking that if I could do what he's doing, I'd be a real chick magnet. And I mean the right sort of chicks.'

'I can take you to a henhouse.'

'That's exactly what I didn't mean.'

171

I feign innocence, but I wonder if there is something behind the light-hearted wish to use magic for getting dates. As much as the Circle of Shamans is a respected authority within Old London, there is a general consensus that Shamans, due to the limited scope of their magic, are at the bottom of our social hierarchy. Mages from the old bloodlines are looked upon as natural leaders, the Paladins of Justice are respected as the keepers of peace, and the Feykin are too divided as a group to claim social standing. Individually, they often rub shoulders with the Mage aristocracy. As for the Wild Folk, we are the uncultured savages from the tales of old, known for dressing in animal skins and eating our kills raw.

We take the stairs up, past the level specialising in spell books, ritual instructions and ancient lore. The level after that houses the food court, which caters wholly to the tourists. No Old Londoner would purchase witch bubble tea, mandrake root protein shakes or squid brain pate. When a young woman offers us free samples of belladonna ice cream, we shake our heads and climb yet another set of stairs to the workshops.

The top floor of the shopping centre smells of ozone, true silver and soldering line. Hairs on the back of my neck prick up from the thrum of power. A great many spells are cast here: mana stored in gadgets and gems.

While we look at the shop fronts, two Paladins in full battle armour complete their circuit of the floor and head back down. They subject us to intense scrutiny. We must not look like criminals for they murmur a greeting on their way past.

'I think that's it,' Karrion says and points at a shop to our right.

The shop sign reads "Thaylor's Tinkerings" and the window is lined with shelves containing metal devices of all shapes and sizes. Tinkers are known for their ability to meld spells into machines, to augment technology with magic. Such items are valued by Old Londoners and purchased by humans as quaint curiosities. The Tinkers' talent lies in crafting the items in a way that allows humans to activate their abilities. They understand that as much as humans lack magical blood, they still possess an innate craving for power. That is why humans flock to Old London and One Magic Change: they search for some potion or device that will allow them to feel special, to share a connection with the magical world at their doorstep. Humans may, at times, fear or hate us, but they also want to become us.

As we reach for the door, I note that amidst the brass and steel machines on display is a small jade statue of a cat with eyes that gleam emerald in the pulsing light emanating from the workshops. I push open the door and bells chime once, then again in a different, discordant tune. I look up and see that the bells hang next to the door, but they are not connected to it.

The shop is crammed full, and from the chaos of the shelves, I pick out an old-fashioned telephone, a doorbell and various lamps. Metal animals of all kinds hang from the ceiling, including a snake that stretches half of the length of the space, its body decorated with gleaming rivets. Next to it, a golden head of a dragon puffs tiny clouds of purple smoke. What its purpose could be, I can only guess.

At the back of the shop is a low counter, and a woman straightens into view behind it. She is diminutive, with grey hair pulled back in a tight bun. A leather apron is pitted with burn marks, droplets of metal and a variety of stains. Thick goggles enlarge her already huge eyes, giving her a gnomish appearance. She looks up and down at us, then grins, revealing sparse, stained teeth.

We approach the counter, and I inhale. Beneath the sweat, grease and metal shavings, I detect moss, frost and autumn leaves. She is a North Mage.

'Awaque,' she says and taps the tail feathers of a brass wren perched on a branch on the counter. The bird comes to life, hopping into flight with a blur of gleaming wings. After circling the shop, it lands on Karrion's outstretched hand and bursts into song. Karrion responds with a tiny exhale of magic, and chirps back. He rarely alters his voice box to sing like a bird, but when he does, it is always a pleasure to witness.

'I can give my creations the power to fly and to sing, but I cannot give them life. Still, even a metal bird recognises kin in a Bird Shaman.'

'Tinker Thaylor, I presume,' I say.

'Indeed. As for you, my machine didn't know what to make of you.'

I nod. 'Most detection devices in Old London struggle with my kind.'

'That narrows it down. You're too young to be Lady Bergamon, but you have an edge of wildness about you. My guess is you're one of the Wild Folk. The PI living in Old London, perhaps?'

'Yannia Wilde.' I offer my hand. Her grip is strong; her hand calloused and bony. 'Fria suggested that we come to see you.'

'Did she now? What mischief is she up to this time?'

The question throws me. There must be a subtext I am missing.

'I don't know. We ran into her outside the shopping centre, and when I mentioned we were looking for a Tinker, she gave us your name.'

'I see. All is forgiven. How can I help you?'

Karrion joins me by the counter, and the bird flies from his finger back on to its perch. I introduce Karrion.

'We are looking for a device that would allow us to identify a spell in effect and trace it back to its caster.'

Thaylor makes a clicking noise at the back of her throat. 'Tracing is tricky. For that to work, the spell must retain a link to the caster.'

'Don't they all?' Karrion asks.

'No. Say someone casts a ward against remote viewing. Once it is up and running, the caster's involvement ends. But if an alarm ward sends a silent signal to the caster when the ward is breached, a link remains.'

'What about illusions?' I ask.

'Depends on the illusion. Are we talking Mage or Feykin in origin? Is it targeted at a specific person or an area? Does it include the caster? Can the illusions be interacted with?'

'We think all of the above.'

Thaylor lifts her goggles and rubs the bridge of her nose. 'As I said, tracing is tricky. If you had something belonging to the caster, a lock of hair or an item of clothing, that would help. But if you're looking to trace him, I'm assuming you don't know the caster's identity.'

'We know very little, except there are two casters and one of them is likely to be a woman.'

'I have nothing in stock powerful enough to both

175

identify illusions and trace their caster. Building something would take a week or two, and it would be costly.'

Karrion and I exchange a look, frustrated by another dead end.

'Time is of the essence,' I say, worried that we have wasted too much of it by coming to One Magic Change.

'If that's the case, would a simpler device be of help? It will tell you if a spell is cast by a Mage, a Shaman, a Paladin or a Feykin, and in the case of Mages and Shamans, it will identify the type. You can even store a caster signature within the memory and see if it matches other spells you come across.'

'What sort of a caster signature?' Karrion asks.

'Each person has a unique way of casting spells. Like fingerprints or handwriting, no two are alike. Every person has a different way of speaking the words of a spell or making preparations for a ritual or for brewing a potion. Just like a fingerprint, a casting signature can be identified and recorded.'

'That sounds brilliant,' Karrion says. 'Do the police use devices like that?'

'No. As far as I know, it is only me who has been developing that particular merging of magic and technology. Even if the police and the Paladins knew about it, they wouldn't touch a Tinker's device.'

Karrion runs a hand through his hair. 'That sounds like an odd prejudice to have.'

'It's always been the way with Tinkers,' Thaylor tells him. 'We are hated by many, and yet our customers keep coming back. The only thing that has changed over the centuries is that we no longer travel around, peddling our wares.'

'It sounds like the police are missing out on a vital resource,' I say. 'In any case, I'd like to purchase the device you described.'

'Just a moment.'

Thaylor disappears through a narrow doorway, and I can hear the sound of drawers opening and closing. When she returns, she is carrying a brown leather pouch. In it is what looks like a pocket calculator set within a case of dull metal. Instead of numbers, below the display are two rows of buttons bearing unfamiliar symbols. Thaylor explains their function, how to store a caster signature, and shows a legend of the possible caster results. At the back of the machine is a panel, and Thaylor slides it aside to reveal five black stones.

'These mana gems power the machine. When the magic runs out, come back and I will charge them for you.'

'For a fee, I presume.'

'Of course.'

'There's something else I was wondering. Is it possible to enchant an item to make a person disappear?'

Thaylor cocks her head. 'Disappear how? Do you mean teleportation? Or disintegration? Or invisibility?'

'Any of the three, though I'm more thinking the first two.'

'You'd need a circle for teleportation, and a permanent one at that. It takes a huge amount of power and would likely destroy any object the magic was channelled through. To suggest that a Mage could store a teleportation spell in an object such as a necklace or an orb is ludicrous. The item would implode and take the Mage with it.'

'That's out then. What about disintegration?'

'It's possible, but tricky. Disintegration spells require strict boundaries. To channel one through an object would require the object to cover the person entirely. A body mesh might do it, though everything outside it would remain behind. As would the ashes from the disintegrated parts.'

'And invisibility?'

'It's easier. An object can create a small area within which the spell operates. The carrier would be undetectable by sight, but other senses could find him.'

I nod. This confirms what we already thought, but gets us no closer to finding the casters. 'Can you think of any other way to make a person disappear?'

'Portals. But if you think teleportation is indiscreet, portals shout from the rooftops that magic is happening. You've seen the Paladins summoning a Herald of Justice, haven't you?'

'Yes.'

'It's no different for the rest of us.' Thaylor braces her hands on the counter and cranes her neck to look at us. 'There are plenty of people out there who believe magic is the easy solution to everything. We all know that's not the case. If I wanted to make someone disappear, I'd use as little magic as possible. After all, every spell I cast could be traced back to me. Why take the risk? A discreet illusion to throw people off my scent would be far better than disintegrating someone.'

'And do you know if it would be possible to disguise one type of magic with another?'

'What do you mean?'

'Could a Feykin use a spell to make his illusions appear like Mage magic?'

'If they can, it's an ability they've kept quiet about. It would mean Mages working with New Scotland Yard and the Paladins would be out of a job.'

'What about the other way round? Could a Mage change his magic to look like Feykin glamour?'

'No, our magic doesn't work like that.'

'Thanks. That's been helpful.'

While I pay, Karrion runs his fingers over the brass wren, which has become still during our conversation with Thaylor.

'If you can make metal birds fly,' he says, each word slow, 'could you build wings for a human?'

Thaylor adjusts her goggles and hands me a receipt. 'I could. It would take time and be an expensive project. But the fate of Icarus awaits any man who yearns for the skies.'

'I've lived with that yearning since the day I was born. I should have hatched from an egg, not been born into the body of a human, wingless and flightless.'

Karrion's candour takes me by surprise, and Thaylor looks intrigued. She hands him a piece of leather with a number etched on to it.

'If in the future you still want wings and have the means to pay for them, give me a call.'

His thumb traces over the numbers, and I see longing in the tightening of his eyes and in the press of his lips.

'No, thanks.' Karrion hands the leather piece back.

'Suit yourself.'

After thanking Thaylor, we leave. Outside the shop, I turn to stare at Karrion.

'What?' he asks when he notices.

'Is the desire to fly really that strong?'

Karrion rubs the back of his neck, unable to meet my eyes. 'The way I see it, it's a craving for a drug I've never tasted. If I ever did get to try it, I doubt I'd be able to stop until it killed me.'

He hesitates, his brow furrowing while he finds the right words. I remain silent, waiting for him to continue.

'This is going to sound crazy, but there are times when I envy my father for the death he had.'

'Why?' It does sound crazy.

'Because when he fell off that building, there was a moment when he knew what it's like to soar through the sky.'

'You don't think he was afraid, knowing that he would die?'

'Dad was fearless. It's something Mum both loved and hated about him.'

'Is the manner of your father's death the reason you turned down Thaylor's number?' I ask, beginning to understand.

'Yes. Dad loved his work, said that on top of a skyscraper was the only place where he could feel the wind on his face and be close to the sky. I think he was consumed by the same desire to fly as I have, and he was less inclined to control it. I'm not saying he jumped off that building, but perhaps he didn't take as much care as he should have done.'

I open my mouth to reply, but I am not certain what to say. Since telling me how his father had died, Karrion has not spoken much about him. It is unusual, for he is forever telling me about the antics of his siblings or his mother's conservative views on his appearance.

'As much as I would love to fly,' he says, words rushing

to fill the silence, 'I don't want to leave the people I love like Dad did.'

'You've been a big help to your mum over the years.'

'Well, yes, but I was also thinking about you since you can't even keep your fridge stocked.'

'I'm not that hopeless.' When he says nothing, I revise my statement. 'I'm not always that hopeless.'

'I know.' Karrion grins. 'But that doesn't mean that you don't need someone to keep an eye on you.'

'If that's the case, I'm glad that someone is you.'

I dodge around two young men coming out of a spell bookstore. From the snippet of conversation I overhear, I take them to be students, but I make no effort to find out what type of spell casters they are. The sounds of the shopping centre are beginning to wear on me, and I yearn for the peace of the forest. After my visit to the conclave, my tolerance for crowds and noise is even lower than usual.

'At least this was a successful trip,' Karrion says as we descend to the ground floor. The juggling Mage is still showing off, this time by sending green flames dancing between the people watching him.

'Yes, we got the device we needed. Now all that's missing is an illusion for us to detect.'

17

A DAY OF DISTRACTIONS

The Paladins are too busy inspecting the lunchtime crowds to spare us more than a glance when we leave One Magic Change.

'Do you think people really come here to fence stolen goods?' Karrion asks.

'It's not the first time I've heard the rumour. I could see it being true; for a magic user, finding an excuse to visit One Magic Change is easy.'

'Who do you think the fence is? The belladonna ice cream girl from the food court?'

'I doubt it.'

'Why?'

'What's the most important thing you need if you're going to buy and sell stolen goods?'

'Money?'

'That's given. Think it through, Karrion.'

'Okay, not the ice cream seller. She works at the food court. It gets plenty of footfall, though it's mostly humans who stop there. But... no privacy.'

I nod, pleased with his deduction. 'In order to guarantee no prying eyes, the transactions must happen in one of the shops.'

'That doesn't really narrow it down. It must be one of

the posher shops given how much money there is in the black market.' Karrion looks back as if the glass front of One Magic Change holds the answer. 'So a posh, shifty shop owner. That does narrow it down.'

'Don't forget that the stolen goods may need to be taken apart or modified before being sold,' I say. Karrion's enthusiasm is contagious.

'We could be looking for a shifty Tinker. Not Thaylor, she wasn't shifty or acting suspiciously.'

'I don't think the fence twitches at every noise and stares obsessively at the door. If they did, the Paladins would already have caught them.'

'Still, I think we're on to something.'

'It's a shame no one has hired us to find the fence. Although,' I grin, 'I'm sure Lord Ellensthorne would be delighted if you returned the items stolen from him. He might even say thank you.'

Karrion's expression turns sour. 'On reflection, I'm more of a live and let live kind of man. The fence probably has a wife and a clutch of children to feed.'

'No doubt, though I should point out that the fence could just as easily be a woman.'

'Never let it be said that Old London's criminal under-world doesn't believe in equal opportunities.'

'Exactly.'

What I leave unsaid is that the mystery of the fence's identity could easily be solved by asking Fria.

'What are we going to do next?' Karrion asks. 'It feels like we've ended up in a dead end with the case. As much as I'd love to get on with helping Lord Ellensthorne – not – I worry that something is going to happen to Tim.'

'Me too. Let's head over to Liverpool Street Station

and see if the machine can pick up any trace of the illusion at the second crime scene.'

'But didn't the Mage say in her report that there was too much background magic for her to identify the spell that was used?'

'She did. It'll be a long shot, but we have to try something.'

'I'm all for it. This is just different from last week. We had loads of leads to follow and not enough time to get everything done.'

'The pressure was different. We had a clear time frame. This time, it's as though we're sitting on a ticking bomb without being able to see the timer.'

'If in doubt, cut the red wire,' Karrion says.

We catch a bus to Liverpool Street Station and alight on Bishopsgate. The streets are busy, and our progress towards the crime scene slow.

A whiff of cologne drifts past me, pungent even to my human nose. I recognise the brand, and it sends a chill of fear into my limbs. Whirling around, I scan the crowd for anyone that might be paying attention to me.

'What's wrong?' asks Karrion.

The current of people streams past us, none casting more than a cursory glance in our direction. I sense no depletion of my power, and it is that, more than anything, that settles my nerves. It was a ghost I sensed, nothing more.

'I thought I smelled Jans.'

Karrion straightens his shoulders and lifts his hands, ready to defend me. His magic would be no use against a creature born to drain power from others, but physically he could easily overpower Jans.

'Did you smell a Leech?'

'No, the cologne Jans wore to mask his identity from me. One whiff and I was frozen in my bed with him standing over me, ready to attack.'

Karrion relaxes his defensive stance. 'It's over, Yan. You stopped the attack, and he can never hurt you again.'

'I know.' I lead Karrion to a quiet spot by a bus stop and lower my voice. 'But what's been left behind is a sense that nowhere is safe.'

Looking away, I blink to stop tears that threaten to fall. Karrion lays a hand on my shoulder, but I dare not turn into his embrace. Not yet.

'Jans took that from me. Yes, I'm lucky that he didn't take a lot more, but it makes me angry that I no longer feel safe in my own skin. What right did he have to do that? What right has anyone to do that to another person?'

'I'm sorry,' Karrion whispers. 'I wish I'd been there to protect you.'

'It's not your fault. It's not anyone's fault, except his. I keep hoping that one morning I'll wake up and be me again. I want to live my life without having to fear that Jans will come after me a second time.'

'There's no chance of that happening, is there? The Paladins have him locked up for good.'

'As far as I know. I'd like to think they would warn me if Jans was ever released.'

'Jamie would as well, wouldn't he? Though I don't suppose it would hurt to check. Can I have your phone?'

I hand it to him and watch as Karrion goes through my contacts. Finding the one he wants, he takes out his own phone and dials a number. The call connects, and I smile when I hear the greeting.

It is so like Karrion to want to help, to share the burden

of my trauma. Dearon would kill Jans for what he did. He would kill to protect me. But Karrion wants to heal me.

The moisture from my eyes dries while I wait for Karrion to finish his phone call. When he does, he hands me back my phone.

'Jamie confirmed that Jans is still in prison, waiting to appear before a Herald. He also said that should Jans ever be released, he would certainly let you know.'

'Thanks, Karrion.' Now I do hug him. The smell of him and his magic chases away the lingering threads of fear.

'You're welcome. But I want you to promise me something.'

'What's that?'

'If you ever feel unsafe in your flat, you call me, okay? I don't care what time it is, you can call me. And if you're scared on your own, you can always spend the night at ours. Mum won't mind, and I can sleep on the sofa.'

'The sofa is far too small for you.'

'It doesn't matter,' he says, shaking his head. 'I'll sleep on the floor if I have to, as long as you're safe.'

Touched by the vehemence in his voice, I stand on tiptoes and press a kiss on his cheek. 'Thanks. But shouldn't it be me looking out for you? You are my apprentice after all.'

'Well, yeah, but I'm dependent on you for gainful employment. I'd best keep you safe.'

I laugh, and he joins in. With a hand on his arm, I steer him back into the flow of pedestrians.

'Maybe we'll both watch out for the other.'

There is no sign of Sunday's crash when we reach the correct spot. Even the broken glass has been swept off the road. I get Thaylor's device out of my pocket and switch it on. The screen remains blank. I try again on several spots, even stepping on to the road briefly, and we retrace Tim's steps to Bishop's Square. The results remain the same: the device cannot detect an active spell.

'Maybe it doesn't work,' Karrion says, disappointed.

'Let's test it. Call a bird.'

Karrion's magic unfurls, brushing along the edges of my aura with the softness of down feathers before passing beyond my senses. The sensation distracts me from the task, and it is only when a pigeon lands at his feet that I recall the device in my hand. Taking aim, I activate it. The screen lights up straight away, and I check the symbols for the spell: Shaman, Bird. I lock Karrion's caster signature in the memory while he dismisses the pigeon.

'Sharpen your sight.'

This time, the surge of power is less noticeable, and I watch as Karrion's brown eyes pale to amber and his pupils narrow to those of a bird of prey. He looks towards the sky, and I wonder what he sees. While I, too, have the ability to borrow the keen senses of a hawk, when Karrion does it, he takes on the bird's perception of the world. Does he also get a taste of the primal hunger I feel when I stalk prey in the wilderness?

When I activate the device again, it identifies the Bird Shaman spell and an additional symbol flashes on the screen. It confirms that both spells were cast by the same Shaman.

'The device works,' I say, and switch it off. 'But to detect the illusions, we need to come upon one while it's still happening. How are we going to manage that?'

'Maybe we'll get lucky?'

'Maybe, but I'm not much of a PI if I have to rely on luck to solve my cases.'

'No one could have figured this out from the limited amount of information we have.'

'You don't know that,' I say, sceptical in the face of Karrion's optimism.

'I do. Jamie came to us, remember? In two days, we've already got further than the police did.'

'That's true. Thanks, Karrion.'

We head towards the bus stop in comfortable silence.

Back at home, I check my email and find that Whyte has sent the list of names he promised, together with information on each person named. Karrion takes a look at it over my shoulder and groans.

'That list is endless.'

'True, but think of all the bills we're going to send Lord Ellensthorne for vetting these people.'

The prospect cheers Karrion up, and we begin by creating a spreadsheet for all the information we have. Next, we look for photos of each person online. Members of the High Council of Mages and the Circle of Shamans are easy, but some of the other names are trickier. It would not do to vet the wrong person.

'You must be able to cover a lot of the names in one go if you lurk by the entrance during the Council and Circle meetings.'

'That's a good idea, though I can't just walk up to these people and start sniffing them. But why don't you look up the schedule for the forthcoming meetings, and we can then see which ones fit best with our other work.'

'Yes, boss.'

He soon presents me with a list of scheduled meetings for the next two weeks. They are frequent enough that I should be able to cover most of the Council and Circle members if I go along to a few of them. But while the term "lurking" does not sit well with me, I will need to maintain a certain level of discretion. Perhaps I ought to ask Fria for some lessons in sneaking around.

Still pondering the possibilities of lurking near a council meeting, I become aware of Karrion staring at me. I last for nearly a minute before my patience runs out.

'What?'

'You said last week that Dearon was the golden boy of the conclave.'

'Yes. So?'

'I was just wondering... do you envy him for the power he has?'

'No!'

Karrion says nothing, and eventually the silence gets the better of me again.

'Maybe.' I look away. 'Yes.'

'Why?'

'Because it irritates me that he has it so easy. He comes to the conclave, grows up to be the most powerful individual other than the current Elderman, and everyone loves him. He never had to work for any of it.'

Karrion nods. 'Whereas every day is a struggle for you because of the EDS.'

'Yes.' I pause, trying to find words for the honest truth. 'It takes so much effort, hiding the pain and the fatigue. And that's before I've done any of the endless tasks each day is made up of. Sometimes, I look at people and wonder if they realise how easy their lives are, how much they take for granted.'

'I don't think anyone's life is as easy as it looks to an outside observer,' Karrion says.

'Perhaps not, but some lives are a lot harder than others.'

'Point.' Karrion hesitates. 'You said Dearon came to the conclave. Is he one of those children adopted to a different conclave to diversify the gene pool?'

'Yes. He's from a family known for their strong blood, and our Elderman felt he would benefit the conclave.'

'It can't have been easy for him, being taken from his parents and sent to live with strangers.'

'His adoptive parents adored him,' I say, and cross my arms.

'That's good, of course it is. But I was just thinking, imagine growing up to find out that your parents sent you away for the betterment of another conclave.'

'It can't be too terrible since he's been brought up to be the next Elderman.'

'Perhaps not. Did he replace his biological family with lots of friends?'

'Mmm.'

'What's that?'

'I guess he has some friends, perhaps more now he's an adult.'

'But not growing up? Was he a loner?'

'No,' I say, unsure whether I like the direction of his questions. No point stopping now. 'He spent most of his time with me.'

'He did? You were friends?'

'Yes, of sorts. I suppose the Elderman ordered Dearon to keep an eye on me.'

'Did he tell you that?'

'No, I just figured that's the way it was. Dearon did know about the Elderman's plans, after all.'

'Or he could simply have considered you a friend.'

'Are you sure you didn't study psychology instead of fine arts?'

Karrion grins and spreads his arms. 'Maybe I'm just gifted in more ways than one.'

'Or perhaps you've taken a leaf out of Wishearth's book.'

'What do you mean?'

'You're meddling.'

'I'm just curious, and you don't often share as much as you did just now. It seems to me like something changed while you were at the conclave.'

'Like what?'

'You're less tense than before, but angrier.'

'I'm not angry,' I say, puzzled.

'Whenever the conclave or Dearon comes up in conversation, I can see it simmering just below the surface. You've told me a little about your past, but I keep thinking that someone must have done something terrible for you to be that angry.'

I flinch, once again surprised by his perceptiveness. Thinking back to the conversations I had with the Elderman, I recall all the things I was unable to say, all the emotions hidden. The only person I could express my anger to was Dearon. It has always been Dearon.

The thought threatens to take me back to the night I spent with him. Embers of our time together are still smouldering in my belly, and I dare not stoke them for fear of being engulfed in the flames.

'Back to work,' I say, my tone weary, and Karrion takes the hint.

The list Whyte provided forms a good basis for the task, but there is plenty of groundwork for us to do. By researching each name, we are able to build an image of not just the listed individual, but also their family and background. While I intend to check each name in person, our work allows me to begin assigning risk levels to them. Those who come from recognised bloodlines and whose offspring all have magical blood are low risk. But there are others who are relatively new to Old London politics and whose background is little known. They are a much higher risk of being Leeches, though there is nothing to say that living as a Mage or Shaman could not be a tradition passed down the generations.

I send Karrion home around five despite his protests that he does not mind another late night. There will be plenty of opportunities for those, I remind him, and bid him goodnight with the promise that I will call him if something comes up.

An hour later, a whisper of magic nearby pricks up the hairs on the back of my neck. My first thought is that Jans is back, but the aura I sense does not belong to a Leech. My armchair is next to the window, and I set the laptop down, making a show of stretching. As I do so, I sharpen my sight and look out.

I spot the tortoiseshell cat before Fria. While she is hiding in the shadows by the shed, the cat appears less concerned about being spotted and is sniffing at the low hanging branches of a blackberry bush. I get up and set the kettle to boil. When two cups of tea are brewing, I open the window.

'How do you take your tea?'

The silence lasts long enough that I wonder if Fria has slipped away. Then she steps out of the shadows.

'Milk, no sugar.'

'Of course.'

By the time I am carrying the mugs to the lounge, Fria and the cat have entered through the window. Fria is examining the room, and I am willing to bet that little escapes her notice. There is not much she can learn about me from my simple home, but I would be inter- ested to hear her conclusions.

'Can I help you with something?'

Fria shrugs and sips her tea. 'I was curious.'

'About?'

'You. How you live. Who you are. Why you are here instead of in the wilderness.'

Her words are statements, not questions, and I remain silent. We watch each other, and this time, I believe the curiosity is mutual. More than that, she is an attractive woman.

'I still owe you a favour,' she says, and sets her mug on the mantelpiece. It may be my imagination, but her hand seems to linger on the stones of the fireplace. Does she follow the old ways?

'There may come a time when I need your help or advice.'

'You know where I live.'

Fria returns to the window and swings her leg over the windowsill. The cat leaps on to her shoulder.

'You know, I half expected you to have a Catwoman poster downstairs.'

They slide back into the shadows while I laugh. Did she break into my office while I was here? Or did she crouch on the street, peering in through the narrow windows? The former seems more her style.

I continue working until my eyes sting from staring at the screen. An ache has crept into my legs while I have been curled up in an armchair, and the pain throbs in time with my heartbeat. I debate whether lying with my back to the fire will provide enough relief for me to fall asleep, or whether I should fix myself something to eat so I can take pain medication. Convenience wins, and I settle for pushing the mattress closer to the fireplace. With the chill of the autumn seeping into the walls, heat will be a blessing.

I am kneeling on the hearth stones, watching an offering to Wishearth burn with a crackle of sap when my phone rings.

'Yannia,' Jamie says when I answer, 'it's happened again.'

18

THIRD BLOOD

'You're up to something,' Lizzie said.

They had eaten at a family-run Italian restaurant near New Oxford Street and were now walking past the British Museum. The spotlights on the façade cast a bright glow against the darkness of the October night. A street vendor selling roasted chestnuts was packing away his cart, and the stream of tourists had slowed to a trickle.

'What do you mean?'

Tim turned left to Montague Street.

'For one, you've been grinning all evening. And now you look like you're walking with a purpose.'

'Can't I just be happy to spend time with you?' Tim put on a mock pout.

'You can, but you're even more cheerful than usual. What's going on?'

'You'll see,' he said, and winked.

Lizzie laughed, a little uncertainly.

The whitewashed buildings took on pallid yellow hues from the street lights, while the shadows cast from the wrought-iron fences gave the homes a hostile feel. From the heavy flower pots to the wide pavement, everything about the area spoke of affluence, and such a residential street was all but deserted after the British Museum had closed. The few pedestrians around were hurrying to or from Russell Square, oblivious to the world around them. A door banged shut behind them, and Lizzie shifted closer to Tim.

Once the street opened to Russell Square, Tim steered Lizzie across the road at the traffic lights. A homeless man was settling down on a bench atop layers of cardboard, and the fountain at the centre of the shaded square was switched off, leaving an empty space where children, dogs and teenagers frolicked during the warmer months. Glass breaking nearby had Lizzie inching closer to Tim's side, eyes wide as she looked for the source of the sound. Tim did not appear to notice anything was amiss.

Lizzie's steps slowed next to the cafe at the far end of the square. The building was dark and empty, creating deeper shadows amidst the outlines of bare branches that swayed in the breeze.

'What's really going on?' Lizzie asked. 'It's getting pretty late, and I have work tomorrow.'

'I have a surprise for you,' Tim said and pressed the button by the pedestrian crossing. When the lights changed, they continued diagonally across the road and away from Russell Square. 'It's not far.'

'Okay.' The uncertainty in Lizzie's voice was more pronounced, but Tim did not notice.

They took the next right and then a left before Tim stopped next to the front steps of the Ardent Hotel.

'Here we are.'

'A hotel. Why?'

'It's part of the surprise.'

'And what is the surprise?'

'You'll see upstairs.' Tim held out his hand. 'Come, please. I promise you'll like it.'

Lizzie glanced over her shoulder towards the way they had come before taking Tim's hand. He grinned as he led her up the steps to the door, seemingly oblivious to her hesitation.

Inside, the reception hall was decorated in reds and gold with dark wood furniture. A fire was alight opposite the reception desk, and Lizzie turned towards the flames to breathe in the smell of wood smoke. Tim waved to the man behind the desk and steered Lizzie to the stairs in the far corner. Their footsteps were muffled by the thick carpet, and the brass bannister was cool under Lizzie's palm.

On the first floor, Tim opened a door to a large double room that was dominated by a four-poster bed. In the low light from the lamps, the golden bedspread and decorative pillows added a soft glow to the room. On a low coffee table was a box of chocolates and a cooler bucket with a bottle of champagne. A vase of red roses was positioned next to a flat screen television.

'What's all this?' Lizzie asked, hovering in the doorway.

'You're always saying what a shame it is that I have to catch a train home at the end of the evening. I thought I'd surprise you by booking us a hotel room.'

'Us?'

'I was rather hoping you'd join me for a drink, and we'd have a chance to really talk without being interrupted by waiters and overheard by other diners. And maybe, if you wanted to, you could spend the night with me.'

'This feels like a big step.'

'We've been dating for a while now, and I wanted to show you that I'm serious about us.'

'I don't doubt that. But we agreed to take things slow.'

'That's exactly what we've done. I love you and I want to show that to you.' Tim lifted the champagne bottle out of the cooler and dried it on a hand towel that was draped over the back of a nearby chair. 'Can I pour you a glass of champagne?'

'Not right now.' Lizzie crossed her arms. 'Look, I already know that you love me. If there's any way you can demonstrate that, it's by allowing this to progress at a pace I'm comfortable with.'

'Don't you want to keep moving forward?' Tim asked and set the champagne bottle down, unopened.

'Yes, but at my pace.'

A door slammed in the corridor and the sound startled her. She twisted her head, but silence had returned to the floor. When she turned back, Tim was standing in front of her, and she jumped.

'Don't you love me?'

'Tim,' Lizzie began, but Tim let her get no further.

'You don't, do you?'

He reached past her and closed the door. Lizzie backed away along the wall until her legs touched the edge of the bed. Her eyes darted between the door, Tim and the dark windows framed by burgundy velvet curtains.

'It's not that simple,' she said, trying to calm her breathing. Tears were pooling in her eyes. In the warmth of the radiators, the smell of the roses was cloying, sickly sweet. 'You know what happened with Wayne.'

'I'm not him.'

'I know, but I need time to feel safe.' Her voice cracked and a tear got caught in her eyelashes.

'There's no way I'd ever treat you like that bastard did.'

'If that's the case, why are we here?'

'I love you.'

'Then let me go!' Lizzie's knees buckled, and she slid to the floor with her back against the bed. Her body shook with the force of the sobs, and she buried her face in her hands.

Tim stood by the door, startled by her reaction. The sound of her sobs unfroze him, and he hurried to kneel by her side.

'What's wrong, love?' He rested his hand on her shoulder.

'Don't touch me!'

Lizzie slapped his hand aside and shuffled away from him, still keeping her back to the bed. Mascara had formed dark circles under her eyes, and her cheeks were red. Her tears ran freely.

'Don't touch me,' she said again, her voice cracking.

'What did I do? I don't know what I did wrong.' Tim tried to shift closer, but stopped when Lizzie made to move away.

'You're just like Wayne.'

'That's not true. I'm nothing like him and I'm everything he's not.'

Lizzie wiped her cheeks, eyes burning with anger. 'Then why am I trapped here?'

'You're not. You can go anytime you wish.' Tim rose and walked to the window to show there was nothing between Lizzie and the door.

It took several minutes for Lizzie's crying to abate. When her breathing calmed, she used the corner of the bed to pull herself up. Beyond the bed, the bathroom door was open, but she took a handful of tissues from a box on the nightstand. Once she had wiped her face and blown her nose, she stuffed the used tissues in her pocket.

'I'm sorry,' Tim said. 'I didn't realise.'

'You should have.' Lizzie kept her eyes on her shoes.

'I wish I could turn back time and make this evening what it was supposed to be.' He walked to the coffee table and picked up the champagne bottle before setting it back down, still unopened.

Lizzie took three unsteady steps to the vase by the television and brushed her fingers along the edges of a rosebud. Her words were all but lost in the folds of her woollen scarf.

'You can't. And I can't be what you need me to be. I've tried falling in love with you, but I can't.'

'Can't you try harder?'

'No.' She whirled around, tears yet to fall glistening in her red-rimmed eyes. 'And pressuring me into doing things I'm not comfortable with isn't sweet, it's exactly what Wayne used to do.'

The silence that followed echoed the words spoken in anger, twisting the earlier banter into accusations and deflections. Lizzie shifted, her right hand rising to run along the row of familiar lines on her left wrist, while her gaze was drawn to the door. She began to move, but Tim spoke before she had taken a step.

'What happens now?' he asked. All traces of anger had gone from his voice.

'I'd like to go home.'

'What about us?'

'I think it's best if we take some time apart to think about what we want and whether this relationship is a good idea.'

'In my experience, taking a break doesn't lead to anything except growing distant and losing our connection.'

'If that's the case here, then I guess we weren't meant to be.'

'No.' Tim shook his head and approached Lizzie, who raised her arms to keep him back. 'I won't accept that. This is far too precious for me to give up.'

'Tim, you can't force a relationship, just like you can't force someone to fall in love with you. Emotions are involuntary.'

'I don't know what I'd do without you. You're the first and last thing on my mind every day. The only time I feel complete is when I'm with you.'

'I'm sorry, Tim. Hurting you is the last thing I want to do, but I have to be true to myself.'

'If that's the case and you hurt me anyway,' Tim's hand dipped in and out of his coat pocket, 'then I don't think I want to go on without you.'

Lizzie clapped a hand over her mouth as she backed away from Tim. 'Why do you have a gun?'

Tim's grip on the revolver was awkward, and although it was pointed down, he kept adjusting the angle and running his thumb over the hammer. Sweat beaded on his forehead. The air in the room grew suffocating.

'To protect you from Wayne,' Tim said as if it was the most obvious thing in the world.

'He's in prison.'

'How do you know that for sure?'

'They'd let me know.' Lizzie hugged her torso and inched sideways towards the door. 'How did you get a gun?'

'From the brother of my colleague. He has quite a collection.'

'Can you hear yourself? Never mind that handguns are illegal, but you carry one around London in your pocket. That's madness.'

'It's not as though I was going to whip it out in public and start shooting strangers.'

'I don't know what you were intending. But I can't help wondering if you were going to use the gun to force me to spend the night.'

Tim's eyes widened, and he took three strides towards Lizzie. 'I would never threaten you to get my way. You know that.'

Lizzie's hand found the door handle and closed around it. 'No, I don't. It's clear I never knew you at all.'

Noticing the downward progress of the door handle, Tim felt his shoulders slump.

'You're leaving.'

'Yes,' Lizzie whispered. A breath of cooler air tickled the shell of her ear.

'And you're not coming back.'

'No.'

'Then I might as well go too,' Tim said and raised the gun.

Lizzie's scream began a second before the shot rang out.

19

MID-ILLUSION

I meet Jamie outside the Ardent Hotel, and Karrion jogs into view from the opposite direction. He takes the steps two at a time and pauses next to me, a hand on my shoulder while he catches his breath. An ambulance and two police cars are double parked.

'A hotel is different,' I say as Jamie holds the door open for us.

When I step over the threshold, a ripple of magic brushes against my skin, delicate as the touch of ferns. I look around for the source. The reception area is deserted, save for a frightened man sitting behind the desk and a police officer standing next to him. Dark woods and the glow of the fire create a cosy atmosphere, but something seems off in the room. A glance at Karrion and Jamie indicates that they sense nothing wrong. Fatigue and pain blur my vision, and I rub my eyes.

'There's more,' Jamie says in a low voice as he steers us upstairs. 'This time it appears to be a suicide.'

'A suicide? That's odd.'

We pass paramedics on the stairs, and they confirm that the victim is deceased. With little else to do at the crime scene, they are heading off to respond to another call out. On the first floor, a police officer is guarding a door to our right. After a brief word with Jamie, she steps aside and we enter the crime scene.

Tim is lying on a rug in the middle of the room. A bullet hole in his right temple leaves no question regarding the cause of death, and the gun is on the floor next to him. The sumptuous room has all the accoutrements for a night of romance. A cloying scent permeates, too strong to be from the roses alone. Underneath it, there is a floral undercurrent I cannot place. Perfume, perhaps? Trying to identify the elusive smell draws me to a different realisation.

'Can you smell that?'

'Smell what?' Karrion asks. 'The roses?'

'We are two yards from the body. Why can't I smell the blood?'

Jamie frowns. 'You're right. It should overpower everything else.'

The sight of the body disturbs me less than I expected. No primal hunger rises from within. My instincts are not whispering that there is meat, urging me to partake of the carcass. Perhaps the wilder side of me recognises the illusion even as my five normal senses deceive me. There is no power there, no release of energy from the decay of flesh and blood and bones.

As much as I am unperturbed by the sight, I notice that Karrion hovers in the doorway, his eyes wide. This is the first time he will have seen a dead body, and his brain is not distinguishing between reality and illusion. When his nostrils flare, I wonder if he is going to be sick.

Shifting closer to him, I squeeze his hand. 'You okay?'

'There's so much blood.' He keeps his voice down; self-conscious in Jamie's presence.

'You don't have to look.'

'I just need a minute.'

'That's fine. When you're ready, photograph everything in this room. If I'm not mistaken, this will all disappear soon.'

'Will do.'

After a few deep breaths, he gets to work, while I crouch next to the body. There is stippling around the entry wound, indicating that the shot was fired from a close range. A glance at the hands reveals no defensive wound, nor are there any other signs of struggle present in the room. Everything points to a suicide.

Even with the damage done by the bullet, there is no question about the man's identity. It is Tim, looking exactly like he did when I saw him this morning. I frown. His clothes are the same. The way his hair sticks out at the back is the same. The tie tucked into his shirt pocket is the same. It is as if someone has taken a snapshot of him as he was today and applied it to the illusion.

Excitement takes root within me. This narrows it down. Whoever the casters are, they must have seen him this morning and committed his appearance to memory. I need to meet up with Tim again, to walk through his morning routines with greater attention. Whatever I missed this morning, I cannot afford to miss again.

Conscious that my time with the body is limited, I take out Thaylor's device and switch it on. It picks up a spell signature straight away, but the screen remains otherwise blank. I save the caster signature over Karrion's and refresh the screen. No change.

'This is odd,' I say and shake the device.

'What's that?' Karrion asks while photographing the

roses. His face is pale, and he is looking everywhere but towards the body.

'This machine picks up a caster signature, but cannot identify the caster type.'

'That's impossible, isn't it?'

'Apparently not.'

'What machine is that?' Jamie asks.

'Something we got from a Tinker at One Magic Change. It's meant to be able to identify active spells and even the signature of the caster. We tested it earlier on Karrion, and it worked. I don't understand what the problem is now.'

'I didn't know such machines existed. Can anyone use it?'

'Yes. You don't need magic to activate it. As for why you don't know about them, most Mages don't think much to Tinkers and this device has limited function. But given that Karrion and I are not Mages, it's better than going around blind.'

'I might have to get one for myself.'

'But why isn't the device picking up traces of a Mage or a Feykin spell?' Karrion asks. 'It should be one or the other.'

I tap the corner of the metal case against my chin. 'What if the Mages were wrong?'

'Which Mages?' Jamie asks.

'From the previous two crime scenes. What if there were never two spell casters, but only one?'

'You read the reports, Yannia. The Mages identified clear traces of Mage and Feykin magic at the separate scenes.'

'Yes, but what if they didn't?'

Jamie frowns. 'Are you saying they lied in their reports?'

'No. What if they were wrong?'

'Just because you hear howling doesn't mean it's a wolf,' Karrion says and uses his elbow to switch on the bathroom lights. He peers in.

'Explain.' Jamie gets a pair of latex gloves out of his pocket and puts them on, crouching next to the body.

Having lost interest in the bathroom, Karrion returns to us, though I note that he keeps his back to the body.

'Assume you came to a crime scene where magic had been used, but the remaining traces were not enough for identification. If everything else pointed towards a Mage illusion, which sort of spell caster would you conclude was behind the casting?'

Jamie nods. 'A Mage.'

'Exactly.'

'And this scene disproves their reports how?' Jamie asks.

'Thaylor's machine does,' I say. 'If this illusion was created by a Mage or a Feykin, the machine would be able to identify the type of magic. That it doesn't, suggests we're dealing with something different.'

'If you exclude both Mages and Feykin, you're not left with many options.'

'Could the illusion have been created by an atypical spell caster?' Karrion asks. He has moved to inspect the bed. The smooth cover indicates no one has touched it since it was made.

Jamie checks Tim's pockets. 'Like what?'

'We know little about Leeches, and yet they exist. Perhaps there are others out there.'

'It's a possibility to bear in mind.' I turn back to the body. 'What can you tell me about what happened here?'

'The room is registered in Tim's name, and he paid cash for it,' Jamie says. 'According to the receptionist, he came in earlier this evening with a bouquet of roses and a couple of bags. He returned later with a woman, and they went straight up. The occupant in the next room heard a gunshot and a scream, and he called reception. They alerted the police and the paramedics. I got a call about this because I had flagged Tim's name in our system.'

'Are we sure this isn't the real Tim?'

'I tried calling him, but he didn't pick up. He's probably asleep. What I can do is get the local police to check up on him. I haven't yet because I assumed he was fine.'

'Let's wait to see what happens here. If the body is still on the floor in an hour or so, we can start to worry.'

'From what he said about his life the other day and the weariness in his tone, maybe it wouldn't be inconceivable for him to commit suicide,' Jamie says.

'I disagree. As much as he may feel trapped in his life and feel like all his dreams are on hold while he looks after his mother, he cares for her deeply. If he's not willing to put her in a care home, he's certainly not going to commit suicide and leave her without a warning.'

'Good point.'

'Let me see if I can get hold of him.' I select the number and listen to the dial tone until the call is diverted to his voicemail. Choosing not to go into detail, I ask him to get in touch as soon as he gets the message.

'Have the scene of crime officers and a Mage been already?' I ask.

'No. I requested a SOCO team and a Mage, but we're short staffed and they haven't got here yet. I thought it best to alert you as soon as I was called. If the previous two instances are anything to go by, this body isn't going to be here for long.'

'I appreciate it. Any information we can glean from this scene will help us track down the caster or casters behind all this.' I put away the machine.

'Is there anything here that would prove what kind of caster created the illusion?' Jamie asks.

We all look around the room. There is a body, the roses, a box of chocolates and a bottle of champagne. Moisture has run down the bottle and created a wet patch on the coffee table. Were it not for the fact that we know the victim to be a version of Tim, there would be nothing in the room to indicate the presence of any kind of magic.

I reach over and touch the back of Tim's hand. It feels warm. I search for a pulse and find no sign of life. He is dead, though of course, the bullet wound already told me as much.

'When was the shot reported?'

Jamie checks his watch. 'Just over an hour ago.'

'If Tim has been dead for over an hour, why is the body still warm?'

Prompted by my question, Jamie also touches the body. His confusion matches mine.

'I have no idea.'

'And look at the blood pool. Shouldn't the edges be congealing and drying by now?'

'They should. Yet the blood looks fresh.'

'Also, take a look around. If Tim was standing when he shot himself, and I assume that was the case, there should be blood spatter on the walls. The bullet went through his head, and yet there is no sign of brain matter anywhere. Karrion, have you spotted a bullet hole?'

'No.' He comes to stand next to me. 'From the way Tim is lying, I'd guess the path of the bullet would have taken it somewhere near the television and the roses. But the wall is clean, I can't see a single drop of blood on the screen, and the roses look pristine. It's as though the bullet killed Tim and then vanished in mid-air.'

'Which is impossible,' Jamie says.

'Plenty of things in this room seem to be impossible.'

'Something is off here.' The body feels solid under my hand, but when I pat down the pockets, I find no wallet, keys or phone. 'I feel like I'm looking at a glossy photo, but scratch the surface and you find nothing but blank paper underneath.'

'Isn't that what illusions always are?' Karrion asks.

'Perhaps, but here the inconsistencies strike me as odd. Tim on the floor is exactly like Tim was this morning, down to the pattern of his tie and the way his hair was combed. But he doesn't have any of the personal items I'd expect to see. Also, where's his coat? He had one this morning, and I doubt he'd been walking around London without one.'

Karrion shrugs. 'He could have left it somewhere. At his office, perhaps?'

'There's something else I don't understand,' I say. 'If the shot was reported an hour ago, why is the body still here?'

'Didn't the previous illusions linger after Tim died?' Jamie asks.

'Not for long. The first time, the body faded away

immediately. The second time, it was maybe a minute or two later. Why is this time any different?'

Neither man answers straight away. Karrion looks at the body, his lips pressed into a thin line.

'Could it simply be that the caster is growing more powerful every time she creates an illusion?'

'Jumping from the body remaining for a minute to an hour is quite a power shift,' I say.

'And there has only been three days between the deaths.'

'Is it possible for the spell caster to grow in power so rapidly?' Jamie asks.

'If they used mana gems, probably. We'd have to ask a Mage to be sure.'

'There could be another explanation,' Karrion says. 'Maybe the death wasn't the point?'

'What do you mean?' I ask.

'With the last two illusions, it seems that the accidents were the climax of the events. Could it be that this time, the point of it is different?'

I nod. 'Like what?'

'I have no idea.'

'Look,' Jamie says, pointing down.

What was a solid body is beginning to fade along the edges, blurring into nothingness. The brightness of the blood becomes brown carpet, and I feel the same brush of magic as before. Turning a full circle, I see no apparent source for the magic. The cloying scent of roses intensifies, and I fancy that there is an undertone of noonday heat. Then the scent dissipates, only to be replaced by air freshener and bleach.

Karrion gasps. 'What just happened?'

Gone is the four poster bed with its golden bedspread and decorative pillows, gone is the wallpaper with its pattern of roses and lilies. There is nothing luxurious about the room we are standing in, and while everything looks clean, the furniture and the decor are drab and worn. The body and all the makings of a romantic evening have vanished.

Standing up, I turn to Jamie. 'You might want to cancel that Mage and SOCO team. The crime scene just disappeared.'

20

INSUBSTANTIAL CLUES

We end up having to wait at the hotel until a Mage arrives to declare there are no active spells in the room. From the traces of the illusion that remain, he is unable to determine the type of illusion. It comes as no surprise after what we learned from Thaylor's machine. Whatever the caster is, it is something unusual.

'Wait,' I say as the Mage says his goodbyes to Jamie and prepares to leave, 'I know the spells you use can identify Mage, Shaman and Paladin magic, but what about Feykin?'

'Broad brush, yes.' Upon seeing my expression, he continues, 'Feykin magic is different. It comes from the caster's spirit and is shaped by their personality, experiences and even agenda. If two Feykin called upon the same glamour, we would identify it as different spells. But we would know it was Feykin magic and the broad type.'

'What if a Feykin cast the same glamour on two different occasions? Would you be able to tell it was the same caster?'

'Only if the two instances were close together and the circumstances of the caster had remained much the same. Magic isn't like fingerprints or DNA, Ms Wilde. It cannot be tied back to an individual with absolute accuracy.'

'I see.'

Next to me, Karrion opens his mouth, but my pointed look silences him. If Thaylor wants to make her discoveries in that area known to the police, she will do so.

There is nothing further we can glean from the hotel room, and we follow the Mage downstairs. There, another surprise is waiting for us. The warm, inviting reception area has transformed into a pale and chilly space. Two old computers are tucked in a corner with a sign charging two pounds per fifteen minutes of internet usage. Where before my attention was drawn to the fireplace, now only a bare wall remains. It appears that the illusion had a greater range than I initially appreciated.

One thing that has not changed is the frazzled looking receptionist. When Jamie goes to explain to him that the suspected suicide was all a false alarm and that the police are leaving, he leaps to his feet.

'No, I won't accept that! False alarm, my arse. I went upstairs, I saw the body. People don't blow their brains out and then change their mind and walk away. You're either dead or not. What are you bastards hiding?'

I can sense Jamie's hesitation as he takes his time deciding the least inflammatory explanation. In the end, he settles for the truth.

'It appears that magic was involved. Didn't you notice the room looking different when you went upstairs?'

'I was too focused on the man bleeding on to my carpet to notice the furniture.' He slams his fist on the reception desk. 'Fucking magic. Can't the freaks stay in their part of London, away from us normal people? Them and their bloody spells are bad for business.'

214

Karrion bristles, but I lay a hand on his arm and he settles for glaring at the receptionist with the haughtiness of an owl. Jamie chooses the diplomatic route of apologising for any inconvenience while ushering us out. Once the door has closed behind us, Karrion makes a rude gesture at the hotel.

'Humans can be such morons,' he says and then seems to remember that Jamie is standing next to him. 'Present company excepted.'

Jamie pats Karrion's shoulder. 'No offence taken.'

'That attitude goes both ways,' I say. 'You only need to go into certain pubs in Old London on a Friday night to hear the same sort of sentiments, or worse.'

'Like the Open Hearth?' Karrion asks.

'No. Funja wouldn't stand for it. Neither would Wishearth.' I glance back toward the door. 'That the receptionist didn't notice the reception area changing suggests Feykin glamour to me. They have a way of trapping the unwary in an illusion strong enough that the victim can't tell the difference between the glamour and reality.'

'What's your next step?' Jamie asks.

'Take a look at those photos Karrion took. Maybe we can learn more about Lizzie if we study the things included in the illusions.'

'Who's Lizzie?'

'The woman Tim has been with every time he's died in these illusions.'

'I thought the car crash was the only other time a woman was present. How do you know her name?'

'Sorry, Jamie, I need to bring you up to speed.'

Keeping my voice low, I tell Jamie about Bob's

involvement and about the woman Tim was supposedly dating. Once I get started, I explain our progress and what little information we have found out. Jamie seems impressed even though we are still in the dark about plenty of things.

'I knew it was a good idea to refer Tim to you,' he says.

'We haven't solved the case yet.'

'No, but I have every faith that you will.' Glancing at his phone, Jamie bids us goodnight and reiterates his offer of help.

'Back to yours?' Karrion asks after Jamie has left.

'Do you mind? I'd like to look at those photos as soon as possible.'

We take a taxi back to mine, and Karrion transfers the files from his phone on to my computer while I brew a pot of coffee. Side by side, we click through the pictures. When we were within the illusion, the details were sharp and looked real. On the screen, the hotel room appears blurred, like the faces on the CCTV footage.

'I was thinking,' Karrion says, 'that the illusion being in a hotel room changes things.'

'In what way?' The same thought has occurred to me too, but I am interested to hear Karrion's reasoning.

'If it was just Tim and Lizzie in the hotel room, then Lizzie must be the illusionist.'

'Are we sure there was no one else in the room?'

'The receptionist said he only saw Tim and Lizzie going up.'

'But who's to say the illusionist didn't pass through the reception earlier. If Tim had been to the hotel earlier in the evening, the illusion lasted for a long time. We don't know what happened when Tim paid for the room, for instance.'

'I hadn't thought of that,' Karrion says, worry clouding his expression.

'There's nothing to say the caster couldn't hide outside the illusion and watch as it unfolds. It could be a voyeuristic fantasy.'

Karrion grimaces. 'Who'd get off on that?'

'People are into all sorts of things. But I think you're right, Lizzie is likely to be our caster. That would explain why she was able to talk to Bob and why the person next door heard her screams tonight.'

'Now all we need to figure out is who she is and what sort of magic she possesses.'

'Perhaps the answer is in these photos. Jamie said that Tim was seen going up to the room earlier this evening with the flowers and a couple of bags. What's likely to have been in them?'

Karrion gets a notepad and a pen from his pocket and finds an empty page. Looking through the photos again, he makes notes in an illegible scrawl. For someone with a fine arts degree, his handwriting is terrible.

'The flowers were in a vase. Assuming the hotel didn't lend it to him, he probably brought it with him,' says Karrion.

'The vase vanished when the illusion ended. It must have been his.'

'Okay. The roses were wrapped when he took them in. I found the clear cellophane in the bin under the desk. The strange thing about it was that there was no indication of where the roses came from. I'd expect a flower shop to at least put their sticker on a bouquet.'

'That is odd. What else was there?'

'The champagne.' Karrion zooms in on the label, but it is too blurry to read. 'I remember the brand: Veuve-Clicquot. Nice, but not posh.'

'You're now an expert in champagne brands, are you?'

'Not even a little. Mum bought us a bottle for my graduation ceremony. It was nice enough, although champagne isn't really my thing. That particular brand is available at supermarkets and won't bankrupt you.'

'The cooler also disappeared. And there was a wet ring on the table under the bottle. It must have been in ice to generate that much condensation.'

Karrion has zoomed in on another photo. 'The cooler looks to be made of plastic. It's nothing fancy, and my guess is that it, too, was bought from a supermarket, probably at the same time as the champagne.'

'And the ice.'

'What else? There was a box of chocolates, Black Magic.'

'Do you think the spell caster has a sense of irony?' I ask, the corner of my mouth lifting.

'Who knows? But you can get them from a super-market as well. Could that be the theme here? We could canvass the shops near the hotel and see if a woman came in to buy those items at some point today.'

'But it wasn't real, Karrion. All those things were merely components of the illusion. That said, I do think you're right about the supermarket being the common element. Could the flowers have come from a supermarket?'

'I don't think so. They'd definitely have put their sticker on the packing.'

'Okay, flowers came from elsewhere. That's as far as we'll get with them. It would be impossible to distin-

218

guish one bouquet of red roses from the next. Was there anything else in the room that couldn't have been bought at a supermarket?'

'I'm pretty sure Tim didn't buy a four poster bed from a supermarket. The only other item I can think of was the gun.'

Karrion finds a close up of the weapon. There is fine blood spatter on the barrel, just visible on the blurry shape. At the conclave, guns are regarded as unnecessary and dangerous. To me, it looks like a simple lump of metal.

'If the American police procedurals I've been watching are correct, that's a revolver,' Karrion says.

'Does it make a difference what type of handgun it is?'

'I don't know. Maybe if you're a cowboy?'

I laugh, and Karrion joins in. It pleases me to note that all the paleness has gone from his face and he appears to have returned to his normal self.

'Are you okay?' I ask, just to be sure.

'Fine. Why wouldn't I be?'

'You came across your first dead body today. It's not an experience that should be taken lightly.'

'It was the sight of all that blood. I didn't expect there to be so much of it. The rest of it didn't seem real, and I suppose it wasn't. You said it yourself, the body wasn't even cold.'

'You will let me know if you ever want to talk about it, won't you? Or about anything else?'

'Of course. Thanks, Yan.'

What I leave unsaid is that I am glad his first corpse was so fresh. Had he seen Brother Valeron's body last week, he might have had second thoughts about wanting to be my apprentice. As much as he is intent on protecting me, I too am determined to keep him safe. He is family, if not by blood, then by bonds of love and friendship.

'Do you think we can attempt some sort of profiling on the woman based on the items she included in the illusion?' Karrion asks when the silence has gone on for too long.

'We can give it a go, though neither of us is an expert. Let's leave aside the flowers and the gun for now and focus on the other items.'

'What I don't get is if you're going to build an elaborate illusion like that, why not go all out and have top of the range champagne in a silver cooler with handmade chocolate truffles? Why settle for stuff you can buy from the shops?'

I ponder the question at length, fingers drumming against my chin. It is impossible to put myself in the woman's position when we know next to nothing about her. A few minutes of CCTV footage is not enough to form an impression about anyone, at least not for someone like me, who is unaccustomed to observing human behaviour. If this case was about animals, I would stand a far greater chance of being able to offer certainties.

'All I can think of is that illusions are like lying,' I say.

'What do you mean?'

'What's the foundation for any good lie?'

It is Karrion's turn to think, and his nose scrunches in concentration. 'I'm not sure.'

'Truth. If you want to construct an effective lie, you must include as much truth as possible.'

'Are you saying that she based the illusion on a true event?'

'Maybe. I was more thinking about constructing the

220

details. Could you picture a bottle of top-of-the-range champagne, down to the wording on the label? Or those handmade truffles you mentioned?'

'The truffles, maybe. I once bought some for a girl I was trying to impress.'

'Did it work?'

'She was impressed, but not enough to agree to a second date. Apparently, my lip piercing was unhygienic and creepy.'

'Her loss,' I say and pat his arm.

'I thought so too. But to answer your other question, I have no idea what a posh champagne bottle might look like.'

'My guess is, neither does Lizzie. If I'm right, the reason most of those items are the kind found in a supermarket is that she's seen them there. Black Magic as a brand is posher than the supermarket's own chocolates. And everyone understands the inherent value of champagne.'

'What about the roses and the gun?'

'Red roses are so universal they aren't hard to imagine. As for the gun, perhaps Lizzie too is a fan of American police procedurals.'

'Does that get us any closer to figuring out who she is?'

I sigh. 'No. None of that narrows it down. There are plenty of supermarkets in Old London stocking all those items, and just because she has magical blood doesn't mean she lives here. Who knows, she might commute in like Tim does.'

'Despite worrying about another death, it hasn't helped us at all,' Karrion says and sets his mug down with more force than necessary. 'We're still at a dead end.'

'Not quite. Tim's appearance is a significant clue.

Lizzie must have seen him this morning in order to create such an accurate version of him.'

'Are you sure it was this morning?'

'Yes. Tim would have put his tie on when he got to work and probably even smoothed down that tuft of hair on his right temple when he looked in the mirror.'

'But you said you couldn't spot anyone paying attention to Tim who smelled like a Mage or a Feykin.'

'True, but I wasn't even sure I was there at the right time of day. Now I am. Tomorrow morning, I'll try again. And I won't restrict my search to Mages and Feykin, given that she may not be one.'

'Lizzie can't hide from you forever.'

'I hope not.' Rocking my coffee mug until an eddy forms within, I stare into its depths. From the feel of the clay against my fingers, the contents of the mug have gone cold. I set it aside. 'One thing that bothers me about tonight's death is the fact that it was a suicide. It doesn't seem in keeping with the other two.'

Karrion nods. 'The real Tim wouldn't kill himself because of his mum, but from what we've seen of the illusion Tim, he'd have even less reason to do it.'

'While I agree, I don't know how far the illusion extends. Does this other Tim go about his life all day long, or are the illusions just snapshots?'

'Wouldn't it take an enormous amount of power to maintain a spell on a semi-permanent basis?'

'Yes, I think it would. So my question is this: why a suicide? What changed?'

'Something about her relationship with Tim.'

'But they don't have a relationship. Tim doesn't know who she is.'

'Which means that her perception of him has changed. What happened? Did he upset her inadvertently?'

'That's something for me to ask him tomorrow. Though I'm not sure how to phrase it. "Hi, Tim, did you say something mean to a girl you don't know that might have caused her to want to kill you?"'

Karrion pulls his knees up and rests his chin on them. 'He's been dying all along.'

'Yes, but the violence was always external. Not accidental, given that Lizzie controls every aspect of the illusion, but tonight was the first time Tim himself became violent.'

'Are we sure it was a suicide? Couldn't Lizzie have killed him and made it look like an accident?'

'Why would she shoot him if she can make him die in any way she wants? As much as she may cause the deaths, they're all removed from her. Tim is the puppet whose strings she pulls while she remains in the shadows.'

'Could she be related to Lord Ellensthorne?'

'We could visit him and ask?' I force a weary grin.

'He's a busy man, best not disturb him.'

'I do think you should have chosen to study psychology instead of fine arts. With a case like this, I'm way out of my depth.'

'We both are.'

Frustrated by all the unanswered questions, I take our mugs to the kitchen and pour the cold coffee down the drain. A glance at the faded plastic clock on the wall tells me it is gone midnight. The pain from earlier re-establishes its hold on me, and I rub my face to ward off rising nausea. Heat alone will not break the back of the agony, which means it is time to eat something.

A survey of the fridge contents reminds me once again that I ought to shop more often, but I take out a jar of tomato sauce and a block of cheese. Dried pasta and a can of tuna from the cupboard follow and I fill the kettle. From the medication drawer, I select a foil strip of pills and set it on the counter.

'Can I help?' Karrion asks, leaning against the kitchen doorway.

'You can grate some cheese,' I say.

'Sure.'

Karrion has spent enough time in my kitchen to know where everything is, and he gets what he needs from the cupboards. I put pasta on to boil and prepare a simple sauce. Once he has grated a small mountain of cheese, Karrion finds bowls and cutlery for us. As a final touch, he places a glass of water by my elbow. With a grateful smile, I take my meds and put the rest of them away. I divide the pasta between our bowls.

'You can make me a midnight feast anytime,' Karrion says over his shoulder as he takes his pasta to the chairs in the lounge.

'Given my limited cooking repertoire, I'm not sure that would be a good idea.'

The pasta is hot and filling. If it lacks a bit of salt and pepper, neither of us comments on the fact. When our bowls are empty, Karrion carries them back to the kitchen and washes up. Alone in the lounge, I flick through the crime scene photos without any real focus or intention.

'Should we look through them once more, in case we missed something?' Karrion asks as he comes in, drying his hands on a tea towel, which ends up in a wad on my bookshelf.

'Let's.'

For the next hour, we make a concentrated effort and examine each photo in detail, zooming in and out. We spot nothing new, and towards the end, my eyes are slipping shut. When Karrion yawns widely enough to crack his jaw, I switch off the computer.

'That's more than enough work for one day.'

'I'm too tired to even think about objecting.' He stretches and misses my head by an inch.

'Do you want to spend the night here?'

'Would you mind? I'd hate to wake up Mum or the brood.'

'Not at all. The bed is plenty big enough for both of us. I'll get you a pillow and another blanket.'

'I don't need another blanket. Sleeping makes me hot.'

'There must be a joke there somewhere, but I'm too tired to figure it out.' I stand, and the press of opiates in my system causes me to sway.

Karrion goes to the bathroom while I get a pillow from the cupboard. When he returns, I am kneeling on the hearth stones, adding logs to the fire. Once the flames are spreading along the dry wood, I reach for an offering and speak the dedication.

'You're still asking for his protection, even though I'm here.' Karrion drops his hoodie on the chair.

'It's a different kind of protection. I'm not sure I'd know how to fall asleep without having gone through the nightly ritual.'

'Fair enough,' Karrion says, but I think I detect an edge of jealousy in his voice.

Having brushed my teeth, I change into a loose shirt and yoga pants. The floors are chilly, and my legs are aching by the time I have returned upstairs. I leave my socks on as I crawl under the blankets and face the fire.

'Good night, Karrion,' I say, sleep dragging me under.

'Night.'

The last thing I am aware of is an arm coming to rest on me and a sense of safety lulling me to sleep.

THURSDAY

21

RAISED STAKES

A phone ringing yanks me awake, and I grope around the hearth stones until I find my mobile. Next to me, Karrion groans while I answer the call and mumble something incoherent by a way of a greeting.

'Yannia, it's Tim. What the hell happened last night?'

'There was another death.'

'That explains the gun.'

Now I am wide awake. 'What gun?'

Karrion sits up, rubbing his face, and reaches for his phone. When the screen lights up, I see it is five thirty. We have been asleep for just under four hours.

'I woke up next to a bloody pistol.'

'Are you okay?' I ask. My mouth feels like a dormouse has nested in it, and a line of drool has dried on my cheek. I wipe it off while I kick the blankets aside.

'My head is killing me, and I have a bruise on my temple. Any idea what happened to me?'

'Which temple?'

'Right. Why?'

I root around in the dark for my jeans, give up and switch on the light. Pain lances into my skull at the brightness of it.

'Yannia, what the hell is going on?' Tim asks, anger

colouring his voice.

'The illusions are beginning to bleed into reality.'

'Does that mean what I think it does?'

I hesitate, but opt for the truth. 'If they continue long enough, you're going to die.'

'Then you better hurry up.'

'I know. Is the gun loaded?'

'I wouldn't know how to check.'

'Don't touch it. I'll call Jamie, and we'll be there as soon as we can.'

'Look, I can't wait forever. I have a meeting with a client this morning.'

'We'll give you a lift to work if we delay you.'

'Driving isn't going to be quicker than taking the train.'

Movement catches my eye, and I turn to watch Karrion pulling on his jeans, hopping on one foot to straighten a bunched up trouser leg. His t-shirt is back to front, and I motion it to him. He pulls his arms out of the shirt and rotates it, flashing his nipple rings in the process.

'Jamie has sirens.'

'Fine, whatever. I need to get Mum up and dressed. Call me when you get here rather than ring the doorbell. Mum gets anxious about strangers in the house.'

I promise to do so, and we end the call. As soon as I have pulled on a fleece, I dial Jamie's number. When he answers, he sounds as groggy as I did.

'We need to get to Tim's,' I say without preamble. 'He woke up next to a gun.'

Jamie lets out a string of curses. Something falls in the background, and Jamie swears again.

'Is he okay?'

'He said he has a splitting headache and a bruise on his right temple.'

'That's where the entry wound was last night.'

'I know. How long before an illusion will kill him?'

'I'd rather not find out. We need to get that gun.'

'I told Tim we'd be there as soon as we can. He's anxious to get to work, but he can't leave a woman suffering from dementia alone with a gun.'

'Of course not. I'll pick you up in half an hour.'

'See you soon.'

When I put my phone away, Karrion is sniffing his socks. He grimaces and then shrugs.

'They'll have to do.'

'You should consider bringing a change of clothes to keep here, given that you're making a habit of spending the night.'

'Not a bad idea.'

Karrion uses the last of my bread to make us toast, and we eat while we wait for Jamie. Fatigue causes a dull throb behind my eyes, but at least the pain in my legs is not as bad as last night. I blink rapidly, trying to clear the blurriness.

'When does the glamorous side of this job start?' Karrion asks and yawns.

'That being?'

'Those high-speed car chases I mentioned last week. Playing blackjack with beautiful women who are foreign spies in disguise. Gloating while the police arrest a villain who was intending to assassinate the Queen. You know, cool stuff.'

'I seem to recall warning you that my job isn't all that glamorous.'

'You did, but I figured you were being modest.'

'Alas, no.'

Jamie arrives as we ascend the stairs to street level, and we get in the car. I have loaded Tim's address on to my navigation app and I attach my phone to the bracket on the dashboard. While Jamie navigates through the sparse morning traffic, I fill him in on my conversation with Tim and on the thoughts we had regarding the crime scene last night. He has little to add, but his expression darkens. In his haste to get to us, he has not shaved and he keeps rubbing his jaw.

'We don't have long to figure this out before Tim ends up with more than just bruises,' Jamie says.

'I'm aware of that. We're doing all we can.'

'It wasn't my intention to suggest otherwise. I worry about him.'

'We all do.'

With fatigue weighing us down, none of us is inclined to engage in small talk. By the time we leave Old London, Karrion is snoring in the back seat. My eyelids begin to droop, and my head sinks towards my chest. The car slows, and I jerk awake, but soon the exhaustion gets the better of me once more.

Jamie parks behind Tim's car on the drive. Grateful to stretch my legs, I allow the cool morning air to chase away some of the drowsiness. After a pointed look from Jamie, I make the call to Tim, and in no time, he opens the door.

'Come in,' he says, speaking in a low voice. 'Go straight upstairs. Mum's in the lounge. She gets confused by strangers so I won't introduce her.'

Tim is dressed in jeans and a faded green cardigan. He looks pale, framed in the light spilling out from the house, and the bruise on his temple is violent purple. I notice that his big toe is poking out of a hole in his sock.

At the far end of a narrow corridor is a kitchen. The counters are bare, and there are locks on the cupboard doors. A door to our left is closed, and I can hear music from the far side. The song ends and an advert begins. In front of the stairs, a wheelchair is folded against the wall under a line of coats. An umbrella stand is tucked in the corner, and the walking sticks it contains are all covered in a layer of dust. The air is thick with the smells of stale urine and burnt toast.

I lead the way upstairs, and by instinct, go through the only door that is open. The bedroom is Tim's. If the gun on the floor did not give it away, the briefcase and laptop on the small desk would. There is just enough room for a single bed and wardrobe in the corner. An ironing board leans against the wall.

As interested as I am in the gun, I hang back while Jamie puts on a pair of latex gloves and picks it up. Straight away he huffs, partly confused, partly irritated.

'This doesn't make any sense.'

'What's that?' I ask.

'The gun isn't real.'

'What?'

'See here,' Jamie shows me the cylinder, 'this should move so that the gun can be loaded. But it's fixed, and there are no bullets in the cylinder. If the gun was fired recently, I'd at the very least expect to see the shell casing for the bullet that went into Tim's head.'

'And that means what? That the gun is a replica?'

233

'If it is, it's the shoddiest replica I've ever seen. I'm more inclined to think that the gun continues your theme of this Lizzie creating items she can imagine. Guns may not be her strong suit, which is just as well. At least we can reassure Tim that there's no way this revolver could be fired.'

'But how was Tim killed in the illusion if the gun is a dud?' Karrion asks. He has been content to stand in the doorway and watch.

'Am I right in thinking that illusions aren't constrained by the laws of mechanics or physics?' Jamie turns to me, and I nod. 'If Lizzie imagined a gun capable of being fired, then within the spell that's what happened.'

'And that makes Lizzie dangerous,' I say. 'With each illusion, the power of her magic is growing. Soon, she could imagine a bomb and make it go off.'

Jamie shudders. 'I hope she doesn't have that sort of imagination.'

'We already know she's violent. What we don't know is whether that extends to people other than Tim.'

Steps approach on the stairs, and Karrion backs out of the doorway to allow Tim into the room.

'What's the verdict?' he asks.

'The gun is harmless,' Jamie says.

'Not harmless enough.' Tim points to the bruise. Up close, I see that it forms a perfect circle and I am willing to bet that it matches the size of the revolver's muzzle exactly.

'Do we still have time to catch your usual train?' I ask.

'Just, if I hurry.'

Glancing at Jamie, I say to Tim, 'Perhaps it's best if Karrion and I accompany you on the train. We can keep an eye on the other passengers, in case Lizzie is someone who also commutes to London. From the crime scene last night, it's clear she saw you yesterday.'

'Fine.' Tim hesitates. 'How did I... I mean, how did *he* die this time?'

'Suicide.'

Unable to hide a flinch, Tim starts to take a step back and catches himself. He nods, the movement jerky, and I am reminded of the comparison between him and a puppet.

'I see.'

During the silence that follows, Jamie puts the gun in a brown evidence bag and I wince at the rustle the bag makes when he rolls it up and puts it in his pocket. My headache intensifies.

'I know I've already asked this, but have you noticed anyone paying attention to you in the past couple of days?'

'No. I've tried looking around, but there's been no one.'

'Okay.' I turn towards the window and watch as a man across the street carries recycling boxes to the end of his drive. I wish I could spot someone spying on the house through binoculars or a car with tinted windows driving by. But nothing looks out of place along the street, and my instincts tell me that I am more likely to find the answers in Old London than in a quiet neighbourhood in Essex.

'I best get ready,' Tim says.

Jamie nods. 'We'll wait outside.'

Tim sees us downstairs, and he unlocks the door with two different keys. There are a total of four locks on the door. When he notices my astonishment, he glances towards the closed door.

'Mum had a habit of wandering off. The last time she did it, we had half the town out looking for her. And I told you about the fire next door. It's best if I make sure she doesn't go out by herself anymore. She's grown frail in the past couple of months, but I don't want to take any chances.'

'I understand.'

We wait by Jamie's car. I draw the cold, damp air deep into my lungs. Hopefully, the station will have a coffee shop.

An Asian woman walks towards us, a heavy bag on one shoulder. Under her coat, I see the hem of a nurse's uniform. Casting a curious glance in our direction, she walks to Tim's door and lets herself in.

'That's odd,' Karrion says. 'Tim didn't mention anyone else living here.'

'I doubt she lives here. But he needs someone to look after his mother if her dementia is so severe she's taken to wandering out and getting lost.'

'Yeah, I didn't think of that. She didn't look like Lizzie.'

'No, she didn't.'

Tim steps out soon after, a briefcase slung over his shoulder and still zipping his coat. He has combed his hair to the side in an attempt to hide the bruise.

'Ready?' he asks.

'Yes.'

'Hop in,' Jamie says. 'I'll give you a ride to the station if you tell me where to go.'

I offer to let Tim sit at the front, but he insists on taking the backseat with Karrion. Leaning between the front seats, he navigates us to the station, choosing a different route from the one Karrion and I walked two days ago. On the way, Tim explains that he mostly walks.

The station is busy, which is to be expected. I promise to call Jamie the moment I find something out, and we follow Tim inside. He buys our train tickets, pointing out they are one fewer expense I will need to claim when I present him with my invoice. The train to London arrives as we go through the turnstiles, and we have to run to get in before the doors slide closed.

There is standing room only. By an unspoken agreement, Karrion and I move away from Tim in opposite directions. This allows us to observe the other people in the carriage. Most are absorbed by their phones or e-readers, but several are reading a book or a newspaper. Here and there, people are talking, either to their co-travellers or on the phone. None appears to be paying attention to Tim.

While we keep an eye on the other passengers, Tim gets a thin booklet out of his briefcase and begins reading it, oblivious to the jostling of people around him when the train stops at the various stations. He holds on to a handrail, only letting go to turn the pages, and he does not look up until the train stops at Liverpool Street Station.

Karrion fights through the crowd to me and speaks low enough that only I can hear him.

'I didn't see anyone taking an interest in Tim.'

'Neither did I. I'm going to walk him to his workplace and see if I missed anything. You shadow us. Keep well enough back that it's not obvious, but get a good idea of whether anyone notices us.'

'Is that a challenge?' Karrion grins.

'It could be.'

'I'll do my best.'

He drops back while I hurry to catch up with Tim, who is looking around the platform for me. We go through the turnstiles together, the press of people steering us along the concourse.

'Do you always travel in the same carriage?' I ask once the crowds begin to thin.

'No. I normally try to aim towards the front of the train, where there is more space, but otherwise it's whichever carriage looks the emptiest. If I'm running late, I'll have to make a mad dash for the nearest doors.'

'How about your fellow passengers? Do you ever speak to them, or have you made friends on the train?'

'I recognise people who do the same commute as I do, but not really. I tend to either prepare for the day ahead or bring a book. The journey, particularly on the way home, is a chance for me to unwind and relax, even if I end up standing most of the way.'

Some of my frustration must show on my face, for Tim says, 'I'm sorry. I wish I could give you an easy answer.'

'If there was an easy answer to all this, you wouldn't need me.'

'That's true.'

Tim leads me on the same route as before, out of the station and to the right along Bishopsgate. I keep my eye on everyone we pass, concern and fear fuelling my sharpness. At the back of my mind, I know I am on the knife edge of exhaustion, but at present, it does not seem to matter. If Karrion and I cannot figure this out soon, Tim is going to die. That is all the motivation I need to ignore a headache sending spikes of pain through my skull with each step. I am in dire need of caffeine so it is just as well we are heading for Amici.

The smells of coffee, chocolate muffins and steamed fruit greet us at the door, but I ignore them in favour of looking around. The Feykin I noticed last time is not there, and I recognise none of the people seated at the tables. I am tempted to enhance my smell with magic, but there are too many people. They, coupled with the scents of the cafe itself, would overwhelm me.

What good are my powers if I cannot use them to solve this case?

Behind the counter, the same woman as before is taking orders. This time, she is wearing a tag that identifies her as Mel. She spots Tim as we join the queue and smiles. Her expression falls when she notices me, and then her attention is diverted back to the customer she is serving.

Two young Horse Shamans join the queue behind us, close enough that I catch the scents of horse hair and fresh hay without resorting to my powers. They chatter about riding lessons and working for a jockey whose name means nothing to me. I envy them for their easy laughter and the joy with which they regard their lives.

When we reach the counter, Mel's smile returns, though she looks pale and feverish.

'Hi, Tim. How are—' She gets no further before she spots the bruise on his temple. 'Oh my God. What happened to you?'

'Nothing, just an accident. I'm fine.'

Mel says nothing further while Tim orders latte and porridge, but her expression grows troubled.

'Yannia, do you want anything?' Tim asks.

239

I request a double espresso, and having put the order through, I notice Mel's right hand rising to stroke a row of wooden bangles adorning her left wrist. Our eyes meet, and she yanks the sleeve of her shirt down.

While Tim pays, I turn to the rest of the cafe. Pavel is clearing a couple of tables by the window, and when he notices me, he grins. Too tired and concerned, I cannot force a smile. I let my attention roam and I am struck that I am going through the same motions as yesterday without getting any closer to figuring out who Lizzie is or why she is intent on hurting Tim. What more can I do?

Tim nudges me when our drinks are ready, and I turn back to the counter. The hesitant smile is back on Mel's face when she hands Tim a bag and a drinks holder.

'I... I put some extra fruit in your porridge. Feel better soon.'

'Thanks,' Tim says.

At the door, the Feykin man from yesterday enters the cafe. When he passes us, I see a pointed tongue darting out to sample the air next to Tim's shoulder. Today, the man is wearing a top hat in addition to a morning suit. When he notices I am watching, he raises the hat in greeting and continues to the counter.

'Are you okay?' Tim asks.

I find he is holding the door open for me and I step out. When I glance through the window, I see the Feykin man taking measured steps – a throwback to a dance he recalls, perhaps – while he waits in line. My fatigued mind idly wonders whether he has a tail.

'She likes you,' I say and thank Tim for the coffee he hands me. I take a long sip and burn my tongue. Wishing

I had ordered an iced coffee instead, I remove the plastic lid and blow into the cup. Steam tickles my nose: a promise of sharp energy and wakefulness. I take another sip and wince as the pain in my tongue intensifies.

'Who?'

'That girl in the cafe, Mel.'

Tim glances over his shoulder and shakes his head. 'I hardly think so.'

'Trust me, she wouldn't put extra steamed fruit on just anyone's porridge.'

Longing flashes across Tim's features, but it is gone so quickly I am left wondering if I imagined it. Does he return her affection, or is it the thought of a romance that appeals to him? His steps slow down as he turns to look back a second time, but then his shoulders stoop.

'Even if that's the case, I doubt she'd still be interested if she knew what my life was like,' he says, voice laced with bitterness.

I shrug. 'Maybe you should give people a chance.'

'What's the point? I don't fit into anyone's picture-perfect life.'

Caffeine has set my pulse tripping, and I frown at Tim, something about his words troubling me. The more I grasp for the meaning, the more it eludes me until the feeling slips away. Perhaps it will come to me.

We walk the rest of the way to his office building in silence. There, instead of going in, he turns to face me.

'Please, help me,' he says, weariness and desperation in every line on his face. 'Mum won't cope if something happens to me. And... my life may not amount to much, but I'm not ready to die either.'

I bite my lip to keep my expression from crumbling into grief. Jonathain Marsh pleaded with me to help him, using similar words, and yet I failed him.

'I will do everything I can.'

Tim nods. 'Thank you.'

He walks away, and I watch his retreating back, rooted to the spot. My promise was earnest, but I am not certain I can keep it.

Will Tim share Marsh's fate?

22

A SHOW OF STRENGTH

'How come you got coffee and I didn't?' Karrion asks.

The question startles me, and the cup in my hand tilts at a wild angle. A hand steadies my wrist before the coffee spills, and Karrion chuckles.

'I did better than I expected.'

He is right. In the twenty minutes since we stepped off the train, I have forgotten about him shadowing us. I curse myself for the lapse in concentration. Tim's words continue to bother me, and I still cannot figure out what was so important about them.

'Did you see anything? Notice anything?'

Karrion huffs. 'No, sorry. There was no one who looked at him except in passing. Whoever this Lizzie is, she's discreet.'

'She may not even be here.' I drain my coffee, the last mouthful cold and bitter, and pace away to bin the cup.

'She's got to be somewhere.'

'Yes, but where? How are we supposed to protect Tim if we can't find Lizzie?'

Karrion rests a hand on my arm. 'We'll figure it out.'

'How? We're no closer to solving this case than we were two days ago. Meanwhile, Tim is in increasing danger of getting killed by a woman he doesn't even know.'

'We're going to keep working at this until we find her. And I know for certain that we're going to succeed.'

'How can you possibly know that?' I ask, not bothering to hide my scepticism.

'Because neither of us is willing to witness a repeat of what happened to Jonathain Marsh,' Karrion says, and from his expression, I can see that last week's events still haunt him. After my initial attempt to console him and remind him that what happened was not our fault, we have spoken no further about Marsh's execution.

'Well, whatever miracle we need to perform to solve this case, we need to do it soon.'

Even as I speak, my attention is drawn across the road, where the Feykin man from the cafe is waltzing along, a coffee cup in each hand. When he draws level with me, he stops and executes a sweeping bow.

'Wait here,' I tell Karrion and jog across the road.

When I step on to the pavement next to him, the Feykin offers me one of the cups. It feels cold against my fingers.

'Something to soothe the sorrows of a tongue,' he says. There is a slight hiss in his pronunciation of the words.

'How did you know?'

'Doesn't everyone observe?' Without moving a muscle on his face, he raises one of his copper eyebrows in a perfect curve.

'Not like that.'

'More's the pity.'

'In the cafe, you tasted the air next to Tim. Why?'

'And Tim is?'

'The man I was with,' I say, trying to conceal my impatience.

'The human? I was curious.'

244

'Why?'

'His aura is tainted. Unusual for a mortal.'

'We're all mortal here.'

'That's what you think, dear. Animals are close to immortal because they will not contemplate their own mortality. You could have that.'

Unwilling to debate philosophy with a Feykin, I shake my head. 'You said Tim's aura is tainted. In what way?'

'Someone is working magic around him, but not on him. It's a clever spider, weaving its web without ever alerting the little fly.'

His purple eyes seem to glow, and I wonder if this is what a mouse feels like when confronted with a snake.

'Who?' I swallow. 'Do you know who the spell caster is? Do you know what she is?'

'Look around, little fly. There are spiders everywhere.'

He takes another bow and performs a leaping pirouette. My tripping thoughts wonder how he does not spill his coffee, but when I look at his hand, I find he is holding a copper-tipped cane instead of a cup. How did I miss that?

'Wait,' I say, stepping forward. 'Who's behind the attacks on Tim?'

A column of swirling autumn leaves appears out of nowhere, blocking my vision of him. When they settle to rustle at my feet, the Feykin is nowhere to be seen. Several people walking by are looking at me with curiosity, but the Feykin is not among them. A hand lands on my shoulder, and I jump.

'Yan, are you okay?' Karrion asks.

'I told you to wait.'

'Yeah, but then you just stood there. Who were you talking to?'

'A Feykin who was at Amici just now and yesterday morning.' I look at the cup in my hand and peek under the lid. 'He gave me an iced coffee because I burnt my tongue.'

'But why did you continue talking after he left?'

'What?'

'A businessman handed you a coffee and carried on walking, while you stood there talking at thin air.'

'No, he was here. He danced up the road in his morning suit and he changed his coffee into a cane. Or maybe the other way round.' I frown. My memories are blurred and jumbled. 'He said something about spiders and auras and flies. I can't remember.'

'Let's hope it wasn't anything important. It sounds to me like the Feykin put a spell on you.'

'It felt real.' I look down at my feet. It is no surprise to find the pavement bare of leaves.

'Like the illusion last night?'

Rubbing my temples to focus, I think back to last night. 'Last night, there was a smell of roses. It wasn't present now.'

'But there were roses in the room.'

'It was the wrong kind of smell, like you get when the roses are past their prime and the water they're in is getting stagnant. Sweet and unpleasant at the same time.'

'Could you have missed it just now? It's harder to notice smells outside.'

'Not for me.'

'In any case, it's probably best you don't drink that,' Karrion says and points at the cup chilling my fingers. 'Who knows what he put in it.'

'True.' My tongue could do with the ice, but sense wins, and I throw away the cup untouched.

'What's our next move?' Karrion scratches his chin. It and his neck are dark with stubble.

'Go home, take a shower and have a proper breakfast.'

'What about you? Shouldn't you take a break too?'

'I will. But first I'm going to see a Hearth Spirit about a fire.'

At the Open Hearth, Wishearth is leaning back in his chair. The collar of the mariner's pea coat is raised around his face, and his combat boots poke out from under the table. Even though the pub is not yet officially open, he has a pint of Guinness in front of him.

Funja is nowhere to be seen when I call a hello to the familiar staff and walk around the bar, but his Irish Wolfhound rises from his spot by the fire to greet me. I pet Boris and continue to Wishearth's table.

'Long time, no see,' he says and pulls his feet back. I sit opposite him.

A heady mixture of ash, wood smoke and pine branches engulfs me, and I relax into the familiar scents. Ever since I was a child, I have found the smell of wood fire reassuring, but only after moving to Old London did I come to appreciate the protection offered by a Hearth Spirit. In my home, making offerings to Wishearth is an integral part of each day.

'It's been less than a week.'

'Has it, now? You still look terrible.' Wishearth grins and sparks fly from his black eyes.

'And you haven't lost any of your charm.'

'Why would I? Am I not perfect as I am?' he asks, and raises his pint.

'Isn't it a little early for a pint?'

'A little early, little late, what's time to a spirit?'

What indeed? As a spirit, Wishearth is close to immortal, but he rarely refers to his longevity and he never speaks of the things he has seen during his life.

'Perhaps nothing. But doesn't Funja have to follow the laws for serving alcohol?'

'In my experience, Funja can be flexible about the rules when it suits him.'

Just like Wishearth, Funja also rewards loyalty. A few pints a day is a small price to pay for having a Hearth Spirit guarding his home and pub.

'Which reminds me, I have something for you. Here.' Wishearth hands me a small pumpkin.

I turn it in my hand. The surface is smooth, the colour somewhere between green and orange. 'Thanks, I think. What am I supposed to do with this?'

'Find someone to turn it into a carriage. Isn't that what fairy godmothers are supposed to do?'

'You were listening in on our initial meeting with Tim.' I grin. 'Are you keeping tabs on me?'

'That's for me to know and for you to wonder.'

Does he know how much I wonder about his doings, especially in connection with me? Every time I speak to him, I raise more questions than answers. He is watching me now, an enigmatic smile on his face. The baiting and teasing is part of our friendship, but it does leave me wondering whether there is a subtext I am missing or whether I am reading too much into every smile and every touch.

'I was hoping to ask you something regarding a case I'm working on,' I say before the silence becomes too tense. I cannot seem to maintain eye contact with him for long.

'Ask away.' If he is curious, he hides it by taking a sip from his pint.

'Are you aware of all the working hearths in London?'

'Yes,' he says without hesitation.

'Would you detect one created by an illusion?'

He sets his pint down, and my attention is drawn to his long, slender fingers. His hands are beautiful. It is a strange thought to have, for I have never held much of an opinion on anyone's hands before. Except Dearon's.

'That depends on the fireplace's function.'

'What do you mean?'

'If the fireplace was integral to the illusion, if someone made an offering to a Hearth Spirit next to it, I might catch a glimmer of it.' When I say nothing, he asks, 'Why?'

'We went to a crime scene last night with a major illusion in place, and it involved a wood-burning fireplace. I wondered if you might have been able to glimpse into the illusion through the flames. An unwitting eyewitness, so to speak.'

'Where was it?'

'On Herbrand Street in New London.'

Wishearth shakes his head. 'There are no wood-burning fireplaces in New London. It's part of the city's attempts to deal with the air pollution.'

'How is it that we can have them?'

'If I'm not mistaken, the argument had something to do with protecting the ways of the magical folk, some of whom are dependent on wood-burning fires for spells and potions.'

'Fair enough. How about the illusion, did you notice it?'

'I noticed nothing out of the ordinary last night. Perhaps if you had invoked the old rituals, I might have heard you despite the fire not being real.' My expression must fall, for he covers my hand and sends a wave of warmth deep into my bones. 'I'm sorry, Yannia.'

'It's fine. Talking to you was a long shot anyway.'

'How is the case with a human client going?'

Fatigue wars with caffeine in my system, and I tap my finger on the table edge. 'Badly. If I don't catch a break soon, my human client is going to die.'

A mortal might express concern for Tim's wellbeing, but not Wishearth. All he does is shrug.

'Sometimes, I find that in order to move forward, I must walk away.'

The movement of my finger stills while I consider his words. 'That makes sense, I guess. Find fresh perspective.'

'Something like that.'

'Thanks, Wishearth,' I say as I rise and force a smile.

'You're welcome.' He narrows his eyes, and I can see flames deep within them. When he leans forward, I bend down, my palms flat on the table. A wisp of smoke caresses my cheek. 'Don't forget to wear a seatbelt.'

I am still pondering Wishearth's warning when, fresh after a shower, I am driving towards the Guildhall where the High Council of Mages will have a meeting in an hour. It is not my habit to take chances with road safety. But knowing Wishearth's penchant for melodrama and cryptic utterings, he could be referring to something altogether different. I just wish I knew for certain.

Karrion agreed to meet me back at mine after lunch when I texted him to say that he should take his time. I too need the rest, but the thought of failure drives me on. My choices were either to attend a Council meeting or to pace around my lounge until I go mad.

The Guildhall is a long building clad in white marble kept gleaming with the aid of spells. It is the administrative centre of Old London, just like the Brotherhood of Justice on the bank of the Thames is the centre for upholding peace and justice. The High Council of Mages has been meeting here for centuries, and the name of every Mage who has sat on the Council is recorded in the oak panels that decorate the walls of the meeting room.

While Mages meet behind closed doors, the Circle of Shamans has their meetings in plain view of Old London. Outside the Guildhall is a square with multi-coloured stones set in geometric patterns. Karrion once told me that it was designed by a famous architect, but I have long since forgotten the name. At the centre of the square is an irregular circle of black stones. Any Shaman wishing to be admitted to the Circle must show that the animalistic life force within them is strong enough to raise a stone pillar from the earth. When the Circle meets, each Shaman demonstrates their continued worth by raising their seat until the entire Circle sits high above the square.

Whatever is said during the meetings can only be heard by those seated within the Circle, but I have heard the groans of the earth when it relinquishes its hold on the stones, and I have seen the grim determination on the faces of the Shamans while they prove their power. The task is by no means simple, and I know that plenty of young Shamans have tried and failed to obtain a seat within the Circle.

The Guildhall is busy with Council members and other officials, and the wide entrance hall echoes with numerous conversations and greetings being called out.

Beneath the din, I detect a low buzzing sound, but it disappears when I look around for its origin. My steps slow as I wonder at the enormity of the task set to me, but soon I realise that the situation is not as challenging as I first judged it to be. The Council members are all wearing official silk cloaks embroidered with the colours and insignia of their respective schools of magic, and the sheer volume of people in the entrance hall means that I can call upon my powers unnoticed.

When the crowd parts briefly, I spot Lord Ellensthorne in conversation with two of his fellow Shadow Mages, their black cloaks creating pockets of darkness in the marble hall. He notices me. Our eyes meet, and then he turns his back to me and resumes the conversation.

The message is clear: in this task, he grants me no aid. It is just as well, for I need none.

I have come prepared with a wide-brimmed hat and a loose scarf that loops around my neck several times. Once I get close enough to a couple of Council members, I drop my eyes to the ground and call upon the nose of a badger. Straight away, my senses are assaulted by dozens of competing scents, each more pungent than the last. I can smell several perfumes and aftershaves overlapping, the earthy aromas of sweat and musk, and beneath it all, the identifying signs of magical races. My eyes water and my nose burns while I struggle to make sense of it all.

Severing the threads of my power, I rub my nose until the desire to sneeze dissipates. I need to learn more care. It was for this very reason that I did not invoke my magic at Amici this morning. Why did I think I could do it now? Fatigue is clouding my judgement, and at this rate, I am going to miss something crucial.

With a growing sense of disappointment, I head for the doors. I have no business coming here until I have a better idea of how to complete the vetting process. Otherwise, all I am doing is wasting my time and the Council's money.

I have just stepped outside when the sound of footsteps draws my attention to three Mages running towards me. Their cloaks billow behind them, shimmering pearly white in the pale autumn sunshine. Using the brim of my hat to shield my face, I reach for my inner reserves of power and inhale.

The stink of cars reaches my nose first, but as the Mages pass me, I catch the refreshing scent of new dawn. All three are the Light Mages their cloaks proclaim them to be. I recall each face from the dossiers Karrion and I have compiled, and it reassures me to know that I can at least cross three names off the list. My coming here was not a waste of time after all.

My phone buzzes when I reach my car. Karrion has texted to say that he is on his way, and I tell him that I am likewise. The roads are getting busier with the lunchtime crowds, but it should take no more than half an hour to get home. The buzzing noise returns, and I shake my head to dislodge it.

I am halfway home when a mirage of a knife flashes across my vision and a searing pain burns down my arm. The shock jolts my body, and my foot slips off the accelerator and hits the brake instead. The driver behind has no time to react, and their car collides with my back bumper. In the moment before my head impacts with the steering wheel, I notice that the sleeve of my left arm has turned deep red. Then pain explodes with a blossom of light behind my eyes, and I slide into darkness.

23

FOURTH BLOOD

'Lizzie!'

She allowed the heavy door to bang shut behind her and waved at Tim striding towards her. He picked her up and spun her around until she was giggling and begging to be allowed down.

'What was that all about?' she asked, gripping Tim's coat while she waited for the world to stop spinning.

'I was just glad to see you.'

'You'll be less glad about it if I throw up on your shoes.'

'Yes, you might be right.' Tim brushed his fingers along Lizzie's cheek. 'Feeling better?'

Lizzie straightened her back. 'Much better.'

'Good. I was just about to come ring your doorbell.'

'I spotted you from my window and I thought I'd come down to meet you.' Lizzie smiled. 'Which is another way of saying that my flat is a mess and I want to tidy it before I invite you in.'

'Do you really think I'd notice? I am a boy after all, as you're so fond of pointing out.'

'I'd forgotten the difference between a man's perspective of a tidy house and a woman's.'

'While I wonder if I should feel a little insulted, I

suppose I'm going to have to let it slide. There's no rush to invite me to your place. You haven't seen my place yet either. Hoovering once a month is good enough, right?' he asked with a wink.

Lizzie groaned. 'Oh dear God, what have I let myself in for?'

'Interesting times, I hope. Didn't you want a project?'

'Don't be silly. I want you, not some project.'

Tim leant in to press a kiss to Lizzie's cheek. 'I thought women liked projects.'

Lizzie brushed a lock of hair from her face. 'Maybe some do, I don't.'

They shared a laugh, and Lizzie bit her lip, her cheeks heating.

'What did you have planned for us today?'

'There's an artisan food market on the South Bank. I thought we could have a look through it, grab something for late lunch and then walk to Leicester Square to see if we could get last minute tickets to a show.'

'A musical?' Lizzie nudged him with her shoulder. 'But I thought you didn't like musicals.'

'I didn't. But a fantastic lady showed me that I should keep an open mind about musicals, like many other things.'

'A lady? Way to make me feel old.'

'Sorry.'

'I'm kidding, silly. And your plans sound wonderful.'

Tim took Lizzie's hand, and they turned to head towards the bus stop while he listed the different stalls at the food market he had read about. His wide grin slipped when he noticed a figure walking towards them.

'Yannia, what are you doing here?'

The woman was dressed in faded jeans and a green

woollen coat that had seen a few too many washes. Her hair was tied back, but strands of it had escaped the braid and hung untidily around her face. Thin lips, pressed into a severe line, cracked into a smile when pale, watery eyes found Tim.

'There you are, love. I've been looking all over for you.'

'Love?' Lizzie asked.

'You promised to take me out for dinner, remember? We talked about it this morning. I thought we could go to Burger King.'

'No, I told you about the plans I had with my girlfriend.'

'That's right,' Yannia came closer, a brighter smile lifting her plain face. 'Our plans.'

'Tim, what's going on?' Lizzie asked, her hand slipping from Tim's.

Yannia appeared to notice Lizzie for the first time, and she frowned, her expression hardening into a scowl. When she reached up to brush strands of hair behind her ear, Lizzie saw her coat sleeves were caked with mud.

'I don't know,' Tim said, stepping forward to put himself between the women. 'Yannia seems to be operating under the illusion that she is my girlfriend.'

'But I am. We have such fun on the morning commute together. It's the highlight of my day. You must think so too – why else would you offer to buy me coffee each morning? Don't think I haven't realised it's a ruse to spend a few more minutes with me.'

'I've done it twice. That's hardly a declaration of love.'

'I thought she was a colleague of yours,' Lizzie said.

'No, we share a part of the commute and occasionally we exchange pleasantries on the train.' He looked at Yannia. 'That's all.'

'Then what's with all the offers to buy me coffee?' Yannia asked, crossing her arms. 'And what about the times you've suggested we have dinner together?'

'I've never done that,' Tim said, losing patience. 'You've mentioned a restaurant you liked, and I've said that I need to give it a try.'

'Yes, with me.'

'No, with Lizzie. Or on my own. But not with you.'

'That's not the impression you gave me.'

'Maybe you're just seeing romance where none exists,' Lizzie said.

Yannia glanced at Lizzie past Tim's shoulder. 'Maybe if you were the sort of girlfriend Tim needs, he wouldn't turn to me.'

The sound of a souped-up car engine echoed between the buildings, but they all ignored it.

Tim raised his arms in an effort to placate both women. 'Look, there has clearly been some sort of a misunderstanding. Yannia, I'm sorry if you have miscon-strued my attempt to be polite as romantic advances. Nothing could be further from the truth. I'm with Lizzie. I'm very happy with Lizzie.'

'If that's the case, why flirt with me?'

'I haven't been flirting with you!'

The sound of the engine was growing nearer, and Lizzie glanced towards the road. Her attention was drawn back to the confrontation when Yannia approached Tim, her face twisted in anger.

'You're an arse.' She punctuated each word by prodding Tim's chest. 'Why make me think you liked me if you didn't? Why all the smiles and lingering looks and all that shit?'

'It is not my problem if you choose to read something into situations that are completely innocent. I have not once tried to flirt with you or entertained any sort of romantic ideas towards you. You and I are just friends. In fact, we're not even that.'

'What are you saying?' Yannia's eyes filled with tears.

'I'm saying that I think it's best if, in the future, we choose different carriages on the train. My priorities are Lizzie and my relationship with her. Whatever you're offering, be it a romance or a friendship, I'm not interested.'

Yannia's tears fell just as a rusty bright blue Subaru rounded the bend and rolled up the hill. A wing at the back of the car had been painted in a pattern of neon yellows and oranges, and the car's suspension had been lowered until it was inches from the ground. "God Save the Queen" by the Sex Pistols was blaring from the stereo, the bass so loud that those standing by the car felt the vibrations through their feet.

Behind Tim, Lizzie gasped; a desperate, strangled sound. She backed away, but tripped on the edge of the front step and fell, the skin of her palms rubbed open by the stony ground. Tim turned towards her, concerned at the sight of her terror. Yannia shifted to remain behind Tim.

'Lizzie, what's wrong?'

The music cut off mid-lyric, and the silence that followed echoed in the car park. The driver's door opened.

'Miss me, bitch?'

Jagged sobs shook Lizzie's body, and she scooted back, oblivious to the smears of blood she left on the ground beside her and on her jeans. When her back collided with

258

the door to her building, Lizzie's feet continued to kick against the ground, although they achieved little more than a continuous rasping sound.

'Lizzie?' Tim asked again, crouching in front of her and reaching for her bleeding hand. She drew it back, pressing both arms tightly against her chest.

'No,' she managed between sobs, 'it can't be.'

'What the fuck is this? Have you moved on?'

A tall man dressed in a leather jacket and faded jeans slammed the Subaru door shut. After a final drag from a cigarette, he crushed the stump under a steel-capped boot.

Lizzie's mouth opened, but no sound came out. Large tears dripped from her jaw and were absorbed in her scarf. She drew her left hand up and bit the knuckles, exposing a row of scars on the wrist.

'Did you wait even a day before whoring yourself out? Huh? Can you remember how many blokes you've shagged while I've been rotting in a cell?'

'Hey, back off.' Tim stood, blocking the man's view of Lizzie. 'You've got no right to talk to her like that.'

'No right? She's my bitch.' He walked closer, stepping sideways around Tim. His fingers stroked his metal belt buckle. 'I reckon she needs a reminder.'

'Please, Wayne, don't.' Lizzie twisted to push the door to the building that housed her flat, but it would not budge.

'You're Wayne?'

Wayne grinned. 'Just got out, I did. For good behaviour. Now piss off, the missus and I are going to discuss how much she missed me while I was gone.'

'I know what you did to her,' Tim said, moving to stand between Lizzie and Wayne again. 'You're not going to hurt her.'

'Oh yeah? And who's going to stop me?' Wayne stepped close enough that Tim could smell alcohol on his breath. 'You?'

'Me. I promised to keep her safe and that's exactly what I'm going to do.'

'Tim, maybe you shouldn't get involved.' Yannia had remained silent since Wayne's appearance, but now she wiped the tears from her cheeks and tugged at Tim's arm to draw him away from the confrontation.

'Yeah, listen to the broad. Keep your nose out of things that aren't your business.'

'Yannia,' said Tim, 'I don't know what you're doing here, but just stay out of this. Please.'

'I'm not going to stand by and watch while you get hurt in an argument that doesn't concern you.'

'Lizzie is my girlfriend. Of course it concerns me.'

Wayne pushed Yannia out of the way. She yelped, but regained her balance before she fell.

'Girlfriend? You make a habit of banging my missus?' He shoved Tim, who took a step back.

'Please, Wayne,' Lizzie whispered. 'I'll do whatever you want, just don't hurt Tim.'

'Is that how it is?' Wayne advanced on Lizzie, who shrank back against the door. 'Like him, do you?' He glanced over his shoulder. 'Does she tell you she loves you? Does her pretty little mouth spew lies while her eyes look for the next gullible bloke? News flash: she don't care about anyone but herself.'

Grabbing the front of Lizzie's coat, Wayne picked her up and shook her. She screamed. Wayne brought their faces inches apart.

'You're mine, you filthy whore. Don't you forget that.'

'Leave her alone.'

Tim aimed a punch at Wayne's cheek. It was a glancing blow and only angered him further. Wayne dropped Lizzie, who landed on the ground in a heap.

'Wait there, love. I've got to teach the posh boy some manners.'

Backing away, Tim raised his fists. From his stance, it was apparent that he had no experience of boxing or fighting. When Wayne approached, Tim threw a punch. Wayne dodged it without breaking his stride. With a cocky grin, he feigned a blow to Tim's head. When he moved to block it, Wayne sank his fist into Tim's stomach. Tim doubled over, struggling to draw breath. A second punch connected with his jaw and snapped him straight. His eyes rolled back, and he fell, the back of his head hitting the pavement with a crack.

'Tim!' Lizzie screamed.

A rivulet of blood ran from underneath Tim's head, then another.

'What did you do?' Yannia growled and advanced on Wayne.

'Nobody touches my missus.'

From her pocket, Yannia pulled a butterfly knife. A flick of her wrist opened the blade. Wayne's surprise turned to amusement, and he waited for Yannia to approach. When she was almost within reach, he rushed forward, batting her knife hand aside. He grabbed her wrist and twisted it until she was forced to drop the knife. Wayne caught it, heedless of the blade cutting his palm.

'You should've stayed out of this.'

Yannia aimed a kick between Wayne's legs. He twisted his body around, and her knee hit his thigh. Wayne cut a long wound on her left bicep. She fell and scooted backwards away from him, cradling her bleeding arm against her chest.

Drops of blood flew from the knife as Wayne shook it and turned to Lizzie. She was staring past him at Tim, lying motionless on the ground, and at Yannia, who was sobbing nearby.

'Looks like it's just you and me left, babe,' Wayne said, knife ready at his side. 'Just like the good old times.'

Curling into a foetal position, arms shielding her face, Lizzie screamed.

24

THE HUNT

Ours is a collective memory, and in dreaming, the Wild Folk can access the experiences of the generations that have gone before. We share their wisdom and their understanding of the wilderness they inhabit. They teach us, and we, in turn, dream the dreams for those who come after us.

In Old London, I am rarely able to tap into the collective dreaming. But now, fatigue, pain and the shock of the car crash drag me to a different landscape, where I am not me, but we.

The pack is on the move, ascending a steep hillside. Heather brushes against our bellies, our paws finding silent purchase within the undergrowth. Ahead of us, the herd is on the run, and the air is thick with the smell of deer, fear and the acrid undertones of adrenaline secreted from the hooves. We have been loping for hours, but the smell of the prey and the knowledge of the gorging to come spurs us on, heedless of hunger or fatigue.

We crest the hill and are rewarded with a view of the vale, its sides purple and orange and red. Above us, clouds the colour of human weapons roll across the sky and the wind carries a promise of snow. A stream drains to a loch, and the smell of water brings a sharp stab of thirst. But we cannot drink, not while the prey is running.

The Elderman leads us on, and we follow in single file. In every step of the hunt, in every aspect of our lives, we pay him obeisance, and he, in turn, sees that we survive the harsh seasons and the encroachment of strangers. The loyalty is bone-deep, as ingrained within us as the hunger for the hunt.

The herd has turned left, away from the loch, and we pursue it with single-minded determination. Now in full view, each of us assesses the herd, seeking the old and infirm, the young and clumsy. A hind stumbles, and a limp in its foreleg becomes more pronounced. The pack surges on, refreshed by the clear target.

We run on for a mile or more before the hind begins to lag behind. The Elderman speeds up, and the line formation breaks apart as we circle the hind, separate it from the others. It calls out, panic in its shrill voice, but half the pack now stands between it and the herd. We take turns to slump for a brief rest or to leap at the hind's sides.

It whirls round and round, hooves flying to keep the pack at bay. No matter which way it turns, the Elderman is always in front of it, amber eyes fixed on its throat. We launch ourselves into the air, and our teeth make contact above its shank, but our grip is awkward and we slip down. The hind bucks, and pain explodes in our foreleg where its hoof connects. We slash at it again, and our mouth fills with hot blood. Then a second buck sends us flying backwards, and we land in a clump of heather with a yelp.

Others have followed our example, and soon the hind's sides are slick with blood. Its movements are becoming more violent, more desperate, and when it rears to slash down at two of us, the Elderman makes his move. He leaps at the hind's throat, but it pulls down its head and the Elderman latches on to the muzzle instead. The hind screams and falls to its knees, unable to keep its balance with the added weight attached to its face. More of us rush forward, teeth sinking into the throat and slashing open its belly. The smell and taste of blood drive us to a frenzy, and the valley echoes with our yelps and howls.

All fight leaves the hind, and it falls to its side. The Elderman releases his grip and rests his forehead briefly against the hind's. A final, ragged breath is all the hind manages, and then it is still. The pack converges on the carcass, ready to feast. None make the first move, all waiting for the Elderman's signal.

We lie in the heather, licking our forelimb. Pain throbs through it, but no bones are broken. When a nose nudges us, we snarl a warning. Dark eyes watch us, dancing with mirth, and we curl our lips back.

Why has Dearon invaded our hunt?

Heedless of our anger, he nudges us again. We fly at him, teeth bared. He dodges our lunge and uses our momentum to knock us to the ground. Before we have a chance to try again, the Elderman barks a signal and our anger is forgotten.

Time to feast.

The deer intestines have spilt on to the trampled heather, and we find ourselves a spot between the front legs. Hot blood sprays into our eyes, and we close them, allowing instinct to guide our head deep into the chest cavity. The rich iron tang of blood sends our pulse tripping in frenzy, and we growl to keep the others from our prize.

Before my mouth closes around the warm heart, a lance of light stabs into my eyes and arms drag me away from the carcass, the hunger and my family.

25

LICKING WOUNDS

I regain consciousness when the paramedics fit the gurney into the ambulance. The dream of the hunt lingers at the forefront of my mind, and at first, I assume that the blood I can taste is from the deer. Then my teeth find a cut on the side of my tongue, and the source of the blood becomes apparent.

My body is a mass of pain, but after a few jolting moments where the gurney is locked into place, I begin to distinguish between large and small sources of agony. My left arm is burning, while my forehead throbs in time with my heartbeat. Something tight is pressed over my face, and it is digging into my cheeks.

It is my intention to ask what is going on, but all that escapes my mouth is a groan that echoes strangely within whatever is covering my mouth. The lance of light stabs me in the eye again, and I shy away, only to have a strong hand keep my head still while the light brings tears to my eyes.

'Lie still. You're in an ambulance.'

I must convey enough confusion with my limited facial expressions for a paramedic to elaborate.

'You were in a car crash.'

I have no memory of being in a car crash. The last

things I recall are the overwhelming scents of the reception area at the Guildhall and verifying three Light Mages. After that, everything is a jumbled mess of images, sounds and sensations. What happened to me?

'Take it easy now. We're going to transport you to a hospital. You may have concussion and you're going to need stitches.'

There is something I should remember, something important I need to tell someone, but the thought eludes me. I struggle against the confusion until black spots swim across my vision and bile rises to my mouth. The fatigue from lack of sleep that has been dragging me under all morning engulfs me, and my eyes flutter closed.

When I next wake up, I am staring at a blue curtain. I am lying in a bed, a cannula taped to the back of my left hand. The individual pains in my forehead and arm are gone, but I can feel the tightness of bandages against both. My legs retain a faint ache, but it is the familiar pain of my connective tissue disorder, rather than anything indicating trauma.

The curtain hides my bed from view, and from beyond it, I can hear a steady hum of noise. Drawing upon a thread of magic, I sharpen my hearing until the ringing phones, the doctors' instructions, the moans of patients and the soothing tones of nurses come into sharper focus. I must be in A&E.

I hear my name being mentioned and the approach of footsteps. The curtain parts, and Jamie pokes his head through.

'How're you feeling?'

My throat is dry, and it takes me a few tries before I get my voice going.

'Like I was hit by a car?' I attempt a laugh, but it turns into a cough and Jamie passes me a paper cup. I gulp the water down, even though it is tepid and not the shocking cold of loch water. A line of moisture dribbles from the corner of my mouth and wets the collar of my hospital gown. 'Actually, I'm feeling like I just got some sleep I desperately needed.'

'There are easier ways to get sleep, you know.'

'I'll bear that in mind.' The smile slips off my face. 'Do you have any idea what happened?'

'The Paladins are investigating. From the initial reports at the scene, you slammed on the brakes. The car behind hit you, and you collided with the taxi in front of you. No one else got hurt. You shouldn't have either, but the airbag in your car seems to have malfunctioned. Bad luck.'

'I don't remember slamming on the brakes.'

'The doctor said there was something strange about your injuries. That cut in your arm, it's clean. Not as in it's been disinfected, but rather that the edges are clean. I made a call and there was no broken glass in your car. What's also interesting is that your coat was intact, at least until the doctors cut it off you.'

'Wait, they cut through my coat?'

'Yes, you were covered in blood, and they couldn't figure out where the source of the bleeding was. But don't you think you're focusing on the unimportant?'

'I liked that coat.' I reach to rub the sleep from my eyes, but the needle in my hand catches and I switch to my right hand. 'What were you saying again?'

269

'I was saying that you have a knife wound on your arm, but your clothes weren't cut.'

'How can that be?' There it is again, that feeling that I am missing something important.

'Well, following a hunch, I sent a Mage to check out your car. And guess what?'

I realise he is expecting me to guess. The headache returns, and all I want is to curl up on my side and go back to sleep. But Jamie is waiting for an answer.

'What?'

'She found traces of an unidentifiable illusion we've come to know and love.'

I sit bolt upright on the bed, and pain stabs through my forehead. Sinking back into the pillow, I frown as well as I can under the bandages.

'Lizzie did this?'

Those three words open the floodgates in my mind, and I sit bolt upright a second time, heedless of the pain. Now I remember what was so important.

'Tim. Where is he? How is he?'

Jamie's expression grows grim. 'He's upstairs, in a coma.'

'What?'

'He collapsed at work. They rushed him to the hospital, and the doctors said they got to him just in time. Apparently he has a fractured skull and a subdural haematoma. Or something. They were able to stop the bleeding and remove the blood clot, but they are keeping him under close observation to make sure he remains stable.'

'But he's going to wake up, isn't he?'

'Provided that there aren't any unexpected complications, he should be fine.'

I sag back, relief robbing strength from my limbs.

'What about Tim's mother? A nurse is there only when Tim's at work.'

'I've already called the nurse and informed her. She's organising care for Tim's mother.'

'Thanks, Jamie.' Now that my brain has woken up, I remember something else. 'What time is it?'

'A little after four. Why?'

'Bugger. I was supposed to meet Karrion hours ago.'

'I know. He called me when you didn't show up. By then I'd heard about the accident, but I didn't yet know where they had taken you. Once I found out about your and Tim's injuries, I rang him back. He's down the hall.'

'Would you mind calling him in? I think this is a conversation all three of us need to have.'

'Sure.'

Jamie leaves. I can tell when he has spoken to Karrion, for running footsteps approach and the curtain is yanked aside with enough force to send it halfway around the bed.

'Yan.' Karrion looks like he wants to hug me, but his eyes skitter from my bandaged head to the IV stand next to the bed and back. I resolve his dilemma by sitting up and reaching for him with my uninjured arm.

He crosses the distance in a stride and throws his arms around me, but the hug is gentle. His piercings feel cold against my skin as he buries his face in the crook of my neck.

'Thank the spirits you're okay. I was so worried.'

'It's all good, Karrion. I'll be back to normal in no time.'

I pat his back, but the contact triggers a burning pain in my palm and I pull my hand back. My palm is covered in a wide plaster.

'What's this?'

'You have road rash across the palm. It looked like you had broken a fall with that hand. The doctor cleaned it, but none of the cuts required stitches.'

'This doesn't make any sense. I was stabbed, had a car crash, and now I fell too. And Tim is in a coma.'

'What?' It is Karrion's turn to look shocked.

'Sorry, I didn't get a chance to bring you up to date while Yannia was unconscious,' Jamie says. He tells Karrion what he discovered about my crash and Tim's condition. Karrion's expression darkens, and he stands by my bed, clenching and unclenching his fists.

'Lizzie is going to pay for this,' he says.

'Just as soon as you or the police find her,' says Jamie.

'By the way, how is my car?' I ask.

Jamie grimaces. 'It's going to take a lot of work.'

'Fantastic. The insurance company is going to love me.'

'It wasn't your fault.' I must look puzzled for Jamie continues, 'Our preliminary investigation indicates that the cause of the accident was the illusion. If you're the victim of a magical attack, you can't be held responsible for the crash.'

I attempt a smile. 'Do you mind telling that to my insurer?'

'Not at all. When you call them about the accident, you can give them the crime reference number and inform them that the crash is part of an ongoing criminal investigation. They'll then get in touch with us about the details.'

'Thanks, Jamie.'

'Do you want me to call them?' Karrion asks.

'Please. If you can find my phone, I'll email you the policy details.'

Karrion looks through the drawers of the nightstand and finds a plastic bag containing my belongings. He hands me my phone, which has survived the crash intact.

'When can Yan leave?' Karrion asks Jamie. I look up from writing the email, eager for the answer.

'The doctors suspect you have concussion, and they want to keep you in overnight for observation.'

'I can't do that. Lizzie is still out there, and she's expanding her pool of victims.'

'You're no good to anyone if you keel over and pass out,' Jamie says.

'But until I do, I should get something useful done.'

Karrion places his hand over mine, mindful of the cannula. 'That's why you have me, Yan.' When I do not reply, he continues, 'I can do the legwork for you, if Jamie doesn't mind. You can man the command centre here, while you rest and the nurses ask you questions about who the prime minister is and what you had for tea.'

Jamie nods. 'That suits me. Karrion has proven himself to be a great help.'

I can sense Karrion's swelling pride as a blue capercaillie cock showing off his plumage, and he grins. It is infectious, and both Jamie and I join in.

'You just wait, I'm going to be your eyes and ears, your nightjar.'

'A nightjar? That doesn't sound terribly menacing. Wouldn't a Nightwing or Batman be more useful?'

Karrion rolls his eyes and sighs. He takes my phone and does something with it before returning it to the drawer. 'It's a bird, known for being so elusive that people attribute it with mystical abilities.'

'Right. I knew that, of course.'

'I'm sure you did. What's it going to be, boss? Point me in the right direction and I'll get straight to work.'

A nurse walking past gives us a warning frown, and I lie back down, drawing the cover up to my chin. Jamie and Karrion look chastened, and they sit down on the uncomfortable plastic chairs that seem to breed in hospitals.

'We know there has been another illusion, which means that somewhere there is a crime scene and a body. It's likely any sign of the crime has faded by now, but it's possible the police investigated it, or at the very least, it was reported. That's where we'll need Jamie's help. Once he pinpoints a crime scene for us, go there. Find out if there were any eyewitnesses and whether whatever happened was caught on CCTV.'

'Will do.'

'And take Thaylor's machine with you, in case there's something there to detect.'

Karrion goes through the drawer again and pockets the device. 'I hope this will help us figure out who Lizzie is.'

'We're already closer.'

'Are we?' Karrion asks.

'Yes. This time, Lizzie came after Tim and me. For her to have registered me as someone who is part of Tim's life and a potential threat, she must have seen us together this morning or yesterday.'

'Lizzie thinks you're a threat?'

I turn to Jamie. 'Why else would she attack me?'

'What exactly did you and Tim do?'

Ignoring the suggestive tone of the question, I run through our movements on both mornings. Karrion adds a few comments about today, but we both know the morning yielded no breakthroughs.

'If she sees you as a threat, then she must really hate Tim,' Jamie says. 'Killing someone over and over suggests a deep-seated hatred. You'd think that an emotion that intense would be difficult to hide from the rest of the world, and especially from someone who was looking for signs that something's not right.'

'That's what we thought and yet we haven't been able to spot anyone like that.'

'Could she be invisible?' When Jamie and I turn to look at him, Karrion rubs his neck. 'I know, I know. "The Invisible Man did it" is hardly the most original solution in the world. But maybe she is hiding in plain sight? If she has enough magic to create large-scale illusions, maybe she has a way of disguising herself with magic too? That Feykin man was able to fool you completely. If Lizzie is also Feykin, chances are she can do something similar.'

There is a silence while we all consider the possibility. If Karrion is right, our task is that much harder to complete. How are we ever going to find Lizzie if she is using magic to hide from us?

'If someone can hide with magic, it must be possible to see through that sort of spell,' Jamie says, his words slow. 'That is right, isn't it?'

'Thaylor said that invisibility works on sight alone and that the invisible person can still be detected using the other senses,' I say. 'I imagine there must be spells that can also see through invisibility, though I don't know any. That's something for you to ask the Mages that work for New Scotland Yard.'

'I'll look into it when I get back to the office.'

'There's something else you could check,' Karrion says. His tone is hesitant to begin with, but he soon regains his natural confidence. 'As far as we know, the first three illusions happened three days apart. But there has been less than twenty-four hours between the last two. Could you ask one of the Mages how much power it would take to create an illusion like Lizzie's?'

'Sure, no problem.'

'Are you thinking that Lizzie is running low on magic?' I ask.

'Yes, at least I hope she is. It worries me that there have been two attacks in such a short space of time and the severity is increasing. We have less and less time to catch her.' Karrion squeezes my hand. 'And next time, it might not just be Tim and you who get hurt.'

'You should ask your boss for hazard pay.' I attempt a smile, but in truth, I share his concern.

'Hang on, you said as far as we know. What did you mean by that?' Jamie asks.

'We know of these four illusions because they left a body and a crime scene. But who's to say that there aren't many others that don't end with Tim dying?'

I can see where Karrion is going and I nod. 'If Lizzie is creating other illusions we know nothing about, she's more powerful than we had anticipated.'

'Which also makes her more dangerous.' Karrion finishes the thought for me.

'In which case, we gain nothing from just standing around,' Jamie says. 'Karrion and I will head over to New

Scotland Yard. You, Yannia, need to rest before the nurses come after me for disturbing their patient.'

Karrion waggles his eyebrows. 'That sounded like an official order. You best obey, Yan.'

'Fine, but you'll let me know the moment you hear something, won't you?'

'Of course we will.' Jamie looks like he is going to offer to shake my hand, but he ends up giving me an awkward pat on the shoulder. 'Feel better soon.'

'Thank you.'

I watch Karrion and Jamie leave. My headache has increased to a steady throb, but it feels strange to have to sit on the sidelines while the others work on the case. I appreciate in a whole new way how frustrating it must have been for Karrion not to accompany me at all times. In the future, I will need to make sure he does not get left out.

FRIDAY

26

THE FINAL PIECES

I find Karrion asleep on a chair by my bed, his head resting on his arms next to my feet. He was not there last time the nurse woke me to ask inane questions about the Speaker of the High Council of Mages and the time of the year. Apparently I passed, for I was allowed to go back to sleep.

The throb in my forehead has lessened to a twinge around the stitches, and my full bladder nags me. I ease the covers aside and inch myself off the bed without waking Karrion. The IV stand provides support as I make my way to the toilet and back. Rather than getting back into bed, I gently stretch my limbs. Now that I am better rested, my mind is in overdrive, thinking about the case.

When I get my phone from the drawer, I see that it is seven o'clock in the morning. The screen shows several emails, but the phone is on silent. I glare at Karrion, who responds with a snore.

A nurse arriving awakens Karrion, who sits up, wiping his mouth. He blinks at the empty bed and then spots me.

'Morning, Yan.'

The nurse ushers me back to bed and checks my condition. A doctor arrives shortly after and does the same. Together they pronounce that my recovery has begun well and that I have no concussion. The doctor signs my discharge papers while the nurse removes the cannula. They leave, and Karrion hands me a bag.

'I figured your coat and shirt were wrecked and I stopped by your place to get you some clean clothes.'

'Thanks.' I lean over and press a kiss to his cheek. 'You're the best.'

'Can you tell Mum that? Apparently I don't go to church enough and my soul is in danger.'

'I'll write her a letter on the subject,' I say and head over to the bathroom to get changed.

A bandage is covering my left arm from shoulder to elbow. There is a localised ache, but I cannot tell where the wound begins and ends. The cut on my forehead is likewise covered with a bandage, but a bruise has spread down my right temple and under the eye. Standing in front of the mirror in just my underwear, I trace the angry red scar across my shoulder with my fingers. It's healing, but still prominent. If I carry on like this, my body will be a roadmap of scars by the time Karrion celebrates his first anniversary as my apprentice.

What would Dearon think if he saw me now?

I dismiss the thought with a shake of my head. Wild Folk are no strangers to scars.

When I open the bag of clothes, I laugh. Karrion has packed me the darkest pair of jeans I own, and the jumper and wool coat are both black. He has even found my black socks. The simple gesture keeps a smile on my face as I ease into the clothes, mindful of my sore arm. A good night's sleep and the medication have worked wonders, and I find I am hungry and eager to get back to the case.

Karrion grins when I return to him. 'Definite improvement on a hospital gown.'

'I'm glad you approve. Are you trying to turn me into a goth?'

'Nah, way too much work. I just wanted to give you a taste of life on the dark side.'

The warmth of his smile discourages a sarky response, and instead, I drop the empty bag on his lap, letting my hand rest briefly on his shoulder.

It takes another half hour for us to pack my meagre belongings and listen to the nurse's instructions on keeping my wounds clean. She also removes the bandage from my forehead and covers the stitches with a large plaster. When we finally step out of the hospital's front doors, my stomach is growling and I am craving coffee.

'Let's get some breakfast, and you can bring me up to date on everything that happened while I was asleep. And don't think I'm not aware that you switched my phone to silent yesterday.'

'I'm not sorry, Yan. You looked like you needed the sleep.'

'I did, but not at the expense of our client's wellbeing.'

'If we'd had a breakthrough, I would have come and woken you up. I'm not that dense. Or suicidal.'

'Fine.'

We find a cafe and order breakfast. A table in the corner gives us a degree of privacy. The first sip of coffee warms my insides, and I cradle the mug in my hands, enjoying the warmth seeping into my fingers.

'How are you feeling now?' Karrion asks.

'Better. Anxious to get on with the case.'

My words are enough of a hint, but Karrion's account is delayed by the arrival of our plates. I am not usually one for a full English breakfast, but given that I have not eaten since yesterday morning, I dig in straight away.

'Did you find the crime scene?' I ask and take another sip of my coffee.

'We did, after some searching. It's on the Isle of Dogs, on a council estate on Manchester Road.'

'Isle of Dogs? That seems odd, given the other three incidents have taken place in or near Old London.'

'I agree. That's one of the reasons why it took us a while to find it. The incident was originally reported to the police as a domestic disturbance, and an ambulance was called because two people appeared hurt.'

'Two people?'

'Yes, a young man, who was beaten, and a woman with a stab wound on her arm.'

It is one thing to know Lizzie targeted me and quite another to hear that I was there. How it would help to have had some insight into the illusion as it happened. The thought prompts a memory, and I recall an image of a knife flashing across my vision. But it has no context; my recollection of the minutes leading up to the car crash is jumbled and fragmented.

'I was there.'

Karrion appears to share my concern, and he nods, a forkful of beans midway to his mouth. 'You were.'

'Why don't you start from the beginning?'

'What made this incident different from the others was the fact that there was an eyewitness. A woman was waiting for an Argos delivery, and she was watching the car park from her kitchen window. She's the one who called the police.'

'It sounds as though we got lucky. In so far as that's possible, given Tim is in a coma.'

'We did. She said at first, there were two people outside the building, a man and a woman. Jamie and I went to see her last night and showed her photos of Tim and Lizzie. She recognised Tim straight away, but wasn't sure about Lizzie given how poor the quality of the still from the CCTV was.'

'I think we can safely assume it was her.'

'Agreed. The woman stepped out of the building, and Tim was waiting for her. According to our eyewitness, Mrs Benson, Tim seemed to appear out of nowhere.'

'Which is consistent with the beginning of an illusion.'

Karrion nods and butters another slice of toast. While he does so, I steal the mushrooms off his plate and he retaliates by taking my fried tomato.

'Mrs Benson said that it was clear as day that Lizzie and Tim were a couple. They exchanged a few words and were about to head off when another woman appeared, again seemingly out of nowhere. I showed Mrs Benson a photo of you, and she confirmed that you were the other woman.'

'I've never liked the thought of being the other woman.'

'It doesn't suit you,' Karrion says. 'Mrs Benson did mention you looked drab and unkempt. I don't know if that's relevant.'

'Relevant or not, it's certainly odd. Just like so many other things about this case.'

'Anyway, you had an argument with Tim, who was trying to keep himself between you and Lizzie. Whatever was said, you didn't like it.'

'I'd pay good money to know what we argued over,' I say, and pile beans on to my toast. I bite into it, heedless of the tomato sauce clinging to the corners of my mouth.

'Me too. Whatever Tim said made you cry, but before

anyone could leave, another man arrived in a car and things started going wrong.'

'Wrong how?'

'Lizzie fell to pieces, obviously frightened of the man. Tim defended her while you tried to draw Tim away from it all. The men ended up trading blows, but Tim was way out of his league and took a couple of serious punches. He was knocked unconscious and hit his head on the ground. You drew a knife—'

'I did *what*?'

'You drew a knife, the kind that flicks open, and went after the mystery man. He disarmed you and stabbed you in the left arm.'

My right hand strays to the bandage under my cardigan. Once again, I see the vision of the knife, and this time searing pain accompanies the vision.

'You fell, which meant both you and Tim were out of the picture. The man advanced on Lizzie, who was curled on her side next to the front door. Mrs Benson said she could hear Lizzie scream even though her windows were shut. That's when she left the window to call the police. When she came back a minute or so later, you, Lizzie and the mystery man had disappeared. All that was left of the crime was Tim, dead on the ground, and a small pool of blood where your arm had bled.'

'And presumably Tim disappeared right around the time the paramedics got there.'

'Later, actually. They pronounced him dead at the scene and the body vanished while it was being transported to the morgue. He had no ID on him, nothing in his pockets, which is the other reason it took Jamie and me a while to find the right crime scene.'

'Do we have any idea who the mystery man is?'

Karrion grins. 'Yes, we do. Mrs Benson was quite the model eyewitness and noted down the registration of the car he was driving. The car also vanished when she was calling the police, by the way.'

'But is it real? The car, I mean?'

'So far, everything with any detail in the illusions has been based on reality. That's also the case with the car.'

'Who's the owner?'

'Last night, all we had was a name. Wayne Henderson. Jamie is running down everything we know about him, and he promised to call us this morning.'

'Fair enough. You've done a great job, Karrion.'

We have just finished our breakfast when Karrion's phone rings. He shows me Jamie's name on the screen and answers the call. Almost straight away, he moves the phone away from his face.

'Jamie says to answer your phone.'

I fumble for the phone in my coat pocket and see that it is still on silent. With a curse, I switch the sound on and scroll through the notifications. I have three missed calls and a text from Jamie.

Having listened to Jamie for a while longer, Karrion passes his phone to me.

'He's got news for us.'

The cafe is empty enough that I can put Jamie on speaker, and both Karrion and I lean over the table to get close to the phone.

'Like I promised Karrion, I did some digging into Wayne Henderson. There was plenty to uncover. He's a nasty piece of work and has been in and out of the system for most of his life. The charges were, for a time, relatively minor: petty theft, vandalism, drunk and disorderly. But at the moment, he's serving a longer prison sentence for an aggravated assault.'

'Wait, he's in prison?' I ask.

'Yes. I've spoken to the prison warden this morning, who confirmed that he's safely under lock and key.'

'Is the car seen at the crime scene definitely his?'

'He is the registered owner of a blue 2001 Subaru with a registration number that ties in with the eyewitness's account. What's more, he matches the description of the man seen assaulting you and Tim yesterday.'

With every new discovery, the case is getting increasingly confusing and I feel a familiar frustration fuelling my restlessness. I resist the urge to drum my fingers on the table, and try to focus instead on the latest mystery.

'What is the connection between Wayne and Lizzie?'

'Are we sure there is one?' Karrion asks. 'Couldn't it be just another freak accident that sees Tim dead?'

'I don't think so.' I shake my head for Karrion's benefit. 'For Lizzie to have included both Wayne and his car in the illusion, she must have known him well enough to get the details, such as the registration number, right. That to me implies a deeper connection than two strangers passing each other on the street. Besides, how long has Wayne been in prison?'

'A year and seven months,' Jamie says.

'Right. Any random connection had to have taken place over a year and a half ago. Can you remember the registration number of a taxi you took two years ago?'

'No,' Karrion says. 'I take your point.'

'Also, didn't you say Lizzie fell to pieces as soon as Wayne arrived?'

We can hear a rustle of papers through the speaker, and Jamie clears his throat. 'That's right. Mrs Benson thought Lizzie was petrified of Wayne.'

'For a person to be that afraid of someone, they must share history. Could she have been Wayne's victim?'

More rustling of papers follows. My leg bounces restlessly, and it accidentally hits the underside of the table, causing the cutlery on our plates to clatter. I mutter an apology.

'The assault charges were brought by Wayne's partner. According to the case notes, the abuse was extensive and took place over two years. But the victim's name isn't Elizabeth.'

'Who was the victim?'

'Melissa Hall.'

Adrenaline floods my body, and I jump up, my chair scraping back with a loud squeak.

'I know who Lizzie is.'

27

A DISAGREEMENT OF HUMANS

'We need to get to Amici,' I say to Jamie as I hurry out, Karrion hot on my heels.

'The cafe?'

'Yes.'

'Are you sure she'll be there?'

'No, but that's the likeliest place for her to be in the morning, and we need to find her fast. It's been almost a day since the last attack. In the condition he's in, Tim won't survive another.'

'Be careful, Yannia,' Jamie says, his voice resigned. 'Call me as soon as you know something, and I'll alert the Paladins.'

'Will do.'

I end the call and hand Karrion his phone.

'I thought you didn't notice anything unusual in the cafe,' he says, striding to keep up with me.

'Nothing that seemed out of place, but I couldn't use the full extent of my Wild Folk senses. There were too many people.'

'But you think Melissa Hall and Lizzie are the same person.'

'I do.'

'It's an odd nickname for a Melissa.'

'Think about it. What's our sole source for the name?'

Karrion's brow creases while I look around, trying to orient myself. A bus would take too long, and I hail a taxi instead. We get in and I give the driver directions to Amici.

'We heard it from Bob, didn't we? The homeless guy?'

'Correct. But who's to say he didn't mishear Lissa or Lissy as Lizzie? By his account, Tim was bleeding to death. It's possible that Bob got the name wrong.'

'Or Elizabeth could be Melissa's middle name and that's why she uses it.'

'That's also possible.' I peer out of the window, disappointed by how little progress we have made. 'Do you know if Jamie had a chance to ask any of his Mage colleagues about the illusions?'

'Yes. We spoke to a grumpy old git who seemed to think we were wasting his time. But he did say that creating such an elaborate illusion would take a great deal of raw power. If the illusion was repeated, or if it was something very close to the Mage's experiences and memories, the magic requirement would be lessened. Even so, a sensible Mage would use artefacts, or at the very least mana gems to bear some of the power load.'

'Which means that either Melissa is very powerful or she's exhausted by now.'

'Let's hope it's the latter. According to the Mage, the reason illusions require so much power is the amount of detail included. The more you include, the more you need to keep track of. Moving parts, be they animals, people or machines, are the hardest.'

'That could explain why the bullet was nowhere to be found. Perhaps it was one detail too many for Melissa.'

Karrion nods. 'Same with the Thai restaurant. Maybe she was conserving energy.'

'It's possible.'

'The Mage said something else interesting. When we described the nature of the illusion and the fact that part of it becomes reality, he looked at us like we'd grown wings. He claims what we told him is impossible. Illusions are a separate type of magic from the creation of things. The two cannot be combined.'

'But we already know that Melissa doesn't fit into the usual types of spell casters,' I say. 'Could it be that she's figured out how to combine different strands of magic?'

'But what about the traces of Feykin magic at the scene? There's way too much we still don't understand.'

'What I don't get is why she'd want a past abuser as part of the illusion.'

'It makes no more sense than Tim's suicide.'

Once we get past a set of traffic lights, the queues disperse and the taxi attains a reasonable speed. I cannot help thinking how useful it would be to have control over electrical machinery. If I could do that, I could change all the lights to green and grant us easy passage through Old London. But one person playing with the traffic system, let alone several, could cause chaos. It is best I stick to hoping that the driver senses our urgency and drives faster.

'What's the plan, boss?' Karrion asks.

'Get to Amici and stop Melissa before she creates another illusion.'

'That sounds simple.'

'If luck is on our side, it will be. I am hoping we can explain to Melissa the seriousness of her actions and get her to surrender to the Paladins without a fuss.'

'How very British. Welcome to Britain, the country where killers are apprehended with minimal fuss.'

'That could be a slogan at the airports,' I say, but my heart is not in the banter. Karrion senses this, and we lapse into silence.

When we reach Amici, I pay the taxi fare and leave a generous tip, in most part because I am unwilling to waste time waiting for change. We jog across the road, and Karrion pushes the cafe door open, allowing me to go in first.

The cafe is less busy than the previous times I have been there, although about half the tables are occupied. Several people have prams with them. The laughter and gurgle of toddlers add a discordant note to the urgency with which I survey the cafe. Melissa does not appear to be there, but Pavel is stocking a box of herbal teas.

'Hi there,' I say as I stop by the counter, 'I was hoping to speak to Melissa. Is she working today?'

Pavel smiles.

'Yes. She said she wasn't feeling well so she's taking a quick break. I think she said she needed some fresh air. You could check the back door. Or if you'd rather wait, I'm sure she won't be long.'

The thought of any kind of confrontation taking place inside the cafe chills my insides. If Melissa is as dangerous as I think she is, all these people are at risk. Keeping the thought to myself, I nod.

'Thank you.'

We hurry out and down the street. There is an alley running behind the shops for loading and bins. The back doors have no shop signs, only numbers. I have time to worry about not knowing where the cafe's back door is before I spot a woman leaning against a brick wall next to an overflowing blue bin. The stench of rubbish clogs my nose, but she seems oblivious to it.

If I thought Melissa looked ill yesterday, now she appears to be on the verge of collapse. Her face is gaunt and both her eyes have broken blood vessels in them. When she raises a hand to brush a lank lock of hair from her face, her arm shakes from the effort. Although it is a cold morning, she is wearing nothing more than her uniform and jeans.

I have often heard a warning that we must be temperate with our magic or risk burning out, but I've always assumed it meant we run the risk of burning out the magical part of our blood. Looking at Melissa now, I see that it is ourselves we can harm. What is magic, but an essence of who we are? Can we therefore not burn our life force to fuel our spells?

'You.'

Melissa has heard our approaching footsteps and has pushed herself off the wall. She sways, but manages to keep her balance.

'Melissa, I'm here about Tim.'

'You've ruined everything,' she shouts, and her face twists in anger.

'Why do you think that?' I ask and motion for Karrion to stay back.

'Before you, I could talk to Tim, and now he only has eyes for you. You and the coffees and the dinners and the commute you share.' A bead of sweat slides down her temple and lands on the collar of her uniform. Melissa shivers.

'I'm not the least bit interested in Tim, nor is he in me.'

'You're a liar. You're a liar and a thief. Tim cares about me, he does, but you've made him confused.'

Power causes the hairs on the back of my neck to stand. Beneath the smells of the alley, I catch the cloying scent of drooping roses. The air shimmers next to the bins, and Tim appears, dressed as he was yesterday morning. Melissa's nose begins to bleed. She mutters under her breath, and I have to call upon the hearing of a mouse to catch her words.

'Tim, he cares about me and now he's going to tell you to go away.' As she speaks, the image of Tim repeats the words, looking right at me.

'Go away.'

A drop of blood lands on Melissa's upper lip, and she wipes it away. 'But no, you're stubborn and can't accept that he's mine. You have to come and ruin everything.'

Instead of a smooth exhale of power, the second invocation of magic is a juddering gasp. An image of me shimmers into existence. My clothes are those I wore yesterday, now ruined, but I notice subtle differences in my appearance. The colour of my hair is not quite right, and my eyes are more amber than brown. Even the way I move is clumsy and awkward.

'Tim is mine,' the other me says. Melissa's hate is blazoned across her face, twisting my features into those of a stranger.

'You already have him,' Tim says at Melissa's instructions and points at Karrion. 'Settle for that. I belong to Lissy.'

'I'm his. Why can't you accept that?'

'I do, you can have him,' I say, though I am beginning

295

to see that whatever I say or do is not likely to make a difference.

Melissa stares through us as Tim and a version of me step forward to flank her. Balling her hands into fists, she shouts, 'It should have been me. He should have bought me coffee and dinner and taken me home so I didn't have to be alone anymore. Without you, he would have done all of that.'

The illusions turn to her, speaking in unison.

'Without her, he will.'

'I love you, Lissy,' Tim says.

For a fleeting moment, I think the madness has lifted, but then Melissa points at us and bares her teeth in a grimace that cannot pass for a smile.

'Make it so.'

At the sight of the gun in Tim's hand, my pulse speeds up and my palms grow clammy. I recognise the revolver from the hotel room and I am willing to bet that it functions well enough to wound both Karrion and me. That the illusion of me flicks open a knife increases my alarm, but I keep my attention on Tim.

How am I supposed to protect Karrion from a gun? How do I keep myself safe? All my magic is focused inwards, and I doubt the scales of an adder or the coat of a bear can stop a bullet. I have no way of disarming Melissa from a distance, and if I leap at her now, Tim will shoot.

We should have called Jamie and the Paladins. The certainty brings the taste of blood to my mouth; a memory of the car crash rather than the thrill of a hunt. But with Melissa being this unstable, could we afford to waste another minute?

Twisting my head to the side, I speak in a low voice. 'Remember, Tim must not be harmed.'

Karrion does not reply, and I am not certain whether he heard me. I am about to repeat myself when Melissa points past me, at Karrion.

'Him first. I want her to suffer before she dies.'

Fear freezes me to the spot, a thousand undefined thoughts flitting through my mind. All along, I expected to be Melissa's target and accepted it. I must find a way to protect Karrion.

As Tim raises his pistol arm and I prepare to jump between Karrion and the bullet, I sense a flare of magic behind me in a rustle of a flock taking flight. It is not until a shadow passes over Melissa's face that I realise the rustle was real and I look up.

The sky above the alley darkens, the light blocked by countless wings. A murder of crows has arrived, accompanied by an unkindness of ravens, a parliament of rooks and tidings of magpies. Beneath the main flock, a quarrel of sparrows is chirping calls to arms. The birds twist and wheel above us, all natural animosity forgotten. I can feel every one of them on the edge of my senses, each a tiny flicker of wildness.

With each turn, the birds are descending, their formation changing to a funnel. Individual crows and sparrows are beginning to dive towards Melissa, and she raises her arms to shield her head.

'No, no birds in the sky.'

The birds closest to the ground fade from view, only to return almost immediately. Melissa staggers, falling to her knees, but managing to stand back up. Tim and the other version of me are waving their arms at the birds.

When three magpies separate from the rest to attack Melissa, Tim aims his gun at them.

'No!'

It is Karrion's turn to shout, and the birds scatter, expedited by his fear. A shot rings out, and a chip off a brick slices my ear. I feel wetness running down my neck, but I ignore it when Tim takes aim again. Calling upon the strength of the buck I shot, the speed of the hare Dearon claimed, the stamina of the hounds that accompanied us, I launch myself forward. Their wildness is mine, as is the speed of the birds above us, and I borrow their power to beat the bullet that I know will be coming my way. From the corner of my eye, I can see Tim adjust his aim and the other Yannia coming at me, knife raised.

A clap of thunder deafens me an instant before lightning kisses my shoulder blade. Neither fully registers before my palms connect with Melissa's torso and she is knocked back. I can hear Karrion's muffled shouts, but I focus on Melissa, who has fallen to her hands and knees, blood dripping from her nose at a steady rate.

When a hand lands on my shoulder, I whirl around, arms raised to defend myself against a knife or a gun. Karrion takes a step back, alarm written across his face. The memories of the hunt are mixing with the power of the birds, and it takes me some time to realise that Karrion and I are the only two people still standing. Tim and the other Yannia have gone.

'Yan,' Karrion says and takes my hand, 'you can let go of the birds now.'

I feel every one of them: the wind caressing their feathers; the hunger in their bellies; even the whisper of control Karrion has instilled in them. They are me and I am them: all wildness and instinct and impulse. Theirs is a life I understand and one I crave, and this unlikely flock welcomes me as one of them.

Karrion steps closer, and a remote part of me feels the press of his lips against my cheek. 'Let go of the birds, Yannia. You are not one of us.'

I recoil away from him, as shocked as if he had struck me, and my connection to the birds unravels. Straight away, he sends out a tiny burst of magic and the sky begins to clear. My thoughts clear with it.

'Thank you,' I whisper.

28

THE REAL ECHO

We are still staring at each other when Melissa groans. Her nosebleed shows no sign of easing, and I pass her a crummy packet of tissues I find in my coat pocket.

'Call Jamie and tell him where we are. Ask him to get the Paladins,' I say to Karrion. He walks a few steps away before making the call.

The pain hits me then, in my ear, along my arm where the stitches are and down the shoulder blade that was touched by lightning. Or was it? I can no longer tell. I sink to my knees near Melissa, heedless of the muddy water that seeps through my jeans.

'Use the tissues to help with the nosebleed,' I say when I notice Melissa is holding the packet without opening it.

She does as I say, her movements sluggish, and then jerks sideways, retching. From the strings of bile clinging to the ground, it's obvious she has not eaten anything solid today. I feel an unexpected flash of pity.

I shuffle forward to take the tissues from her, pass her one and hold another against my ear. The blood soaks through it in no time, but I am not concerned. Ears bleed a lot.

Karrion returns, pocketing his phone. 'They'll come straight here.'

'Good.'

He helps me up and draws me into a hug.

'There I was, worried about how to keep you safe when you saved us all,' I say.

'Thanks, Yan. I wasn't sure it was going to work, but I couldn't think what else to do.'

'You were brilliant.'

His cheeks are pink when he steps back, but then he looks at his hand and frowns. 'You're bleeding.'

'Yeah, something nicked my ear. It'll soon stop.'

'No, my hand was nowhere near your ear. Turn around.'

I do, and he brushes his hand against the back of my shoulder. The smouldering pain there flares, and I gasp.

'I think you were shot.'

'That's odd. I thought it was lightning.'

'What are you on about?' He shakes his head. 'Never mind, we need to stop the bleeding.'

'Use my coat.'

Attempting to shrug off the coat leaves me breathless, and Karrion tells me to stop. He takes off his leather jacket and his t-shirt and presses the latter against my back.

'This is why I chose black for you, so the blood wouldn't show.'

'Are you suggesting I'm accident prone?' I ask, fighting not to shy away from the pressure that stokes the embers, making the pain hotter than before.

'No, but I do think you're fantastic at getting into trouble.'

Melissa's nosebleed has stopped, but she looks pale and weak. Her closed expression still carries the spark of hatred from earlier, but she has nothing left to attack us with.

'You've worked some pretty impressive magic this past week,' I say to her.

To my surprise, her face goes slack, her jaw hanging open. 'But I'm human.'

Motioning for Karrion to follow, I walk up to her and inhale. Beneath her pheromones and the sickly sweet smell of vomit, I catch a puzzling mixture of scents: roses, sun-baked salt, meadow grass and noonday heat. They are faint, but what gives me pause is the impossibility of it. When two people with magical blood bear children, only one type of magic passes on to the children. To possess qualities from two magical parents, a South Mage and a Feykin, is unprecedented. But perhaps it is the fact that one parent carries the blood of the Fair Folk that allows for a unique magic user such as Melissa. It does explain why the Mages were putting forward conflicting reports regarding the magic at the crime scenes. Hers is a blend of two.

'You are not human.'

Melissa shifts, confused.

'Tell me, have you always worked in Old London?'

'Yes.'

'Why, if you thought you were human?'

'I... I don't know.'

I think I do. My theory has always been that the magic in our blood draws us to converge in Old London. This is further proof of that theory. For even those unaware of their heritage, Old London holds a thrall none can explain. I felt it upon my arrival in the city: a subtle feeling of comfort that comes from being surrounded by others like me. It is not the same feeling as being among the Wild Folk, but an echo of our intense sense of community. Wild Folk are meant to converge, and so, it seems, are people carrying magical blood.

'Did you know you've been hurting Tim?'

'That's not possible.' Melissa shakes her head. 'I would never hurt Tim.'

'And when he was here, when there were two of me, what did you think was going on?'

'Tim was making it right. He was going to fix it.'

'And this?' I point to my bloodied ear. 'How do you explain this?'

'I... I'm not sure. Tim was going to protect me. Only, it didn't go like it was supposed to.'

'That's because you had no idea Karrion and I aren't human.'

Melissa hugs her knees to her chest and begins to rock. I crouch down in front of her and try to maintain eye contact.

'Two nights ago. Did you imagine Tim shooting himself?'

The rocking motion slows and she frowns. 'It was real. How could you possibly know that?'

'If he killed himself two nights ago, how could he protect you today?'

'I don't know!' Melissa pushes me away. 'I don't know. Leave me alone.' She presses her nails around her ears as tears run down her face. 'I want Tim. Where is he?'

'Yesterday afternoon, you imagined Wayne punching Tim. He fell and hit his head. In reality, Tim collapsed at work and was taken to the hospital with a serious head injury. He's still in a coma.'

Melissa's whole body shakes from the force of her

sobs. Karrion and I look at each other, uncertain what to do. This is not the ending I had expected.

From behind us comes the sound of an engine. A door slams, and Jamie runs to us.

'Christ, Yannia, didn't I tell you not to get into trouble?'

'I wasn't sure we could afford to wait,' I say.

'Be that as it may, it looks like you're going straight back to hospital.'

'And I need to pick up more clothes for her,' Karrion says. 'Though she's running out of coats.'

I ignore them both and watch Melissa. 'At least Tim will be okay now.'

Melissa looks up. 'Tim was supposed to save me. Now what will I do?'

There is nothing I can say in return, and she hides her face behind a curtain of damp hair.

Two Paladins in armour join us, their bejewelled swords loosened in the decorated scabbards. One of them is carrying a set of magic-nulling chains, and I step back to keep my distance.

'She can create illusions that become reality,' I say to the Paladins. 'Right now, she's all out of magic, but I suggest you keep a collar on her at all times.'

The Paladins exchange an astonished glance.

'That's not possible,' one of them says.

'It shouldn't be possible, but in her case it is.'

'I'll fill you in on the details,' Jamie says. 'Yannia and Karrion will come in to give statements when Yannia's been to the hospital. Again.'

The Paladins nod. They are gentle, but insistent as they attach manacles forged from cold iron, true silver and heart copper to Melissa's ankles and wrists. A collar made of the same metals follows, and chains attach to links in the collar and the manacles. Melissa looks panicked, and I can imagine that she is feeling the emptiness that comes from being separated from her power, whether she was aware of the magic or not.

Jamie clears his throat. 'Melissa Hall, I hereby arrest you for the assault and attempted murder of Timothy Wedgbury and Yannia Wilde. Since your crimes have been committed with the aid of magic, you will be remanded in Paladin custody until such time as you stand trial for these charges. Do you have any questions?'

Melissa shakes her head, and the Paladins help her up. She is too weak to walk, and the Paladins support her on the way to the armoured van. Once she is secured at the back, one of the Paladins returns to us.

'Has an ambulance been called?' she asks me.

'No, but I think the bleeding has stopped. Jamie can give me a lift to the hospital.' I turn to him, and he nods.

'We have a first aid kit in the van. I can take a look at your injuries if you wish?'

In truth, the pain is bad enough that black spots swim across my vision, but the sooner I get out of the alley, the better. I shake my head and thank the Paladin for the offer.

'There is one thing I wanted to raise with both of you,' I say to Jamie and her. 'When I spoke to Melissa just now about the illusions she's been creating, she couldn't tell the difference between illusion and reality. I think she needs help.'

The Paladin nods. 'I'll see to it that she is assessed.'

I thank her again, and she joins her colleague in the

van. They reverse out of the alley, and we follow. My steps are sluggish, and I stumble on a flattened can. Karrion takes hold of my elbow.

'Now, are you going to tell me what happened while you were supposedly not getting into trouble?' Jamie asks.

'Get me somewhere with lots of painkillers, and I'll tell you anything you want to know.'

'You know, you're lucky they use healing magic at the hospital. Otherwise, at this rate, you'd be incapacitated within a month.'

'Hazards of the job, I guess.'

Before we round the corner, I glance back. Crows, ravens and magpies line the roofs on both sides of the alley, and their eyes are fixed on us. I shiver and with my remaining strength, hurry out of sight.

SATURDAY

29

CALM AFTER THE STORM

I pour brandy into three tumblers and pass them around. Jamie is occupying an armchair while Karrion is perched on the edge of my mattress, his legs stretching out to poke at my feet.

'How's the shoulder?' Jamie asks.

'Healing nicely, thanks.'

Lady Bergamon's tea has supplemented the pain medication I received from the hospital, but most of my body feels bruised and weak. The case took a lot out of me.

'Do you know what's going on with Melissa?' Karrion asks, voicing our assumption that Jamie's visit is more than a social call.

'I met with the Paladins this morning to get an update on her condition. She's still weak from overusing her magic, but the Paladins believe she'll make a full recovery.'

'Will she be able to use her powers again?' I ask.

'No one knows for sure. It's possible that attempting to do so will kill her. But the Paladins are hopeful that it won't be an issue.'

'Why?'

'While she's recovering physically, her mental health remains poor.'

'Was she assessed? In the alley, she didn't seem to know where reality ended and her illusion began.'

'That was part of the problem,' Jamie says. 'The Paladins' mental health team diagnosed her as suffering from acute psychosis.'

'What does that mean?' Karrion asks. 'And is that related to the illusions she was creating?'

'When Wayne abused her, Melissa was left with serious trauma that was never treated. The Paladins think the trauma interacted with the traces of magic in her blood, awakening and amplifying them until she was able to cast illusions.'

I nod. 'And my guess is, the more she tapped into those powers, the worse it was for her psychosis. A vicious circle was born. Melissa accessed her magic because she was ill and doing so made her condition worse.'

Jamie waves his empty tumbler, and I pour him more brandy. Karrion chucks back what is left in his glass and also gets a refill.

'I didn't know magic worked like that,' Karrion says.

'There's a lot we don't know about magic and mental health. In this instance, even the Paladins were surprised.'

'We should be able to operate under the assumption that Melissa's case is an anomaly. But it does present an interesting point about whether magic is a consideration in diagnosing and treating mental health problems.' I wet my lips with brandy. 'I think Karrion and I will leave the exploration of that to the healthcare professionals.'

'Works for me, boss.'

'The Paladins are liaising with New Scotland Yard to make sure that if something like Melissa's illusions crops up in the future, we'll know that it's more than a Mage prank and respond appropriately.' Jamie swirls the brandy in his glass. 'Let's face it, without you two, Tim would be dead.'

'Not just Tim,' I say. 'The way Melissa was looking yesterday, she wouldn't have survived many more illusions.'

'You did good, both of you.'

Karrion grins his pride, but his expression grows serious when he sees I do not share his joy. 'What's wrong, Yan?'

'I can't help thinking that when I rushed into that alley and dragged you with me, I had no idea what I was getting us into. Had Melissa simply wished us gone, we wouldn't have stood a chance.'

'Are you ever satisfied after a case?' Jamie asks, the lightness of his tone forced.

'I'm serious. I never once paused to think whether I was capable of stopping Melissa. Once the illusion began, I was way out of my league and I put Karrion in danger.'

'We did all right,' he says.

'Only because of your quick thinking. You saved the day.'

'I don't know. The way I see it, the birds were just a distraction.'

They were a distraction for me too, but I leave the thought unsaid. When we told Jamie what happened, neither of us mentioned my loss of control, or what Karrion said to snap me out of it. There have been times when I have found Karrion watching me, his brow furrowed and the press of his lips belying sadness. We both want to apologise, but neither knows how to broach the subject, and our regrets cloud the air between us.

Realising I have been staring at my brandy and have lost the thread of the conversation, I shake my head. 'Next time, I'll be smarter about it.'

'Except next time, you'll be faced with a whole new challenge.'

I find my smile. 'Then I'll deal with it using my tried and tested method.'

'What's going to happen to Melissa?' Karrion asks. 'Will she be executed after the judgement? Because technically, she never killed anyone with her magic.'

'She's probably not going to be put before a Herald,' Jamie says.

Karrion takes the brandy bottle from me and refills everyone's glass. I can tell from the set of his shoulders that Jamie's answer troubles him.

'I don't get it. She broke the law.'

'There's no question about it. But because the Brotherhood's doctors have declared her mentally unfit, the barrister assigned to her case is going to propose that Melissa is judged by a process closer to the human courts. If the Crown Prosecution agrees, she'll be sent to a secure mental institution instead of a prison.'

'Do you think the Crown Prosecution is likely to agree?' I ask.

'Yes. Melissa needs treatment, and this way she'll get it. Once she recovers, it's likely that her ability to create the illusions will disappear. Or so the Paladins said. They'll keep her collared just in case.'

'It's good that she'll get help,' Karrion says. 'I know she tried to kill us in that alley, but I don't think she's a bad person. I'd hate to think that past trauma can break someone beyond repair.'

I feel Karrion's eyes on me and I keep mine fixed on my empty tumbler. When did I finish the brandy? Perhaps it is the alcohol that leads me to ignore my instinct to bypass Karrion's words with a joke, and, biting my lip, I find the courage to speak.

'Our past shapes who we become, the good and the bad. There's nothing any of us can do about that. But with the right support, we can ensure that the bad isn't what defines us.'

Karrion dips his chin, affection written across his face. Jamie rests his elbow on the table and is beginning to speak when Karrion interrupts him.

'So, how about this job interview? Did we pass muster?'

'With flying colours. I'd be happy to recommend to New Scotland Yard that they hire you.'

'That's good to know. But you know what? I'm not sure me and Yan would make good police officers. We're damn fine PIs, and it would be a shame to waste that.'

'No arguments from me,' Jamie says.

'Why don't you ask your bosses to sign us up as consultants instead? We can help with cases that need a different approach, and New Scotland Yard can cover Yannia's daily fee.'

I let my pride shine through my smile. Karrion is a better apprentice than I ever imagined.

'I'll speak to the powers that be and get back to you,' Jamie says, the corner of his mouth twitching.

'Good. We would be a valuable asset for the police.'

'I've no doubt about that.'

'But we want to remain independent, take the cases we want and help the people we choose.' Karrion turns to me. 'Did I miss anything?'

'You seem to have everything under control. Soon you'll be running this business.'

'I don't think so. You see far more than I do. But I want to make sure we stay afloat.'

'Sounds good to me.'

Jamie glances at his watch and finishes his brandy. 'I'd best be off. There's a football match on later, and I don't want to miss the kick off.'

'Saturday evening spent watching football on the telly.' I wink at Jamie. 'You're living the dream.'

'You forgot the bit about the takeaway curry.'

We laugh, and Jamie sees himself out. Karrion is looking at his phone, his tumbler resting at a precarious angle on the blankets.

'I need to be off as well,' he says. 'I have a date, and we're meeting near Blackfriars.'

'That explains why you've dressed up.' I point to his shirt, which is half black cotton and half fishnet.

'It's important to make a lasting impression.'

'Are you aiming for good or bad? That shirt could go either way.'

'She thinks goth guys are hot, so I'm not worried.'

'Yes, but does she like pigeons?'

Karrion scowls as he carries the tumblers to the kitchen, but his good mood returns when he picks up his leather coat.

'Are you okay?' he asks.

'Fine. Why?'

'I just wondered after what you said. If you'd rather not be alone tonight, I can postpone the date.'

'No need. I'm going to stop by at the Open Hearth and say hi to Funja and Wishearth.'

'Okay.' He runs a hand through his hair and tugs on the hoop in his right ear. 'Listen, Yan, about the birds... I'm sorry about—'

I cut him off by hugging him. 'I know. Me too.'

'So we're good?'

'Always.'

'Great. I'll see you soon.'

'Don't forget to buy some mints. Otherwise, your date will think you needed a couple of shots to face her.'

'A bit of Dutch courage never hurt anyone.'

'I'm sure she'll agree.'

'Fine. I'll get mints.'

Once Karrion has left, I brush my teeth and comb my hair. My injuries limit how much I can raise my arms, and I have left my hair down. The edges of it curl around my shoulders, and I wonder about cutting it short. When I catch myself dithering between a forest green and a purple jumper, I pick the green one and leave.

The Open Hearth is busy. I spot Funja serving a table of businessmen and wave a greeting. He points to Wishearth's table, and I skirt around the bar. The dog bed by the fire is empty, and I wonder where Boris is.

Wishearth is sitting back, his eyes closed, but he smiles when I sit down. He leans forward, opening his eyes, and strokes my forehead with hot fingers.

'That's quite the fashion statement.'

'Bruise purple is the new black.'

Sparks fly from his eyes as he laughs, and seeing them eases some undefined melancholy within me. I relax back in my chair, content to watch him while my lips return his smile.

'The world is safe again.'

'What?' I frown.

'You saved the world.'

'I saved two people.'

'So, you saved two worlds.'

I am taken aback and I cannot think of a response. Funja's arrival distracts me, and I make a token protest when he sets a plate in front of me.

'Wishearth say you injured. You must eat.'

He has prepared my favourite meal: gammon steak with eggs, pineapple and chips. I thank him and lay a hand on his hairy arm as he moves to leave.

'There was something I wanted to ask you.'

'*Da*?'

'My apprentice and I are planning to start preparing meals for the homeless on a semi-regular basis. I was wondering if you ever have any ingredients that you are going to throw away, but could still be cooked? Perhaps we could have them?'

'The cooked food, we donate here. But ingredients, you may have. Wishearth will bring, yes?'

Wishearth nods, and I thank Funja a second time.

'For the record, you're meant to get drunk at the pub, not before you get here,' Wishearth says.

'I'm not drunk. Jamie, Karrion and me just had a couple of drinks this evening.'

'Case debriefs are important.' He nods.

'Something like that.' I unroll the cutlery from the napkin and squeeze a dollop of ketchup on to my plate. 'Where's Boris? He's usually in front of the fire this time of the evening.'

'He's taking care of something for Funja.'

My curiosity is piqued, but Wishearth appears unwilling to explain. While I eat, I entertain myself by imagining Boris delivering the renewal paperwork for the pub's alcohol licence to the Brotherhood of Justice, or conducting job interviews for a new chef by sampling the steaks they have cooked. Neither scenario is likely, but they bring a smile to my face.

'Why did you send Tim to me?' I ask, once my plate is empty. 'I thought you didn't concern yourself with the lives of mortals.'

'I don't.' He watches me over the rim of his pint glass.

'Then why?'

'Who else was going to solve the case?'

That he thinks so highly of me sends a thrill of pleasure through me. I have no chance to reply before he sets his glass down and rests his chin on his palm.

'But you must take care. No job is worth you getting hurt.'

'A wound or two is a small price to pay for keeping Karrion safe and for saving Tim.'

He shakes his head. 'You must draw the line now, not in the heat of battle. How much are you willing to sacrifice for others? And who will do the same for you?'

The vehemence of his words takes me by surprise. His eyes carry no flicker of flames as he regards me, and I am struck with the feeling that once again, he knows more than he is letting on.

'I'd like to think those I love would do the same for me.'

'What of others?'

'I don't know.'

'You must. One day you must make that choice.'

317

I swallow and nod. A nearby table erupts in raucous laughter, and the loudness startles me. When I look back at Wishearth, he is motioning a waiter to bring us both a drink.

While we sip our drinks, I tell him more about Karrion's suggestion of feeding the homeless and he listens without interrupting. After I have paid, Wishearth's fingers make brief contact with the side of my wrist.

'You're good for Old London. I just hope the city is good for you too.'

His words percolate through my mind as I walk home. Even when I am kneeling on the hearth stones, offering in hand, the warmth of the conversation lingers within me.

TUESDAY

30

CONCLUSIONS

When Tim groans, I close my book and pass him a cup of water. He drains it and asks for more. It takes three cups to quench his thirst.

'Good afternoon,' I say when he settles back against the pillow.

'Is it really?'

'The doctors said that you've been drifting in and out since you woke up in the early hours of the morning.'

Tim's head is wrapped in bandages, and there are dark circles under his eyes, despite him having been unconscious for five days. The bruise on his jaw where Wayne hit him has gone from purple to yellow. I hope the muzzle mark from the gun has faded already.

'Where's Mum?' Tim asks. 'The doctors wouldn't tell me anything.'

'She's fine. I spoke to one of your mother's nurses, Naoko, who organised a temporary place at a care home specialising in dementia patients. After some initial difficulties, your mother settled in well and seems to enjoy the activities and the view of the gardens.'

'Good,' Tim says, his brow creased. 'Did Mum ask after me?'

'I don't know.'

Tim nods, rubbing his eyes. 'Now that she has settled, do you think she could stay there a little longer?'

'Again, I don't know. You'll have to speak to Naoko about it.'

'Yes, I'll do that. Thank you for telling me.'

'You're welcome. I guessed that would be the first thing you'd ask. How's the pain?'

'Fine. I feel like I've been asleep for too long.'

'You needed the rest.'

'Perhaps.' Tim's attention drifts, and I give him time to gather his thoughts. 'What day is it?'

'Tuesday twenty-third of October.'

Tim pats his chest and abdomen, flexes his arms, then his legs. 'I've been here almost a week. Does that mean you found Lizzie?'

'Yes. She's not going to hurt you again.'

'Did she go after someone else?'

While I debate what to say, a sliver of pain runs down my shoulder blade. 'I was collateral damage twice. The second time, it could have been a lot worse.'

'I'm sorry. Are you healed now?'

'No lasting damage.' Several scars, but I choose not to mention that. I have received excellent care and have managed to keep the stitches from bursting. Soon, they will be no more than angry red lines to add to my collection.

A silence settles in the room while Tim rubs his eyes. The hum of hospital life is all around us, and I am drawn to the squeak of shoes on linoleum, the beep of machinery and the rise and fall of countless conversations. It is a reassuring soundtrack to the process of healing; everywhere around this room, life carries on, undefeated.

'Who was she?' Turning back to the bed, I find Tim watching me. 'Who was Lizzie?'

'Melissa Hall. She worked at Amici.'

'Melissa. You mean Mel? The one you said liked me?'

'Yes. Turns out I was right. She liked you a lot more than I or anyone else realised.'

'If that's the case, why has she been trying to kill me?'

Once more, I pause to consider how best to answer the question. Karrion and I have debated the point many times since apprehending Melissa. With everything we have learned about her, the pieces have fallen into place, but the picture that has emerged is open to interpretation.

'This is going to sound crazy, but I don't think she ever meant to harm you.'

'That—' Tim shakes his head. 'I don't understand.'

'When I confronted Melissa about attempting to kill you, she didn't know what I was talking about. In fact, she kept insisting that she'd never hurt you. I was left with the impression that she was in love with you.'

'Do you know how I got this?' Tim points at his bandaged head.

'You were protecting her from a man who once made her life a living hell.'

Since last week, Jamie has discovered that the reason the fourth illusion took place on the Isle of Dogs was that Lizzie and Wayne used to live there.

'She was abused?'

'Yes, that triggered a psychosis which in turn allowed her to access the magic in her blood. Her illusions were unique because they combined two kinds of magic.'

'I thought Melissa was human.'

'So did she until we caught her. Apparently, she was abandoned as a baby and has no idea who her real parents are. Under different circumstances, it's likely she would have lived her whole life without knowing about her magical heritage.'

'I'm sorry she's had a difficult life,' Tim says. 'But what does it have to do with me?'

'From what we could gather, you were safe. You were friendly and polite, perhaps even kind in your encounters with her, and she developed a crush on you. Asking how you were no longer met her needs, and she began imagining conversations with you, first over coffee and then over dinner. Those friendly conversations grew until, within the safety of her imagination, you were dating. You were everything Wayne was not, and when she was with you, she too became a different person.'

A nurse comes in with a trolley and serves Tim tea and biscuits. I recognise her from the previous times I have stopped by to check Tim's condition. She must also have made the connection, for I too am presented with a cup of strong, milky tea.

Tim dunks a digestive into his cup, but he is preoccupied and half the biscuit disintegrates without him noticing. 'At the risk of repeating myself, I'm still not sure I understand what was going on. Surely everyone imagines scenarios and rehearses conversations in their mind. But as far as I know, that's never led to anyone being hurt.'

'Melissa's psychosis spun her innocent daydreams out of control, bleeding the violence from her past into everything she imagined. She used her own life force to fuel her magic, and the last illusion nearly killed her.'

'Will she be able to use her magic again?' Tim asks. In the softening of his mouth, I see traces of the same pity I feel for Melissa.

'I don't know. But she won't get a choice. She'll be collared while she receives the treatment she needs. After that, her daydreams should return to normal.'

Tim finishes his tea, a frown creasing his brow. There is more he wants to ask, and I wait while he searches for the right words.

'I wonder... what was I like with her?'

'From the CCTV I've seen and from what Melissa told the Paladins, you were relaxed, outgoing and the perfect boyfriend for her. She said you were going to save her.'

'That doesn't sound like me,' he says, and this time the pity is reflected inwards.

'No, and that's an important point for you to appreciate. The man she created in her imagination was an idealised you. I've been thinking about what you said last week about fitting into someone's picture-perfect life. Melissa created not just an echo of such a life, but also an echo of you to live in it.'

'And now it's over.'

'Yes. Your life will return to normal. But there are always opportunities for change.'

Tim looks away, and then back at me. 'Thank you for figuring this out. Thank you for saving me.'

I smile, and some of the lingering disappointment from the Marsh case eases away. 'You're welcome. This is what you hired me to do.'

'I don't know how long I'm going to have to stay here, but if you send me your invoice, I'll settle it as soon as I get home.'

'No rush.' Lord Ellensthorne's assignment will cover my expenses and Karrion's wages for some time. I rise. 'I hope you feel better soon.'

I am turning away when Tim calls my name.

'Do you think I should visit her?'

'No. It's best for both of you if your paths don't cross in the future.'

Tim nods and closes his eyes. I see myself out.

31

A Bargain Met

As I round the corner to my home street, I spot Lady Bergamon ahead of me. I call out to her, and she turns, smiling. Dressed in an ankle-length red cloak and carrying a wicker basket, she once again reminds me of Red Riding Hood, although she is far from a naïve girl caught in a wolf's trap.

'How lovely to see you, Yannia,' she says and reaches for my hand, pulling me close to press a kiss on my cheek.

'Lady Bergamon, how are you?'

'Very well, dear.' She lifts her basket. 'I have the potions for your father.'

I invite her in and lead her upstairs. In the past few days, I have had a chance to tidy my home and the fridge is stocked. Lady Bergamon accepts my offer of tea, and I set the kettle to boil.

'Wishearth tells me you solved your latest case. Congratulations.'

'Thanks,' I say. Wishearth and I shared a drink again last night, and I told him a little about the case. 'It was the outcome I'd hoped for.'

'He also tells me you were injured.'

Fingers that are simultaneously rough as spruce bark, smooth as acorns and soft as marigold petals run over the stitches on my forehead. The wound has healed well, and thanks to the remaining salve I received from her two weeks ago, the bruises have gone.

'The case had its dangers. My car suffered the worst damage.'

'Still, I trust you'll tell me if the healing offered at the hospital is not sufficient.'

'Of course. Thank you.'

I prepare a pot of tea and serve it with a coffee and walnut cake Karrion's mother baked for me. We sit in the lounge, and after a sip of tea, Lady Bergamon sets down her cup.

'Why don't you tell me about your case?'

Over the next half an hour, I give her a summary. Lady Bergamon listens with great attention, interrupting only to ask questions. When I have finished, the teapot and our plates are empty.

'It sounds as though your detective friend made the right decision in directing Tim to you.'

'It wasn't all Jamie. Wishearth meddled.'

'You know, he does that more than he ever admits.'

We share a laugh, but concern clouds Lady Bergamon's expression when she reaches to place a hand on mine.

'The Fey are dangerous, far more than most people realise, even we who have magic. By association, the Feykin are likewise. You must remember that in your future dealings with them. Treat them with the utmost caution.'

'I will,' I say, puzzled by the vehemence of her words.

'Good. Your allies are your greatest asset, but I believe you already know that.'

'Yes.'

'Especially young Karrion.'

My thoughts return to the birds and how Karrion helped me regain control of my magic. I owe him, but it occurs to me that he is not one to keep score. Neither am I.

Unperturbed by the lull in the conversation, Lady Bergamon clears away our plates and cups. I hurry to follow with the teapot. While I wash up, she tells me about the hen harriers I saw in her garden last week. When the dishes are put away, she sets her basket on the counter.

'Let's look at these potions,' she says.

My imagination has jumped to bulbous flasks with green smoke billowing out. Instead, the basket contains eight normal bottles wrapped in brown paper. Lady Bergamon unwraps one, and I see that the amber liquid is not smoking.

'The healer must give your father a spoonful, four times a day. It would be best if the bottles were kept somewhere cool.'

'Will an earth cellar do? We don't have fridges.'

'That will be fine. These bottles should last just over five weeks. Unless I hear otherwise, I will prepare a new batch next month.'

'Thank you.' I transfer the potions into an empty rucksack. Lady Bergamon regards me as I do so, a crease between her eyebrows belying her concern.

'I added ginger and feverfew to the mixture to ease the pain,' she says. 'But your healer will need to supplement it. The ginger will also help with nausea, which is a common side effect of the brew.'

'I'll convey all this to our healer.'

She nods. 'Come see me when you have returned from your trip north. We can wander through my garden.'

'I'd like that.'

'Then it's settled.' Reaching into her basket, she hands me a muslin cloth tied into a pouch with a length of twine. 'I thought you might be running low on my pain-relieving tea.'

'I have one dose left. Your timing is perfect.'

The jar is on the counter within easy reach. I have used Lady Bergamon's tea several times a day while I have been recovering from my recent injuries. The pouch opens with a tug of the cord, and I empty the contents into the jar. Lady Bergamon takes the cloth and the twine and returns them to her basket.

'I will see you soon.'

She collects her cloak, and I see her to the door. Her smile conveys an implicit understanding that I am eager to get on the road. The sooner I deliver the potions to the Elderman, the sooner my immediate future in Old London will be secured.

Once we have said our goodbyes, it takes no more than a few minutes for me to get ready for the journey ahead. My car is still undergoing repairs following the crash, but my insurance company has provided me with a hire car. Pausing next to it, I glance, out of habit, towards the windows of the flat above me, but the curtains remain shut.

Tilting my head back, I savour the pungent smells of sea and silt and sand. When I left Old London, instead of taking the motorway north, I drove to the coast and my beach. I have been sitting on the flat expanse of sand, staring at the swell of grey waves and wondering at the sense of ennui preventing me from honouring the promise I made.

Why is it that I am putting off returning to the conclave when the sole reason for doing so is to cement my freedom?

Next to me, sheltered from the restless sea breeze by my body, is a small fire. Bits of driftwood crackle and hiss as the flames consume them, and I find the heat reassuring. This time, the offering I have prepared is not a length of fir. When I scoured the beach for dried seaweed, I came across a birch branch, the leaves shrivelled and brown. Using dune grass as bindings, I wove together the birch and the seaweed: a reminder of my torn existence. I yearn for the one place where I cannot be the person I wish to be.

I stroke the flames with the offering and watch as it alights. When only smoke and ends of grass dancing in the hot air current remain, I choose a different sort of dedication.

'Thank you, Wishearth.'

A gust of wind picks up the smoke from my fire and engulfs me in the smells that have become so familiar. Even here, my prayers are heard and received.

The wildness of the beach recharges my magic, though why I choose to linger until I am filled with power, I am not certain. Dearon saw me utterly depleted a week and a half ago, when he came to Old London, and I have little to hide from him. Little, except the turmoil raging within me.

I sit here until the driftwood has reduced to smouldering embers, and only then do I force myself to move.

The spot I chose is near the water line, and I carry handful after handful of wet sand to smother the last trace of the fire. While the beach appears deserted, I can hear people on the far side of the dunes and I resent the intrusion. This is my beach, my haven. What place have humans here?

But the world is not for Wild Folk alone, or else nature would not have created other races. I must accept that everything is shared: space, resources and power alike. My kind does not yet see it, but I fear one day they, too, must.

Delaying my departure for a little longer, I turn my face to the breeze. To my Wild Folk senses, the sea pulses with power. It is filled with my kin, as are the dunes around me. When I open myself to the magic of the wilderness, even the humans form a part of the weft that makes the world. But around them, the threads are frayed.

Will life in Old London have the same effect on me?

The cries of seagulls high above me remind me that time is passing and I have a long drive ahead of me. Turning from the sea, I open the rest of myself to the weave of magic and run. My feet take the form of hooves and paws; my arms become wings that get the lift of the wind beneath them. Hair no longer streams behind me, but rather seaweed, dune grass and threads of sea mist.

I am free.

My euphoria lasts until I crest the dune in a wild leap and catch a glimpse of my car. The power dissipates with the abruptness of a summer downpour, and my landing sends shooting pains up my shins. As tempted as I am to look back, I choose instead to limp to my car and begin the long drive up to the conclave.

*

The healer is with my father when I walk in, and his face registers surprise at my presence. My father's expression does not change. He may be dying, but he is still the Elderman. Little happens in the conclave that he is not aware of, and he will have known that I was coming the moment I crossed the border, if the sentries had not given him warning even before then.

'Yannia,' my father whispers as I kneel by his cot. 'You have returned.'

'I've brought you the medicine I promised. It will slow the disease, but it's not a cure.'

My father coughs. His face has grown thinner in the week I have been away, and it is clear that as things are, he will die soon.

'I am beyond a cure and I have accepted that.'

'Fine. But you must understand that these potions will cause you additional suffering. They are not for treating pain.'

'I am not frightened of pain,' he says.

I flinch and look away to hide my shock. Were his words intended as a criticism, or are they a statement of fact? I cannot tell.

To avoid having to think of a response, I hand the bottles to the healer and repeat Lady Bergamon's instructions. He clarifies a few points and takes all but one of the bottles to the earth cellar by the communal larder. As soon as he has left the cabin, I turn back to the Elderman.

'Our bargain?'

'You may resume your temporary exile while the potions prolong my life. But when I die, you must fulfil your obligations to Dearon and the conclave.'

Old anger resurfaces, but I keep all trace of it from my face. The Elderman's concession has bought me time, and that is good enough for now. Until nature gets the better of Lady Bergamon's healing, I have a chance to evaluate my life and the threads that bind me to the conclave. It is time to stop pretending the old promises were not made, and decide for myself how my life will be woven. Life here is not what I imagine; I am forever viewing it through the bias of anger and rebellion. How much of the way I see the conclave is a product of convenient interpretations? I must find the truth in my choices, just as I must choose what kind of life I want for myself. Do the old promises matter, or can I forsake my past and that which makes me who I am, to be free? Tim has lived for others and now has a chance to think about himself again. Which kind of life is more meaningful? Which can I live? And would forsaking the conclave be a truly selfish act? I have none of the answers, only questions, but that will change.

'Feel better,' I say, and rise. It is an empty platitude, but I have little more to offer to the stranger who has dictated the course of my life until now.

I am reaching for the door when I hear the Elderman call my name. He has risen to his elbows to look at me, the effort deepening the lines on his face.

'Your mother would be proud to see you now.' A flush of pleasure brings heat to my cheeks, but my father has not finished. 'She often remarked what a great match you and Dearon were. It was a source of deep regret to your mother that she would not live to see Dearon taking his place as the next Elderman and you taking your place by his side.'

'Why is it so important to you that I do my duty?'

'Because then you will be the daughter I always wanted.'

Teeth sinking into my lower lip draw blood as I grope for the twist of wood serving as a door handle and stumble out. Ollie is waiting for me by the cabin, and I kneel by his side. He is gentle when he rests his head against my cheek, and it brings out my tears. I cling to him while his rough tongue wipes away the moisture from my cheeks. His presence reassures me until the initial rush of emotions has subsided to a cloud of turmoil roiling around my mind. There is much I do not understand, memories that do not seem to reconcile. I must, in time, take stock of them all. But not now.

Whispering a thank you to Ollie, I hug him and choose the shortest path to the cover of trees. When I chance a glance back, Ollie is standing where I left him, tail between his legs and his head drooping. I wish I could take him to Old London with me, but he is not my dog and I have no right to separate him from his master.

Throughout the long walk to the car, I expect to hear footsteps behind me. I am reaching for my keys when I hear a whisper of movement and I turn to see Dearon approaching, wolf paws shimmering back to human legs. Anger, disappointment and frustration war in his eyes as he stalks closer, and it saddens me that they are all my fault. In his expression, I see a question he will not voice.

Had I really planned to visit the conclave without seeing him?

The answer is yes, that was what I had intended. It would have been easier for both of us, or that is the excuse I use to try to ease the nagging of my conscience. But I see that in him, too, I have imagined a man who may not exist, and I must find out the truth for myself and for him.

Dearon does not stop until we are mere inches apart. His power is a dark aura around him. Already he has magic I can only dream of, and he will grow stronger once he assumes the title of Elderman. My blood yearns for his power just as my heart and body yearn for him.

Together we would be extraordinary.

The emotions in his eyes lessen, perhaps because he guesses something of my thoughts, or perhaps because my inner conflict is plain to see. Our eyes lock, and I could not look away even if I wanted to. Just as I think I will lose all of myself in him, his lips crash into mine. I surrender myself to the kiss as he yanks me closer. His arms around me are tight enough to cause pain, but all I do is grip his shoulders until my finger joints protest at the tightness of my hold. We kiss until nothing exists in the world except his lips on mine, his scent in my nose and his hold anchoring me to the conclave life.

Even when we have to break apart for air, we remain close. He pants against my lips, dark fire in his eyes, but the fingers caressing my cheek are gentle.

'I wish this was enough for you,' he whispers.

So do I. The words do not come, and I do the only thing I can and kiss him again. All I want is to get lost in the sensation of him for a moment longer. I will need this memory to sustain me through many lonely nights when my doubts and fears deny me sleep. As if sensing this, he pulls me closer and his power envelops me until I feel all of him.

Eventually, I am the one to step back. His head remains bowed, locks of hair hiding something of his expression, but I see enough to know he too is committing the moment to memory. My hand trembles when it traces the curve of his jaw, my thumb ghosting over his lips, but neither of us says anything. For both of us, actions are easier than words.

Dearon remains rooted to the spot as I drive away. I watch him in the rear view mirror until a bend in the road carries me out of sight. But there is a presence in the seat next to mine, so tangible I could reach out and touch him.

He stays with me through the long hours of driving in the dark. It is only when I cross the invisible border into Old London that I glance to my left and find that I am alone.

ACKNOWLEDGEMENTS

Once again, a big thank you to Louise Walters for continuing to see the potential in my work. With her guidance, the series is going from strength to strength. Thank you to Team Wilde Investigations: Jennie Rawlings, Alison Jack and Leigh Forbes, who turn my pages into stunning books. You guys are awesome!

Thank you to Andrew Rogers, my first reader. You are what keeps me grounded and inspired. This, like all my books, was written for you, with my deepest affection and gratitude.

My long-suffering flatmate Johanna Saariluoma had to put up with months of my insecurity while I was writing the first draft, and calmly reassured me when I needed it the most. Thank you for all your support and help with the early drafts. And sorry about all the weird tweets and blog posts.

Thank you to my family and especially my niece, Ada-Sofia, for her enthusiastic support. My family may live in a different country, but they've walked every step of this journey with me.

To my friends, near and far, thanks for being there for me and for being your weird selves!

To the man behind Wishearth, thank you for the spark of inspiration.

I'm indebted to Paul Craddock for his patience in answering endless questions about deer stalking and tracking. Any mistakes in the book are mine and mine alone.

To the readers who bought a copy of Fallible Justice, left reviews and who believed in the series, thank you. A book without readers is only a half a book.

Finally, as ever, thank you to Sinta and Halla for making each day worth it.

LWB Interviews Laura Laakso...

When did you decide to become a writer?
I'm not sure it was something I consciously decided. By the time I turned thirty and wanted to pursue writing more seriously, I was already hooked. The choice I made was about wanting to become a published author. But I was already a writer and had been long before I had anything approaching publishable to show for it. Everyone who writes is a writer, but not everyone becomes an author, and that's okay.

What kind of books do you enjoy reading?
I like a mixed bag. It comes as no surprise that I read a fair bit of paranormal stories as well as crime and murder mysteries. I always appreciate a good thriller and occasionally dip into literary and historical fiction. These days, I follow a few authors, but most books I pick up are recommendations from people I know.

Apart from writing, what are your passions?
Definitely my dogs! My old Corgi has retired now, but my young Australian Shepherd and I compete in three different disciplines. It takes a lot of training, but all the work has helped form a wonderful bond between us. I also run an informal pet dog training class. Many of the

dogs who come are rescues, and it's wonderful to watch them transform into happy, relaxed pets.

If I have any spare time left, I play boardgames and table-top role-playing games. I'm a huge geek at heart, so any excuse to game will do me fine.

How did you conceive the Wilde Investigations series?
It all began with a notion of a justice system built upon otherworldly beings looking into a person's soul to determine guilt or innocence. And me being me, what interested me the most was how such a justice system could be fooled. As soon as I figured that out, I knew I had to write the story. Not long after, I had an image of a woman running on a beach, borrowing aspects of nature with unbridled joy. That scene later became the opening chapter of *Fallible Justice*. The more Yannia revealed about her backstory, the more it became clear that she deserved more than one book. Lucky for me, I've had plenty of ideas for the series!

Do you have a favourite among your characters?
Shhh! You're not supposed to ask that! I love writing Yannia and Karrion working together. They make a great team, and the affection between them is wonderful. Besides, who doesn't enjoy teasing Karrion about pigeons! Of the supporting characters, Lady Bergamon and Wishearth hold a special place in my heart. They don't get many scenes where they interact directly, but writing them is pure delight. My first reader recently suggested that Lady Bergamon and Wishearth need a spin-off story, and I'm a little bit tempted...

Can you tell us anything about book 3?

It combines Samhain traditions, plant magic, the Fey and gruesome murders in a breathless race to stop a killer from claiming any more lives. Yannia has to face her greatest fear, decide who she can trust when faced with damning evidence and discover how much she is willing to sacrifice for those she loves. I've often thought of it as a project in which I inflict as many awful things upon my characters as I possibly can. It's been so much fun to research and write, and not just for the misery!

Who are your favourite writers, and why?

Nicholas Evans for his ability to invoke deep feelings with his words. Agatha Christie for being the queen of murder mysteries. Kelley Armstrong for writing strong female characters in a paranormal setting. Michael Crichton for his amazing thrillers. Terry Pratchett, Douglas Adams and Neil Gaiman all for their sense of humour, wit and attention to detail.

What are the highlights so far of being a published author?

I found the process of getting published hugely exciting and in describing it, I've been throwing around superlatives with wild abandon. One thing that stands out for me is that becoming a published author has lent a certain credibility to my writing. I don't mean in the eyes of others, but for me personally. I can develop the series and characters with a different kind of confidence now I know they and their stories will see the light of day. The more I work on the long-term plots and character arcs, the more pieces fall into place to form images different from those I expected. Every time that happens, I pause to remember how lucky I am.

Another thing that's been brilliant fun has been readers contacting me to tell me how much they loved one (or more) of my characters. A few names keep cropping up, but it's great to see that all the usual suspects are covered. My first reader keeps predicting interesting fanfiction, and I'm actually rather looking forward to seeing if that happens!

And what are the lows?
English comma rules. They make no sense! Every time I think I've got the hang of them, something else crops up and gives me a headache.

Do you have any advice for readers who are also writers?
Don't be afraid to experiment in different genres and narrative styles to find your voice. I wrote two novels and numerous shorter fiction pieces before I found what worked for me. And despite so many people repeating the advice that you should write every day, I think it's more important you write with self-compassion. Looking after your mental and physical wellbeing is more important than meeting a daily word count target.